My Life in Love

Aditya Powar is a Freelance Writer, and a Short Filmmaker. Aditya Likes making short films based on the current issues that are raised throughout the country and bring it to the people through his artistic motion work. He currently lives in Hyderabad and is being pursuing his Film and Media Degree from Akkineni Nagarjuna's *Annapurana International School of Film and Media*, famously known as AISFM. Aditya loves writing short stories, blogs, and motivational essay's. Traveling around the world is one of his finest hobbies. Aditya originally lives with his parents in Kolhapur with his parents and younger brother Atharva. Aditya can be also contacted on his Official Facebook page http://www.facebook.com/adityapowarofficial or he can be also reached at his Official Twitter Handle http://www.twitter.com/@imadityapowar

My Life in Love

ADITYA POWAR

adittia
Publications

Published by **Adittia Publications** 2016
342/2 23B Shahu Sena Chouk,
Jawahar Nager, Kolhapur.
www.adittiapublications.com

ISBN 978-9352915859

Fiction

Typeset by **adittiaStudios**
Printed and bound by **CS**

Visit www.adittiapublications.com for any further information.

To Pranavi, who also made me happy with a smile…

Prologue:

'*P*ass me the bread here' I said as I lifted up the butter bowl and placed it in front of me.

I really didn't like having my breakfast without bread and butter served to me. I have few of my old host at my place. Actually they were not my host's although, they were my best friends. Me, Sam, and Priyanka. We both are best of friends.

'Here' Sam said as he passed me the butter bowl.

I shrugged my shoulders.

We finished our breakfast within a few minutes later. We really had a heavy breakfast today. It was just 8:00 am and we fools has filled our stomachs as if we were having an afternoon lunch.

'Such a heavy breakfast it was? I really had no more space for the lunch!' Priyanka said.

'Hmm' followed Sam.

There was a different love relationship between these both. I knew them from past ten years. We both were very close to each other. The intimacy between us was a bit different from those others.

'Shoo... don't be a spoilsport, I'm sleepy. Let me sleep at my rest.' Priyanka said as she used full of the sofa as she slept off.

Sam and me exchanged 'what's-wrong-with-her' glance as we both smiles at each other.

'Who sleeps when the world gets up?' Sam said as Priyanka signed him with the middle finger. I really didn't understood what was that.

Sam sign me to take off the extra pillow from Priyanka as it was hurting her. I leaned forward as   I pulled out the extra pillow. I still remember the inception of the love life of these both was as romantic as now. Sam could not just see Priyanka hurt. That's what makes a good relationship.

'Rohit, I think we should also get back to our work'

'Let's have a bath first'

'I'll enter the bathroom first'

'No, I'll go first'

I pushed back Sam as he was perfectly placed next to Priyanka. She caught his hand being romantic. I threw her a flying kiss. Sam threw me a dirty look.

'Enjoy, nobody is going to see you. I'm too going for shower.' I said as Priyanka threw the pillow towards me playfully.

'I think I should stay here' I said.

They both smiled at me.

'Now just leave' Priyanka blunt.

◆

'That is it' Priyanka said pointing towards the monitor.

We sat discussing the dresses for my marriage. I had my marriage in two months with the person whom I loved. That's the greatest feeling ever. When we have something we want or love a lot, and when we deserve it into our life, we have a greatest feeling. She had been here at my place.

'That's also nice baby...' Priya said holding my right hand. I looked towards her as her gave me a world class smile.

I smiled back at her.

'Hmm... control yourself guys, you have the entire life still' Priyanka blushed as Priya hid herself behind me.

'Well Priyanka, they can't control anymore' Sam poked.

Priya sat down onto the sofa as Priyanka followed her. Sam and I turned towards the monitor. We both looked at each other. Sam threw me a *'let's-see-it-afterwards'* glance.

'Hmm'

I sniffed in.

We both took our place at the sofas too. Priyanka signed Sam with making her eyes big. I really didn't understand what she had signed him of. Their eyes were onto Priya. She looked puzzled looking at them. Next their eyes were on me.

'What?' I blunt.

Priyanka smiled.

'Well, Rohit you want to be an author. And as we know that you are going to work onto your first novel soon.' Sam said.

'So?'

I looked up at Priyanka.

'So…. How if you write the story about yourself. About us, I guess' Priyanka said.

I really didn't understand anything. I was floored. I looked at Priya. She seemed as if she knew everything and she had hid it from me.

'Say it clearly guys!' I said.

Sam sat next to me. I looked at him. He placed his right hand on my left shoulder. He brought out his iPhone and switched it off.

'Why don't you write the story about our past?' Sam said. 'Write about how we struggled for our love'

I looked at each of their faces. Priya got up as she placed her hand onto mine. She signed me to be calm. She told me I can do it. I really loved when she does me this thing.

'Rohit, that will be a great idea. A great start.' Priyanka said.

I smiled at her.

'Don't you guys have any problem with it?' I said.

'No' all of them said in unison.

I got up from my seat as I walked towards the balcony. I really was not sure about this one. I really couldn't understand anything about this. 'Should I do this?' I asked myself.

'Sam but…'

'No Rohit, that will be fine' Sam interrupted me.

I looked up at Priya to see what she thinks. She smiled at me as I had got my answer. I should really do this. I should turn my real life story into a novel. I should tell whole world about my life and what all had happen.

'Guys, I think I should do this.' I said.

'That's the sprit man' Priyanka said as she jumped into her seat in excitement.

Priya got up as she ran towards me. She hugged me as that hug felt romantic. I looked at her as her eyes went wet.

'Hey, what happen?' I said holding her face.

She buried her face into my chest.

'Rohit, you has given me the best gift ever.' Priya said.

I held her face again and made her look up at me. She seemed very beautiful. I really wanted to kiss her now.

'Guys, not here. It's a public place' Priyanka said playfully pointing her index finger towards the floor.

I and Priya came back to normal. She sat back on her original place as she threw me a flying kiss.

'That's so romantic' Sam said. 'I think Priyanka, we should hung out for some time and give them some time along'

Priyanka got up from her seat as she held Sam's hand and pulled him towards the door.

'Guys....'

'Hey, Rohit have fun, see you!' Sam said.

'Hmm'

♦

We sat crossed leg onto my bed in my bedchamber. I looked at the each of their faces one by one. All of them felt just da'am excited as I was going to make my real life story into a fictional book. We had gathered at my room as these *all have forced me to start for the story. They all seemed as they were host into my house.*

'What happen Rohit?' Priya said.

I nodded.

'Then why don't you start?' Sam poked.

'Rohit, you should start now.' Priyanka too started. 'Have been waiting'

I smiled at all of them as I grabbed my MacBook from the table next to me. I opened the MacBook as I looked up at them.

Priya threw me a 'please-start' glance. I threw her a flying kiss.

She smiled at me.

'Where should I start?' I asked as I really don't know that where should I really start.

Priyanka smiled at me.

'You should start from when we first began your journey. The classroom' Priyanka answered.

1

'Excuse me!' I said. 'Can you tell me where is the SYJC classroom?' I said as a boy turned towards me.

'There' he pointed towards the right side.

He smiled at me as he left. It is my first day at college. I have appeared for this college for my 12th HSC exams. I had reverence in my heart from the first day about the college. It was my inception at this college. I had made some of the friends too the best one was Chetan, who understood me better and now I'm his cranny. I had convoke my friends in our 12th class. We just started talking to each other making jests, etc. Chetan was a very good and sedate student. He had completed his four years in the same college and had a very good reputation in the class and in the college too. He was fully replete with knowledge and a very imperturbable student. He was very friendly with me and I was with him too. He lived with his mom, dad and a younger brother in Dadar near Shivaji Park or something. But was very fro by my house, mine was in Andheri east. Soon I saw our professor '*Pradhan*' entering the class as all students stood up to wish a *good morning* to him. '*Saying good morning was okay but what's the use to say him, he was such an old person. If there was a hot lady professor then it was okay. At least she had....*' I said to myself. I was presume stand up to but I did not.

'Sit down, students' he said as all students sat down instead of me I was already in my seat.

Mr Pradhan soon asked us all new-comers to introduce ourselves. Pradhan's murphy like eyes panicked me too much. 'This man should never enter our class again' I thought. I saw at the entire class gingerly, I found all Hi-fi facilities available in the class room like digital board, the atomic window panes, computer system attached to each and every bench, Internet 24/7, etc. 'I should handle all this things meticulously.' I thought. The classroom too had a void between each row of benches. I saw a girl entering the class room who had worn turquoise T-shirt and a dark blue denims.

'May I come in professor?' She said.

Professor Pradhan shook his head as she entered the classroom.

'Please introduce yourself' professor Pradhan said in soft and calm voice.

Obviously if a person see such a hot and sexy girl his voice will definitely be low and clam.

'My name is Priyanka Mehta, from Andheri east, Mumbai' she said in a clam voice.

Priyanka I repeated the name in my mind as if I was her PA. She stared at me as I suddenly broke down the eye contact with her. She took her seat at the first row, first bench. Mr Pradhan took out his electrical pen and wrote 'CORRUPTION' on the digital board in bold letters. 'So student's corruption is the main....' He started. His voice was too strong and loud that a Dolby system could waive. I there after pooh-pooh at his voice whenever he talks or teaches us. Our first lecture was finally over as professor Pradhan left our class.

I wriggled.

Few hours later our college ended, we packed our bags as I moved towards the door to get out of the classroom. Somebody pushed me from behind as my books made their place on the floor. I looked back to see the fool who had did this. As I looked back I saw the new-comer girl in front of me. Her name was 'Pri....' something. I could not remember it properly as I got floored.

'Oops! I'm sorry' she said as she bend down to pick up the books fell down on the floor. I too bend down to help her. We both stood up as she passed my books back to me.

'Thanks' I said.

'No, it was my mistake, I'm sorry for that' She said meticulously.

'By the way what's your name?' I asked.

'Priyanka' She replied.

'Rohit is here' I said looking insistent in her eyes.

We both exchanged 'Good Bye' glances as we moved to our own roots. I felt something different about her, something special. I saw Priyanka languidly as if she wants me to come to her and talk to her more. I too passed to the college exit gate. I spurt as I was at the college gate. I don't know why, but when I was talking to her I felt timid. I talk to everybody frankly and calmly, but I don't know when I was talking to her why I had felt timid. I did not twig the concept why I did so. I buried the matter in my mind and started walking towards the college bus.

♦

My college bus dropped me home at 4:32 pm. I started walking towards gate. I reached the door and knocked the door three times. My Mom opened the door as I got into the house I directly moved towards my room as I tucked my college bag onto my bed. And then kept the books on my computer table those were in my hand. I sat down on my bed as I cogitate about the timid-ness I felt in the college today. My Mom entered my room as I looked at her.

'Beta, change your cloths! And how was the first day at college today?' She asked.

I shook my head.

'What?' She said.

'Nothing, it was just fine' I blunt.

She smiled at me as I looked up to my T-shirt.

'Change your cloths and come to the kitchen. I'll arrange your lunch' she said.

'Yeah' I said as I changed my cloths.

I moved towards my kitchen as Mom had already arranged the lunch for me in an American plate. There were multifarious items in my plate. I was floored how to eat too many items at the same time. Retrocede the bowl of *gullabjaamun*, *Dahi*, and a bowl of some sweets. I had my lunch in next few minutes and just had returned to my bedroom. I had switched on my PC as I had no work on it rather than surf the web. I Had opened Google Chrome and had typed the address http://www.facebook.com/ in the address bar and logged in into my Facebook account. I had some new friend request and some of the messages. I had accepted the friend requests and logged out from my Facebook account. I thought over to surf through some of the porn sites. I got up from my chair and went towards the door. I locked it properly so that no one can enter into the room. I sat down on my chair and surfed some of the sites like, XXX, adultfriendfinder, redtube, 89, youporn, etc. I closed the chrome window and switched off my PC. I lay down on my bed as I went off to sleep.

♦

We had been gathered at SDIC (Seven-day International College). I had been sitting on Table No. 6. I had reserved this place for myself. I shun the contact with Priyanka as she was sitting right front of me and I can see her clearly. She wore white T-Shirt and a full black jean, it looked fully modish. I don't understand why do girls were such a modish tog. But its good wearing modern modish togs, they look really beautiful. I saw her getting up from her table and coming close to me. I shun eye contact as she came closer and closer.

'Can I sit here?' She said.

I kept quiet for few seconds.

'Sure' I said as she sat on my table.

The smell of Black Cobra filled into my nose. 'Why do girls use those perfumes and that stuff? They already have such a nice smell naturally.' I thought because I know it because of my acquaintance.

'See, yesterday's matter, sorry for that once again' She said.

'No, it's fine' I said.

'See, today I tried to make some new friends, but I found that if I made friendship with them, I'll spoil my college life. I repose you. I found you to be the senior student and helpful calm one. And I know, I have come here for studies not for enjoying nonsense things with this use-less friends.

'So, will you be my friend?' She asked as she extended her hand to shake it with me.

'Sure' I said as I too extended my hand. Her hands were too soft as a soft cotton.

I felt nice as she was the only girl in our 12th class who was smart and studious. And I was friend with Ms. Best girl. And I know she will be the radiant student in the whole class. I converse with her more for some more time. I think we will soon be friends, the close one…

One Month Later

I sat in my class studying for our first prelim exams. I had my science notes in my hands and science textbook on the bench. I have to slumber now. I have studied the whole last night. I have to retrocede Math's notes to Priyanka which I had borrowed from her yesterday. I sat opposite to Priyanka in third row first bench. Soon our Science professor Ms. Patil entered our class. All of us stood up to wish her as she smashed the books from her hand on the teachers table.

'See, students your prelim has come on your heads, study as much as you can. Do your best and try to get more and more grades in this exam. And listen don't write the paper in hurry-burry, with a good handwriting and your answer sheet should be neat and tidy. So, do your best, All the Best' She said.

'Why does each and every professor have to give the same introduction all the time, as if they don't have any other work to do?' I thought. It was very momentous for me to do well in this exam because I had promised my Mom and dad that I'll cross 96 this time. I found professor's book fallen down as I got up from my bench to pick it up. The professor bend down at the same time to pick it up. I bogged Ms. Patil and gave her the books as I retrocede back to my bench. I needed some of the Economic notes to be completed. I looked at Priyanka. I moved towards her bench as she looked up at me. I found her face delectable as if same good is going to happen with her.

'Excuse me, can 1 get your Economics notes, please' I said in a soft voice.

She kept quiet for few seconds.

'Sure' She said as she handed me her Economics notes. She had handed me those notes as if she doesn't know me and I'm her host. The word 'What's Wrong' was going to imminent from my mouth. But I repress myself vehemently. I silently moved towards my bench and started coping her Economics notes. My cranny was the epitomize example of myself. He too does not do his work himself, but only copy down from others. I would like to tell him that don't do it, because it's his 12th HSC. *I'm telling him as if I'm too adroil. 'Idiot first see yours and then tell the world'* I told myself. I saw Priyanka, she looks solemn in her studies. And I think it's atrocious that I copy her notes. 'You concentrate on your work idiot! You are soon going to be replete of knowledge' I told myself. I'll too glint in class one or the other day. I thought.

I had observed past one month that teachers in this college doesn't work properly. I think they only work for mercenary.

I had repose on all the teachers but I don't understand why my mind think negative always. In case of me, Priyanka was a popsy for me and other males. I think Ms. Mehta had received more male attraction in last weeks. The each and every boy stares at her while walking from the corridor, in class as if she is their wife. I should talk to Priyanka about this, what if she has a problem by this incident. 'The snake is going to think to eat rats', I told myself. I heard the bell which meant the college has ended. I learned over to return Economics notes to Priyanka as I moved towards her bench. I observed her packing her bag as I banged the notebook on her bench.   Priyanka flinched. I exchanged 'I'm Sorry' glances with her as I gave the book to her.

'Thanks for this' I said pointing at her notes.

'You are welcome' Priyanka said in a very soft voice.

'Bye' I said.

I did not find any other work rather than 'Bye' to say to her. I looked at her as she had direct eye contact with me.

'Ba…Bye' She said as we left the class room.

♦

I sat on my bed reading Chetan Bhagat's 'Revolution 2020' my friend Chetan had vehemently handed me this book, to read it. He handed me the book as if he is my foe and wants to mug on me. But the book was really good. I was too sleepy while reading it but I somehow repress my sleep.

I shrugged my shoulders.

Suddenly I thought about Chetan, his kindness, his atmosphere, his nature, his understanding, and etc. I loved his obstinacy as he helped me in my studies. I could repose Chetan too in my personal matters. I thought. I saw my mom coming into my room. I saw her bejeweled as if she was going to attend her own marriage. I want to ask her if she is going out somewhere?

'Mom, where are you going' I questioned.

'Beta, for Sarla aunt's son's birthday at Hotel Chandragupta Crown'

I gave her understanding nod as she left.

I disposed myself to prepare a mail for Ajay. Ajay was my aunt's son which my Mom had mentioned some time earlier. I moved towards my PC as I opened the chrome I logged in into my Yahoo account as I composed the birthday mail to Ajay. I shoot it off to him. A message flashed on the screen 'Your message has been sent successfully' I logged out of the Yahoo account. I logged in to Facebook. I typed 'Priyanka Mehta' into the search menu and hit enter. The profile of hers flashed on my screen. It was her, it was Priyanka. I clicked on the 'Add Friend' button as it flashed 'Friend request sent' on the screen. I logged out of my account as I closed the chrome window. I picked up my CD pouch and flipped of some prominent porn CD's. I took out a DVD printed   'National' onto it. I tucked it into my DVD ROM. I watched some of the porn films for the next half hour. I shut down my PC as I retrace to my bed as I took 'Revolution 2020' in my hand. I started reading topic No. 22. I grinned at a joke as if I have smiled on the world's best joke. Soon the sleep filled my eyes. There is one odd think going wrong with me. Whenever I take a book in my hand and started reading it, the sleep starts filling my eyes. I think I was the first slacker of this world. I kept the book aside as I lay down on the bed. The light switched off as the murk filled the whole room. I got up suddenly as the light resumed. I saw the mango juice kept on the computer table as I poured into the glass and consumed. It felt good drinking cold liquid. I retained the juice as I kept the glass aside. I lay down on the bed as I went off to sleep.

Today was the day which can complete my promise done to my Mom and dad? From today was the prelim exams starting. I had a different panic in my mind. I shun the panic as I entered the classroom. I saw Priyanka studying Algebra. I hate the concepts of Algebra and Geometry. Meanwhile I hate the subjects.

'Have you prepared for the prelims?' I said.

'Just few concepts... else fine' Priyanka replied.

'You?'

'Yeah, almost there' I said.

'So, best of luck'

'Same here'

'Well, you must be getting disturbed, I'll talk to you later' I said as I moved to my bench. I found that my bench was dirty with a curd. 'Who the fuck, had fallen the curd on my bench' I thought.

I sat on Chetan's place as I opened my algebra textbook and started studies. I felt a bit nervousness in my mind in my studies. 'What will be if I get less grades in this prelims' the negative thoughts started entering my mind as if the theft entered our house for robbery. I thought over to ask Priyanka some of the Algebraic problems, but I was inarticulate before her. I found a bit of muster of my mind and I totally concur with it. I will vie my answer sheet on time and I will transact this task with a sedate mind.

My mind was replenished, but let's see what will be the results of prelim after six days.

2

Our prelim results were due today. The heartbeats of mine were as fast as a metro train. Not only mine but of every student who had struggled hard for this exam. We can't say 'to no avail' if they have tried their level best in this prelim, they will be successful in their exams. I was very solemn from the last night when I went off to sleep to when I got up in the morning. Let me tell you that I had a nightmare that I had failed this exam with 34%. I had been dressed into the neat and tidy formal togs. My mom sat in the hall watching TV shows. I don't understand why do elder people like to watch this stupid serial and all that stuff? Dad was too sitting right next to my mom reading a Marathi Newspaper.

'Mom, Dad, Good Morning' I said.

'Good Morning Beta' Dad said.

'I think that your prelim exam results are due today'

I kept quiet for few seconds.

'Yes, they are due today. They will be out today' I said in a nervous voice.

I think parents are more interested in our results then our exams. I had put my best efforts in this prelim exams, so let's see what output comes out. I sat down on the dining table for the breakfast as my mom brought *Allo Ke Parate* in a plate and a glassful of milk. I had my breakfast as I got ready for my college.

I reached college as I saw Chetan mixed with some populace. I took him aside as I asked him about the results.

'Where are the prelim results?' I questioned him being excited.

'They are already displayed on the notice board' he replied.

'And what about you?'

'Passed at least'

'By what grades?' I asked.

'85.44%'

'What a luck' I thought. I was already so excited by listening the results of Chetan. What if I see my own? I accorded my bag to Chetan and asked him to put it on my bench. I rushed towards the notice board. I found two papered pasted onto it. 1. Top 5 rankers. 2. Passed students results. I first took a glance at 'Passed student's results' I did not found my name there. Then I checked the 'Top 5 Rankers' as I found the following results.

Priyanka Mehta	98.66%	Passed with Rank 1
Rohit Deshpande	97.45%	Passed with Rank 2
Aditya Patil	96.14%	Passed with Rank 3
Joy Dsouza	92.00%	Passed with Rank 4
Sammy Kapoor	88.42%	Passed with Rank 5

The gladness filled my mind. I could not believe on my own eyes. I stared at the notice board for few seconds. I was presuming to dance at that stage. I could not believe that the grades printed on that white paper pertain to me. But this was totally true. I rushed to my class to receive my Progress Card (results). As I entered the class professor Pradhan sat on a chair distributing the results as he was our class teacher. I went close towards him.

'What's your roll Number' He said looking towards me.

'Six' I replied.

'Six' he murmured as he started searching my result from the bunch of the report cards. He started flipping through the report card as he got mine. He handed it to me as   I looked at it carefully as it printed 'Overall Grades 97.45%' I was very glad to see it front to me.

'Good, nice keep it up' Professor Pradhan said.

'Thank you, Professor' I said as I left the classroom. I saw Priyanka entering the classroom, the report card was already in her hand.

'Hey, Rohit, how are your grades' she said.

'Good' I said in full excitement.

'How much'

'97.45%'

'Good Score!'

'And you?'

'98.66%' she replied.

'So, first in class ha?' I said.

'And you are second, right?' she said. 'Well yesterday I saw your friend request'

'Have you accepted it?' I questioned.

'Of course'

The image of Priyanka glinting in the class flashed in my eyes. I saw foliage falling down from tree. The mellifluous sounds filled my ears. The day felt delectable as the mountain of thoughts molted in my mind.

'Hey, where have you lost' she said waving her hand in front of my face.

'Nothing, just…' I Retore.

I saw the earring in her ears which have the simon-pure diamond onto it and the gold structure around. It was too delectable.

'Can we, go to canteen and have coffee' Priyanka said.

The word 'can we' got echoed in my mind.

'Sure' I said as we moved towards the canteen, we both sat on the same table. Table No. 6. I saw a page coming towards us he wore a black and white hue togs. 'Why these crows work only in hotels, and in these togs?' I thought.

'Get us two coffees and some snacks' Priyanka ordered. 'Which one? Cappuccino?'

I gave her an understanding nod.

'Cappuccino!' She repeated to the page as he left.

I saw at Priyanka she worn a brown colored dress which had more than fifty buttons onto it. I really need to enumerate them, and a deep black hue jeans, and looked very beautiful like she had never before. A tot came towards Priyanka as he hit a lollypop on her jeans.

'How cute is he no? I hope I should also have the same ilk of child' she said as the mother of that cute but very naughty child ran towards us.

'I'm sorry' the child's mother said.

'No problem, I like him. Such a cute champ' Priyanka blunt as the mother took the child fro with her.

Our coffee arrived in few more minutes. The page placed it on our table and left. We took our coffees and started consuming it. I want to ask her about her family as could not do so. 'Fuck you idiot, you are asking her about her parents, not the last time when she had sex' I told myself. I looked into her eyes as hers were too glint. I gathered the courage to ask her about it.

'So, you live with your parents?' I said.

'Yes, and a sister' She replied.

'Elder or Younger?'

'Younger'

I gave her an understanding nod.

'Have you travelled somewhere?' I said.

'Yeah, like Maharaja?'

'What's meant by that?'

'See, I have read an article, in which they have told 'travel like maharaja' do you want to read it.' she said.

'Sure' I said as she passed me three pages from her hand bag it was handwritten as I started reading it.

I read all the article in next few minutes given to me by Priyanka. I didn't understand a single word from it. 'Why Priyanka had given me to read it?' a question popped out in my mind. I looked up at her as she was busy with her cell-phone. I passed her the article back. It was like a Rajasthan people living like a Maharaja there.

'So, how was it? Did you like it?' she said.

I gave her an understanding nod as I had nothing to do else.

'Rohit, I want to talk to you about something' She said.

I gave her a 'speak' glance.

'Not now on my birthday'

'So, when is your birthday?' I said. 'And you're looking so serious what's so important?'

'Four days later' She said. 'I'm inviting you to my birthday on 24ᵗʰ November.'

I gave her an understanding nod as I thought 'what's wrong with her? Why is she so serious that she has to give me an exposition on her birthday?'

'So, when are you taking me to Rajasthan? Or not?' Priyanka asked.

'Now?' I screamed.

'Not now, after all we are friends lifelong you can take me any time after you get a job' she said.

I gave her a fake smile and got up from my chair getting back to my work. I was just wondering what's wrong with this girl.

3

I reached Priyanka's house on her birthday, it was 24ᵗʰ of November as she had said me earlier. I was there sharp at 7:20pm. I had brought a gift along with me. I had purchased her a golden wrist watch from Titan. There were lots of multifarious kinds of watches but I liked a particular one so I purchased it on my choice. I'm sure about that that Priyanka will like it too. I took a panoramatic view of Priyanka's home, it was radiant and too good. I really like these types of houses. I kept my gift on the gift table as Priyanka came towards me. I saw lots of hosts around us as if Priyanka was a celebrity and all people had come to take her photos and have autographs. I looked at Priyanka she was dressed in a pink colored top and blue shots. And was full of makeup on her face. She looked very beautiful like she had never before. If I say vulgarly she looked very *hot* in those togs. My eyes were now on her ears she had worn the pink earrings which looked like same like a diamond.

'Happy Birthday, Priyanka!' I said smiling at her. Her eyes said something to me.

'Thanks' She said in a shy voice.

'Rohit, I want to make you meet someone'

'Who?'

'My Parents' She said as I gave her a puzzled expression.

'Come…' She said as I interrupted her.

'If they don't bite, I'm ready' I said.

Priyanka hit me on my left shoulder smiling.

'Bitch' She said. 'Come on'

We both moved towards Priyanka's Parents. I looked at Priyanka's Parents the first time. They both were something different. I looked at her father, he looked like someone had raped him recently. He was so weak looking. Then my eyes moved towards her Mother. She was a bit okay but looked like... (I should not speak this) I thought over how can these two create so good? I don't know but I felt unsecured before Priyanka's parents.

'Dad, Mum, this is Rohit about whom I spoke to you my... I told you no!' She said as her parents looked at me as if I was going to kidnap them right now.

'*Hi, if I kidnap you what will I get? I don't want to run a prostitute shop*' I told myself. I gave a fake smile before them.

'Oh, so he is who you told us about?' Priyanka's dad said.

Her dad murmured something to her Mom. I was floored. '*Why this people are looking at me like that?*' I thought. I bend down to touch their feet as her dad bogged me. I accorded him a 'Namaste' glance.

'We both want to talk to you in timely later' Priyanka's Mom said.

I looked at Priyanka she gave me a shy smile 'What's wrong with this people, why are these behaving like this?' I puzzled.

'Mum, I want to talk to Rohit in my room upstairs. I want to talk personally with him with some prominent matter. If you don't mind can I...' Priyanka said as her Mom interrupted her.

'Sure, why not?' her Mom said as Priyanka took me towards her bedroom. I saw into Priyanka's eyes as they glint. I was really puzzled with obstinacy of these people. We soon reached Priyanka's room as she locked the room from inside. She turned towards her balcony as I followed her. I found her playing with some bunches of keys.

'I think, you have definitely not called me here to play with this bunch of keys. Can I know why are here?' I said.

'Rohit, I want to tell you something and ask too.' She said.

'What?'

'The thing is that, that….' She said as she was inarticulate before me.

'See, Rohit I don't know when and how but it happened suddenly when I saw you the first time. I know you will twig it. I don't want to lurk any more from you and from myself too.'

'What do you mean?' I said.

'I Love You!!!' She blunt.

The three words rattled me a lot. I flinched. I looked into her eyes as she too did not break any eye contact with me. I was just… a strong panic passed from my body. I started sweating. I had my own reason.

'Please, try to twig me. I only and mere pertain to you. I had told this to my parents too, that I love you and they too are agreed with it. So, they had asked you to meet them in timely later. They want to talk to you about my life. Will you support and step into my life?' she said as the droplets of tears roll down from my eyes. She thought that my answer was a 'yes' but I did not mean it really. I could not really control myself I sat down on the bed. My both hands were on my head. Priyanka ran towards me as she bends down to match my height. I was really unable to understand anything, At that time. This was only because I love someone else and I had promised her that I will stand by her, her whole life. Priyanka hugged me. I could not do anything. The imaged of me promising a girl flashed before my eyes. 'What have you done Priyanka, I did not accept this from you' I said to myself.

'Thanks Rohit, to step into my life!' she said as she was about to cry. 'Love you'

I kept quiet.

I remembered the six-month earlier period when I met Priya at a train platform and had a talk with her. I didn't know this talk will change into a promise that time. How can I tell Priyanka about this truth? I inarticulate. But at last what can I do, this truth was waiting for Priyanka.

6 MONTHS EARLIER

'Mumbai to Delhi' my Mom read the nameplate on the platform. I was seeing Priya for the last time. I don't know when I will get the next chance to see her again? She will be back in six months but I really don't know that how I could pass this six months without Priya? I, my Mom, Priya, Mr. and Ms. Sharma were with us on the platform. Mr. and Ms. Sharma were Priya's parents. I took a panoramatic view of the railway platform. The exact thing was me and Priya who loved each other like hell and can't live without each other. A worse thing had taken place that time that Mr. Sharma's Transfer had been done to Delhi. Her father worked as a software engineer in that Delhi Company. There was no any earning person in their house. They were four of them, Priya, her mother, her father and a tot with them, who was Priya's younger brother. They were going to return to Mumbai from Delhi after six months. I and Priya had intimacy between each other. Priya was a popsy girl. I met her in a shopping mall and then our families met each other. Soon they became very close to each other. Priya was looking very cute at that day at the platform. She wore red T-Shirt and blue jeans and looked sexually attractive. After all I know that she only pertains to me. But who the fuck will expound this into these bloody parents? It was a pesky task to do it. I myself felt timid to stand in front of my own parents, who will be tucked more efforts to say something in front of them. I looked at Priya as she held my right hand with her left. She stood right front of me.

'Look, that's it!' Ms. Sharma said in an excited voice manner as I saw that the Delhi train had arrived on its platform.

Priya accorded me a piece of paper. She put in my hand directly. I think the god had blessed me that she had given me this cheat in timely otherwise if my Mom had seen this then she had been definitely killed me.

I looked at my Mom she hugged Ms. Sharma and exchanged good-bye glances with Mr. Sharma. Mr. Sharma came forward towards me and placed his right hand on my shoulder. I suddenly touched his feet. I saw the tears in the eyes of Priya, she was contrite of going far apart from me. I too felt same for her.

'So, let's meet after six months Rekha!' Ms. Sharma said to my mother.

My mother gave her an understanding nod.

Priya disappeared from my eyes. The eyes were wet and the heart really cried loudly. Priya had went far from me now but she was still there Yes! She was. The piece of paper was still in my hand.

◆

I sat in my bedroom, this time the droplets rolled down from my eyes. I was almost down without Priya. I replenish with emotions, the emotions which brought tears from my eyes. My face was almost like toasties. I was blaming myself for being regardless while she was talking to me. 'You idiot, why was the fuck you not talked to her while she was there, and not feeling contrite' I scolded myself. I missed Priya a lot.

I trusted her a lot more than myself. I have very revere reverence in my mind regarding her. 'When will this six months pass out?' I thought.

I saw my Mom getting into my room.

'Rohit, you are looking lost?' she said 'What happen?'

'No, just feeling tired so….' I lied. She passed me a glassful of milk as she left the room. I remembered the piece of paper given by Priya. I had kept it in my left jeans pocket. I got up from my bed and brought the cheat to me. I don't understand that why she had given me this piece of paper, Priya always talk to me frankly. This paper had really had something….

Dear Rohit,

'Falling in love is every human being right' yours too, so you fell in love with me. I know you would be feeling a bit aloneness and poignant. You know how our life was languidly when we were together? Rohit, we are populace not to famous or something. I know Rohit I can understand you, you are too sad now no? I know! Why, because I'm not there, what do you think I'm not feeling sad? My nick is the same here. Rohit, we are totally matured now, and I think we understand our priorities now ourselves. I think and I mean it too that we should talk to our parents about our relationship. I will try here to talk to my Mom and dad and

expound them. After all it's our life who are the parents to step into it? No one can intervene us, in any ways. I only and only retain to you and you to me. We both love each other and that's it! I think that you totally acquiesce with me. And don't worry it's just a short time, it's just six months! A half year! Then we'll be together again like we were before. And one thing you don't fret about just take care of yourself. I'll retrace soon. I'll be calling you on each month's twenty-fourth because my Mom and dad has a prominent conference in office and none is in the house. Yes, my Mom will help my dad this six months. Or we'll be chatting on Facebook anytime, you already have my mail ID, better be online.

  I did not want to tell you all this on the platform because my parents were around. I'm really sorry about that. I know you have great reverence in your heart about me and I too have the same for you. So, six months are not more don't keep your mind molted for me. I'll be back soon, and do concentrate on your studies and shun talking with other girls rather than me. Promise me that you will not be involved with any other girl in my absence. I trust you that you will never do like that. But still now you have promised me that you will not. Okay bye for now!!! LOVE YOU!!!!

        Missing you,

         Priya.

 I re-folded the paper as it was and kept it down of my pillow. I was too glad, yes because of this letter. After reading it I felt like Priya was sitting beside me. I think I should meticulously care about myself first. A fly volitant on my nose. I hit my left hand on my nose as my nose was redden. 'I Love you too Priya' I said to myself mentally. I loved her like a hell and will be loving forever. I picked up a banana kept beside me in a fruit plate and started to pare it. I will not lose my faith on Priya still she comes back and be normal. And I have already promised her that I'll not interfere with any other girl rather than her. I got up from my bed as I moved towards my PC and logged into my Facebook account. I found a friend request from 'Ketan Sharma' it flashed on my screen. I really don't know that he knows me or not. But as I was in a glad mood I accepted the friend request. '*Friends*' it flashed.

'Mum, get me some snacks' I screamed.

♦

I wriggled as she un-hugged me and stood before me. Yeah, I was at last back in my present life from my past. Priyanka did not break any eye contact with me. I could not give her any exposition because I was not in that condition. I could not tell her about Priya at this stage. I didn't know why did Priyanka said I Love you and all that. I do not fell anything for her then why she feels for me.

'Come Rohit, let's meet my parents' She blunt.

I stared at her 'is this girl gone mad?' I said to myself. Why she likes me I'm already someone else's. 'Priyanka, there are thousands for boys in this world, then why only me?' I wanted to tell her. She brought her mouth close to mine. Yes, she was trying to kiss me. I pushed her back.

'What are you doing?' I said in a strong voice.

'Nor… Nothing' she said stammering as she caught my hand and brought me out of her room.

'Come let's meet my Mom and dad' she said in an excited voice as she brought me in the party hall. I found all populace around me. I found all the ladies wearing some different type of party wears. It was looking like its less-party more-fashion show. Priyanka was so excited as if her life had been doubled for three hundred years more.

'See, if you can see my parents somewhere!' She said. I really had no interest in her conversations now.

I shook my head regarding a 'no'.

I looked around everyone was just twiddling with each other. I didn't understand why and what this people talk to each other in parties? Priyanka caught my hand in a romantic mood. I did not mean it at all. I hate when she does so.

I shrugged my shoulders.

'See there are they' she said pointing towards the entrance door where they were standing with some hosts inviting them.

Priyanka took me towards them. Priyanka why are you disturbing them, they are greeting their prominent guests let them, don't disturb them' I wanted to say. But finally, I was before them.

'So, Priyanka what's the answer?' Priyanka's Mom asked.

'Mum, it's a *'Yes'*' Priyanka replied.

Priyanka's dad widely smiled at me as if I have offered him two packets of condoms.

'Priyanka, let's move to the dining hall' Priyanka's dad said.

'Sure'

Priyanka looked towards me and threw a 'shall-we-go' glance. I really don't want to go but I didn't have any other choice. I gave her a 'yes' glance.

We moved to the dining hall as we took our places, Priyanka besides me her parents right front to me. It was the 24 chairs dining table along with us four there were other people whom I didn't know. They were Priyanka's guest. Priyanka's Mom poured me some mango juice and passed me the glass. I gave her a fake smile. I looked at Priyanka as her eyes said something.... as if she pertains to me. I suddenly disconnected my attention towards Priyanka. I took a final big sip of that mango juice and finished it off. Priyanka's Mom and dad were beatific.

'Have juice beta' her dad offered.

'No uncle, thanks' I said in a soft and imperturbable voice.

'Mum, talk to Rohit about my life. He had said me a yes few minutes earlier' Priyanka begged.

When I gave her a 'yes'? I remembered. 'Aunty your daughter is lying, don't listen to her. I have not said a word' I wanted to say but…

Priyanka's Mom stared at me as if I was going to talk her for a long drive. I stared at her back.

'So, Rohit what does your father do?' she questioned.

'Aunty he is a businessman' I answered.

'And Mom?'

'She is a professor, English'

I leaned forward to catch some water as my heart beat fast answering Priyanka's Mom.

'My daughter loves you and you too love her, why don't you talk to your parents about it? We are thinking to come to your place next week to talk to your parents about the same. By the way you will talk care of Priyanka no?'

As I listened to it I got a sudden cuff. I placed the glass down. I looked up at Priyanka's Mom 'Aunty it's enough now you will kill me or what' I said mentally.

I kept quiet for few seconds.

'Su…Sure aunty' I said as I was inarticulate before them. I wanted to say 'no' I can't marry her but the condition made me to say 'yes' before them.

I don't understand why do the Indian parent interfere too much in their child's life? As if they don't have any other work to do. Doesn't it make a twaddle? I twig that they are the parents and all that, but interfering in their life so deeply is not so good. 'Some doctors should mend their minds one day' I thought.

'Can you pass me the glass please?' Priyanka's dad said.

'You fool, you don't have to give me a prescript, and I know what to do and what not.' I told him in my mind.

'Sure' I said as I passed him the glass.

I was in tense. Someone placed a hand on my shoulder. I looked up, it was Priyanka.

'Rohit, would you like to hung out somewhere?' She said.

'Where? And it's your birthday party. You should be here!' I said.

'Park' she replied.

'Sure' I said. I did not find any other word to say rather than 'sure'. Priyanka smiled at me. 'Who will transact the task of hanging out with this girl' I asked myself. I agreed to go out with Priyanka, obstinacy of her parents had changed, as if they want us both to be alone.

'Mum, how will if Rohit stays here for today?' Priyanka said.

This girl is definitely going to kill me, by falling into relationship. When I'm refusing the same relationship but I can't tell her the truth at this stage.

'Sure, we'll accommodate him to our guest room' her Mom replied.

'No Aunty, I have to go home today, can't stay here. Actually, some hosts are going to arrive at our place too so…. it's my parent's marriage anniversary I have to go' I lied.

Priyanka's dad gave me an understanding nod.

I shrugged my shoulders.

'Priyanka, we have to move to the party hall, some of our guests are waiting for us there, so please…' Priyanka's dad said.

'No dad, you have to give some time to your family too' Priyanka refused.

'Beta, please try to understand'

'Yeah, Priyanka you have to understand. Guests are waiting to see you. You should go' I said to myself mentally. Actually, I wanted to say to her.

'Okay then, I'll be there, but with Rohit.' Priyanka relented as they left the dining hall. I felt it like Raavan had left the Lanka.

Priyanka brought her hand close to mine and placed on mine. I closed my eyes slowly feeling tart. No romantic feeling or something. I slowly took my hand out of it and kept it aside.

Priyanka stared at me.

'What?' I said.

'What's wrong with you?' she questioned.

'Nothing'

'Then why don't you kiss me?'

That time I really felt that I'm in college and someone is making me rag. Yeah, that was true. A girl is making me kiss her.

I did not answer as I kept quiet.

'It's not prominent to kiss each and every girl. And I don't really understand that why do every girl likes to kiss' I thought.

'So, what is your aim' I said. I asked her so that I can change the atmosphere.

'An airhostess' She said.

Who the fuck had invented the policy 'airhostess' every girl I meet wants to be an airhostess as if they don't have any other work rather than it in the entire world. I mollify my anger and kept quiet.

'Good choice' I blunt. I really didn't have any interest in her becoming an airhostess. I said it only as a formality.

'And you?' She said.

I smiled at myself. I really do love my life. I want something from my life. Yeah, life gave me everything I need, I wanted my life to give me some more. I moved close to Priyanka.

'A Software Engineer' I replied.

As Priyanka heard the words 'Software Engineer' from my mouth she pooh-poohed. I twig that why everyone laughs at my aim; does it mean any jest or something?

'An Engineer is very funny' she said as she started laughing again.

Can somebody sort out that why everyone laughs at my aim every time I tell them my aim? Don't they have any other work to do at that time?

'Just shut-up OKAY' I said in a strong voice.

'I'm sorry, I was just…' Priyanka tighten her lips to control her laugh.

I stared regardless at Priyanka 'you shut your mouth, I shut my mind' I said to myself. And I really want to know that what was so fully to laugh at it?

Priyanka sat down on the chair she signed me to sit too. I sat down right beside to Priyanka.

'By the way, why a Software Engineer?' she questioned.

I smiled at myself. I think life gives everyone everything. My life had given me everything I want. But still I want more from my life. I looked into Priyanka's eyes and answered her.

'I want to develop my India. I want to make it strong in the IT field. I want the whole world should only and only use Indian Software's' I said.

'Interesting'

'By the way Priyanka, can I ask you a question?' I said.

'Sure' she agreed.

'What was so funny, to laugh at it, when I told you about my aim?'

Priyanka smiled at me. I noticed her smile. She leaned forward towards me.

'Look Rohit, frankly I hate Engineers. Yeah really, I do. They are so bore-guys'

'Why it this so'

'Rohit yaar, look at their lifestyles, no joy, no family, and no nothing only just work, work, and only work. They are always submerged under their work. Now take an example, look at their cloths style. You know their cloths are fixed. Always White shirt and black Pants and a bloody tie hanged around their neck. I mean does it mean any sense? No, No? You know the most threatening thing about them? Their big size glasses they look like Harry Potter is himself sitting and working. His wife must be also tired that when is he finishing his work and spending some time. Look like this are the Engineers. I feel them like, someone had put 50% discount sale sticker on them in Big Bazaar. I mean….'

I smiled at her. This time whole heartedly.

'Oh, so this is what you think about the engineers, it's good what you think' I said as she passed me the mango juice. I took a small sip and kept the glass down.

I want to end the rapport relationship between me and Priyanka. I want to tell her the truth!

'Priyanka, I want to tell you that….' I said as she interrupted me.

'Come on, let's go downstairs for the party'

I nodded.

We both moved downstairs as all the hosts looked at Priyanka and me. I don't know why they looked at me. I think I was with the birthday girl? I moved fro by her.

'Hey, where are you going?' Priyanka said

'Washroom' I lied as I was already mixed in the stuff of these hosts.

I would have think hereafter that I have to meet Priyanka or not? I really will have to cogitate about it. I moved to the washroom as I damped my hand with water to wash it. I soon got out of the washroom as a girlie came to me.

'Bhaiya, can you please find my parents?' she cried.

I sat down to match her height.

'What's your name, beta?' I said.

'Neha'

'Have you lost in the hall?'

She started crying again. I really could not control her.

'I'll find them out! First stop crying!' I said.

I thought over to take this little girl to Priyanka, what if Priyanka knows her? My mind vehemently took me to Priyanka. I stood front of her as her eyes rolled down towards the little girl.

'This little girl has lost her parents in this hall, do you know her?' I asked.

Priyanka looked at me and smiled. The smile said 'well-done-Rohit' to me. I suddenly broke down the eye contact.

'Neha, what are you doing here, your Mom is searching you, go to my room she is there' Priyanka said as the girl ran towards Priyanka's room.

'Do you know her' I said bringing the eye-contact back.

'My uncle's daughter' she replied.

I didn't say anything after that just a face smile was enough. Priyanka left me as I too was independent in the hall I met some of the guests which I had known. My father's friends were also present, but I didn't recognize them, they recognized me.

I found a void space in the middle of the hall as the song 'Teri Meri' from the film Bodyguard filled the hall. Soon the couples started dancing salsa. I had a belly laugh in my mind. I peered at Priyanka's dress from a distance. I think she had changed it off. Priyanka came closer to me.

'Have you changed your dress' I questioned.

'Why? Don't you like it? I'm looking beautiful no?' She said.

'Yes' I replied.

I was bored in this party as there were oodles of place available outside this party hall, hotels, Parks, etc. What was there in this boring party?

'Can we hang out, Park or something…?' I said as the party had got over and there was nothing else to do.

'Yeah, sure but I have to ask my parents' She said.

'Then ask No' I said as she moved towards her parents.

I had no interest going out with Priyanka I just want to relax myself. I kept staring placard pasted on the wall 'a lady with rose, her breast almost visible' I felt a bit somnolent in the party hall.

'Rohit, let's go' Priyanka called.

I gave her an understanding nod.

♦

We reached Shivaji Park soon. Priyanka's driver had left us to the park and left. My face was almost like toasties. 'Can we sit there' I said pointing towards the sitter. 'You idiot, you are most silly and you are a slacker' I said to myself.

'Yeah, sure' Priyanka said as we sat down.

I want to start the conversation with Priyanka that I'm not interested in her at all. I want to tell her that I love someone else and I don't want to keep any relation after this.

Just a friend is fine. But a life-partner is something worse. I want to tell her that when she proposed me it poignant me too much.

'Priyanka, I want to tell you something' I started.

'What?'

'Priyanka, the thing is that that I'm…'

'Leave all that, do you know the new film is releasing this weekend?' She interrupted 'Can we watch it?'

I nodded my neck regarding a 'no' but Priyanka thought it was a 'yes' from me.

I think, girls are world intelligent topic-switchers, why the fuck they have to change the topic when the person is talking something very important. I don't understand why they do so.

'Will you like to watch it with me?' Priyanka said.

'Sure' I said as I didn't find any other word to say.

I shrugged my shoulders.

I looked at Priyanka. She was busy adjusting her hairs in a very good way. I wondered if I have those beautiful hairs.

'Priyanka, don't laugh at my aim hence-forth' I dissuade.

4

I clicked login as I logged in into my G-Mail account. I have to mail my oldest and nearest friend Sam. His name was actually Samartha Obiroi but lovingly (at college time) we all his friends called him as Sam. We both were childhood friends as we studied together till eighth grade as Sam went to Kolhapur and settled down there. We had not met for past two and a half years. We both did our each and every work in intimity and clandestine. We had a deep intimacy between us both. I used to share each and every thing with him. He was too radiant with his studies, today I remember after two and a half years. I will like to compose a mail to Sam and if possible converse to him secretly.

To: sam313fighters@yahoo.com
From: rohitdeshpande348@gmail.com
Subject: A friend in need is friend indeed.

Dear Sam,

Today I'm composing this mail to you because of two reasons…

1.) My life is in complete mess.
2.) I miss you here in Mumbai.

Samartha my life is in complete mess. I was trying to mollify myself but I can't be successful into that. I have shroud this matter from you so long. But I need someone to share it. I have to tell you now. I don't want to keep you in murk more. You know that I'm your crany and you'll help me out from this. I'm inadvertent in my studies. I'm inarticulate before my problem. I know you'll be completely busy in your work but I need your help not as a friend but as my own bother. I know that you'll revel on me and try to understand me as your own brother. I'm feeling like whole world is my foe. I know you can understand my problem. Retore me.

Regards,
Rohit.

I clicked the 'Send' button as a message flashed 'Your E-Mail has been successfully send'. I shoot him another detailed info mail. I got up from front of my PC as I went straight towards Kitchen. I felt too hungry. I really want something to eat.

'Mom, what's the Snack' I Said.

'Chocolate Cake' Replied Mom.

I moved towards the fridge and took out one piece of chocolate cake. The next few minutes went attacking on the cake silently. I really don't understand that why do chocolate cakes have so sweet taste. Why do not vegetables have the same? I finished the chocolate cake and moved towards my bedroom. I laid down on the bed as I took out my cell phone. A new message was flashed. It was from Priyanka. I opened the inbox.

HOW WAS THE DAY TODAY?
I HOPE IT WAS FRESH,
HOW WAS THE LOVE TODAY?

I HOPE SWEET – I LOVE YOU!

I deleted the useless message from my inbox as a new one flashed onto the screen.

'MEET ME TOMMOROW AT
11:30 PM AT SHIVAJI PARK...

Why this girl had called me to Shivaji Park tomorrow? I buried the thought into my mind as I sat on my PC again as I had nothing work to do. I saw the Priya was online, I entered the chat room.

Loverohit: Hey…!!!
DancingPriya: Hey… ☺
Loverohit: How come you are online today?
DancingPriya: Time Pass!
Loverohit: Priya, one and a half month had passed away, and you don't have time to at least call me once a week?
DancingPriya: I'm sorry baby, I was just busy with my work.
Loverohit: Leave all that. Tell me, how are you???
DancingPriya: ☺☺☺

Her smile meant whole world to me as she smiles one or twice a year.

Loverohit: So, when are you going to return to Mumbai?
DancingPriya: In one week you and I will be in one room, guess why?
Loverohit: Very cheap Priya, but how come? You were going to come back after six month's no?
DancingPriya: Yeah, or transfer is preponed, so meet you soon.

The gladness in my mind was full, of which I can't handle it a bit. Meeting Priya soon earlier is fun. I'm greatly glad.

Loverohit: ☺☺☺☺ Yheppp!
DancingPriya: I hope you have kept my promise? Yeah.

I did not answer for few seconds.

DancingPriya: Rohit, are you there?
Loverohit: ☺☺
DancingPriya: I hope you had kept my promise?
Loverohit: Yeah! I have.

How could I tell Priya about Priyanka? She would have definitely killed me if I had done so.

Loverohit: Priya, have you done my secret work?
DancingPriya: Of Course.
Loverohit: Thanks, I really want to kiss you!!! ♥ ♥ ♥

I could have definitely like if I could have got a kiss now!

DancingPriya: Kiss! Kiss! Kiss! Kiss!
Loverohit: ☺☺☺
DancingPriya: Can we chat later? My Parents are around!
Loverohit: ☹☹☹
Loverohit: Love You!!!
DancingPriya: Love you too…
Loverohit: Ba...Bye!!!

♦

I reached Shivaji Park at 11:35 am. I saw Priyanka stood near the statue of the lady. I went close to her as she noticed me. She smiled at me. I didn't pay more attention towards her. I gloat at her. She wore red T-shirt printed 'KISS' on it and a dark greenish jean. I don't understand that why girls are so interested in such a modish fashionable tog? No one is going to make a placard of it and going to paste outside the Government toilets. Can't they live like populance? I presume they should do so.

'So, why have you called me here?' I said.

'Just like that, I want to talk to you. Why? I can't call you?' Priyanka blunt.

'Go and fuck your 'Just like that' somewhere. You are calling me as if I am a A/c repairer' I want to say.

I shook my head.

I heard a din from a long distance. Priyanka caught my right hand and took me towards an empty place where I could not find a single fly. 'Why had this girl brought me here?' I thought.

'What are we doing here?' I inquired.

'Can we kiss?' Priyanka said.

'What'

Someone had said a true sentence. 'Understanding girls is too difficult'

'Why do you have any problem? Why can't we? Priyanka said.

'No!' I said 'I mean you can but kiss me on my cheeks for now'

Priyanka smiled at me.

She grabbed my shirt as she pulled me towards her. Priyanka leaned forward to kiss me. She had successfully placed her wet lips kiss on my left cheek. 'I'm sorry Priya' I said to myself mentally. I really should not do this at all.

'So, how do you feel?' Priyanka questioned.

I stared at her as if she had ruined my respect totally. I stared at her few more seconds.

Priyanka soft slapped my cheeks with her right hand.

'Rohit? Where have you lost?' She said. 'How do you feel?'

I shrugged my shoulders.

'Good!' I said as I moved.

We moved out of the park. Priyanka had done her work. Now what's the work was? Walking by, we reached a movie theater. I stared at a billposter on the wall. The picture said 'Enjoy the 3D experience of an adult movie'. I saw Priyanka with her cell phone. She was like messaging someone.

'What are you messaging?' I said.

She kept quite as had not got any answer from her. I stared at her in a puzzled way. 'I should tell her about everything about my life. It's the right time' I thought.

'Priyanka, I want to tell you something!' I said.

'What?'

I sniffed in.

'I can't be in this relationship anymore!'

'In Which... What Relation... What?'

'No, nothing' I said.

This time I had totally lost my confidence and courage. She was happy being in this relationship. If I tell her she would break down. But what to do now or another day I have to tell her!!!!

◆

I sat on my bench studying Geometry gingerly. I saw professor Pradhan entering the classroom. I didn't pay more attention towards him and started doing my own work. My mind had got turmoil, why professor had entered the class during the recess time? I walked towards him as I looked up at him. He wore a white shirt and a black formal pants and was in trim togs. He took his place on my front bencher's desk.

'Can I talk to you something?' Professor Pradhan Said turning back towards me.

Was this something so important? I asked myself. I retreat a little on my sitter.

I wriggled.

'Sure, professor' I said.

'Rohit, your grades are decreasing day by day, you are not able to concentrate on your study works. Is anything wrong???' He said.

Yeah, there is something wrong with me, because of which I cannot concentrate on my study works. 'But how could I converse Professor Pradhan about Priyanka?' I thought.

'No, Nothing Wrong Professor' I replied.

He stared at me as if I have offered him a bottle of vodka.

'Look Rohit, I don't know that why have you lie me few minutes ago, but I know that you are the splendent student of this class. If there is any problem you can share it with me. I can help you to sort it out.'

Yeah, it's like handling over my porn collection to you. (Duffer Professor I can't really share this with you)

I shook my head in no option way.

'See you are a very adroil student and I tell you don't mix with these all students so much. These all people have come near you to bag you down. This world is filled with very evil thoughts today' He said. 'Can I get your rough notebook and a pen please?'

I handed him a rough notebook and a pen as he drawn some diagram.

'Can you see the Cube Rohit' He said.

'Yeah'

'Suppose that this cube is your thought area' He said as he overwritten the cube approximately six times.

'And the line going outside it is the extra thought.' He said overwriting the line once.

'So, you have to think in that way. Always think out of box' He said 'So, are you follow my out-of-box thinking policy?'

I did understand what he said and I totally agreed with it.

'Sure, I will Professor' I said.

We both exchanged 'okay' glances.

5

One Week Later…

'**R**ohit, come down for your dinner' my mom screamed as I got up from my bed. I kept my cell-phone on the computer and plugged the charging in. I moved down towards our dining table.

'Did, you wash your hands?' Dad said.

I nodded.

I don't understand why do every Indian parent is so interested in their children matter's? Don't they have any other work to do? I gingerly saw at the jar of the mango juice as I heard the clink. I don't really know from where it came and all that… I saw a Cyclops ring in my mom's right hand. Has she made a new one? I asked myself. The diamond, it was splendent and a Simon-Pure one.

I shrugged my shoulders.

'Mom, have you made the new ring for yourself?' I inquired.

Mom smiled at me.

Mom pushed my plate towards me. I saw mom serving the food for my dad and herself. I truly want to ask her that why she had served me first but I repressed myself. 'Imperturbable do the same' my mind poked.

'So, Rohit, how are your studied going?' Dad asked.

I kept quiet for few seconds.

'Fine, almost all the portion is covered, only the preparation work is lagging back by us' I said in a soft voice.

'Good then'

My eyes turned towards my dad, looking more serious than never before. I would like to ask him that why he was so serious? This thing was weightless, I neglected it. 'Idiot, thinking on dad's seriousness is useless, let's concentrate on your dinner.' I said to myself.

I stated at the bowl of *gullab jaamun* in my mom's plate as if I want them to eat as early as I could. I saw the goatsucker like flying outside. It was volitant as I thought it was a honeybee.

'Do you need more rice, beta Rohit?' Mom said.

I shook my head.

I heard someone knocked the door. I didn't paid attention towards it. 'Who the hell had arrived too late now?' I thought. Again, someone who was out the door knocked, this time a bit louder.

'I'll see' I said as I got up from my chair. I moved towards the main door. My eyes had replete sleep into them. I opened the main door in that sleepy mood as I saw the impossible thing in front of my eyes. I saw Priya and her Mom standing front of me. The sleep in my eyes was totally flied off somewhere. I could not control my gladness any more.

I shrugged my shoulders.

'Priya!!!' I said in excitement.

She smiled at me. Her smile meant whole world to me as I could see it again after so long.

'How are you doing beta?' Priya's Mom said.

'Fine, Aunty!' I said. 'But how come you arrived today?'

'Err… are you going to keep us here only or take us in?' Priya said.

'Oh! Please' I said as they entered. They both took their places on the hall's sofa as my mom and dad arrived in the hall. I was too glad to see Priya before me as I repressed gladness and stood quietly simply staring at Priya's face.

'Ms. Sharma, when have you arrived in Mumbai?' My mom questioned.

'Just now, Pradip dropped here and he left for home' Priya's Mom said. Pradip was Priya's Dad (Mr. Sharma).

My mom gave her an understanding nod.

'Aunty, have dinner with us no!' I said finally looking at Priya's mom rather that Priya's face.

'No, Beta we have already had our dinner. Thank You!' She replied.

I smiled at her.

'Actually, Priya forced me to visit here as she was missing Rohit a lot. She said she wants to stay here for a night tonight. If you don't mind can she…'

'Are… why not let her stay here tonight' my mom interrupted.

I looked at Priya as I gave her an 'OK' glance.

'So, I think I should leave now!' Ms. Sharma said.

'Why Aunty? Wait no!' I said.

'No beta, it's getting very late' Priya's Mom said getting up from the sofa.

I checked my wrist watch. Yes, it was 11:45 PM, it was already too late night.

'Shall I drop you home?' Dad said.

We all stood up and walked towards the main door. Once we were outside the house I touched my will be 'mother-in-law's' feet.

'No Thanks, I'll take Cab!' She said as she left.

Mom and Dad were back to kitchen. I begged Priya to have dinner with us as she had only one answer with her 'No-Please'.

I vehemently brought her towards our kitchen as she too had interest to have dinner with us. My Mom stared as I looked up at her. Her eyes said 'Where-Will-Priya-Stay-

Tonight?' 'Don't worry mom   I will accommodate her in my room' I wanted to say. In next few minutes we all finished our dinner as I got up from my chair.

'Priya, you can sleep in the room next to Rohit's room upstairs' Mom blunt.

Priya gave my mom a 'yes' nod.

We both moved towards our respected rooms upstairs. ('Towards our respected room' was just for few more minutes. I was going to grab Priya to my room later.)

It was about 1:00 PM late night. I got up from my bed as I silently opened my rooms door. The door was very old that it made noise when I open it. I gingerly opened the door focusing it didn't made any noise. I didn't need to knock Priya's door as I had already told her that I'm going to enter her room at any time later after dinner. I entered her room as she sat up on her bed her back towards me. I moved in front of her as she made a long noise. I rushed towards as I pressed her mouth with my right hand.

'Relax Priya, it's me!!!' I said.

She sniffed in.

She playfully hit her left hand on my right shoulder. I released her mouth as she caught my hand and took me towards my room. Finally, we were into my room.

I caught her shoulders and pushed her onto the wall. I came close to her. What to do next? I cogitate. 'What will be the best thing rather than ask her about her journey' I Thought. I was indecipherable about where to do an inception. I cogitate about it gingerly.

'So, Madam, how was your journey?' I questioned.

She kept quiet for few seconds.

'Fine and interesting' She replied.

I gave her an understanding nod.

'Priya, I really missed you a lot' I said. 'Promise me you will not let me alone again!'

She saw into my eyes as I did the same. We both didn't broke our eye contact for few minutes. She caught my right hand with her left. I looked at her lips. She broke down the eye contact with me.

'I Promise you Rohit, I'll never' She said.

'Come on let's sleep!' She said pushing me back.

I kept quiet.

Priya moved towards my bed.

'Shall we join the beds?' I said.

'Sure'

We both joined both the beds and then sat up. I want to do something clandestine with Priya. I had met her after a long time. I would like to kiss her if I really get to. I accorded her 'what-to-do-now' glance. Priya took me towards my balcony as I thought over to talk to Priya more. As we stepped the balcony the wind felt too romantic.

'So, how are you?' I said.

'Fine and you?' Priya requisitioned.

'Fine' I said. 'I completely repose you'

'I too and I know you will never mug on my faith. You will not no?' Priya said in a childish way.

'I will' I said.

'What???'

'Not' I said. 'I mean I will not!'

Priya punched on my hand playfully as I took her into my arms. I noticed her, she wore extra modish togs and looked beddable. I learned over to kiss her. I caught her both hands and pushed her along the balcony grill. I didn't know what I was doing. I slowly brought my mouth towards her as she pushed me back.

'Rohit, what are you doing? Your parents are downstairs!'

'They won't come up'

'Rohit Please!!!'

'Priya, Please, I've not met you for a long time at least let me kiss today'

'You love me no?'

'More than myself' I said. 'Priya Please'

'Ok but once' Priya Relented.

She closed her eyes as I brought my mouth close to her right cheek. The wind bowled as it brought romance with it. Firstly, I kissed her right cheek, then her left and finally, her forehead. Priya opened her eyes and stared at mine. She hugged me tight as I hugged her back.

'Rohit, lets sleep, it's too late' She said.

I made my hug a bit tighter as I felt that my Priya was back with me. Truly, I felt ashamed of myself. 'Priya had faith on me, what will I tell her about Priyanka.' I thought. I was floored.

♦

I sat up on my bed adjusting my hairs as Priya slept right beside me. I saw her hairs were on the face as I tugged it behind her ears. I brought my right hand towards her right eye as I slowly half opened her eyes. She smiled at me. Priya looks more beautiful when she is asleep.

I shrugged my shoulders.

'Good Morning!' I said.

'Where are you going?' Priya questioned.

'Nowhere, Why?'

'Then why have you worn this party wears?'

'Only for you, you like me in this togs.'

She threw me a flying kiss as it softly landed on my lips.

'So Sweet! You wore then just for me?'

'Ok! Leave all this and get ready?'

'Why where are we going?'

'Madam, I think you don't want your breakfast?'

She smiled at me as I smiled at her back. Her smile was inadequate for me for my whole life. If I get to, I would smile at her my whole life. 'Well, beta it's only the inception, I have planned a date for her today' I told myself. I had a great aroma from Priya's body. Well, there is a fact that, when girls get up from the bed they have a great fragrance.

'Very funny!' She said as she threw me a pillow. I like that play.

My cell-phone rang as it had ballad as the ringtone. I unplugged the charger as I grabbed it form my computer table. The screen printed 'SAM' in bold letters. I had a different beatitude on my face that time.

'Excuse me, Priya' I said as I moved out in the balcony.

'Sam? How come you called me today?' I said.

'Just I was checking my mails and found yours' He replied.

I got a bit panicked. I looked back at Priya.

'So, you have this mess before you and you have no answer for Priya. Right?' Sam Said. I had shoot him another mail telling him about Priyanka earlier.

'Well Priya is with me now. She returned back yesterday' I said.

'What?'

I was floored, that to whom I would give more priority. Sam to whom I was talking at this stage or Priya who had just called me inside. (Priya had called me inside by hand gestures) I would like to choose option two. At least I would get a change to have sex with Priya! (Just Joking)

'So, that's a pesky task to handle' Sam said.

I kept silent for few seconds.

'Rohit! Rohit!' I heard a long scream as I suddenly looked behind.

'Sam I'll call you back later, my problem is calling me' I said.

'Sure' Sam said as we hung up.

I stepped into my room as Priya sat upon the bed. I noticed a different anger in her eyes as it was not immitigable. I sat next to her.

'Rohit, have you...' She said as she stopped 'leave it it's no use talking to you.'

'What have I done?'

'No, don't talk to me, go talk to your friends'

'Okay, I'm sorry' I meliorate her. She looked more beautiful, as she was already a beautiful popsy (of course only for me)

I sniffed in.

We both moved down towards the kitchen for breakfast. I really had no interest in taking my breakfast. I was about to disannul it, but stopped because of Priya. We all took our places as I saw Priya tugging her hairs behind her right ear. I like that movement she does it.

'Good Morning beta' Mom said looking at me then at Priya.

'Good Morning Aunty' Priya said.

I didn't say anything.

We all started having our breakfast. I saw at Priya, her eyes glint and of course she was a radiant girl too. I then thought over my bloody situation. How could I expound Priya about Priyanka? I noticed Priya picking up the water jar as I preclude her and passed her the jar.

'Thanks'

I heard my mobile phone ringing in as I ran into my room. The cell phone flashed 'SAM' in bold and capital letters. I accepted the call.

'Can you meet me now at Padma Park?' Sam Questioned.

I kept quiet for few seconds.

'I'm going for my aunt's place for 2 weeks so...' I said. 'Sure, I will'

I really don't know why Sam had called me there at this stage. I was floored at his talk. I kept down the cell phone and sniffed in.

♦

I stepped into Padma Park. Sam had already informed me to wait near the statue. I did the same I saw Sam entering the park after few minutes. I was finally seeing him after a long time, but nothing had changed into him. I stared at him as he came closer and closer to me. I noticed his hairs standing straight upwards, hope this was his new hair style. Seriously I really didn't like him making this type of hair styles. 'Beta you are not Mr. Bean to do so, you are an ordinary boy who cannot handle his girlfriends' I told myself. I grinned at my own joke. Sam came closer and closer to me as in few seconds he was right front of me. The smell of '*Axe chocolate*' filled my nose.

'How are you?' I said as I raised my hand.

'I'm good, what about you?' he said shaking hands with me.

'Good, Pretty good actually!'

We both looked into each other's eyes. We had smiles on our faces. We hugged. Our friendship made us cry.

'Let's have a sit!' I said.

We sat on the bench as my cell phone played SMS tone. I brought out my cell phone from my pocket and jumped to the inbox. The senders name flashed 'Priya'. I opened the message. I don't understand why girls are so interested in sending messages.

HOPE YOUR MEETING GOES SWEET,
HOPE WE BOTH CAN REALLY TWEET.

I smiled at the message as I placed my cell phone down.

'So, you really understood my problem?' I questioned.

Sam nodded.

'So how can I get rid on this?'

'Simple' Sam simply said.

'How?' I said.

I was really excited to hear my problems solution.

'Tell her that you don't love her. Simple!' Sam said.

'Simple? Have you totally lost it?' I said.

I was really not satisfied by his answer and I was floored too. I kept quiet for few seconds. I was going to say 'But…' but stopped mid-sentence.

'Priyanka will never say no to this' Sam said.

'Sam, you really don't know her, she is Priyanka Mehta not Priyanka Chopra to understand every male animal like us'

'What?' Sam Screamed.

'What?'

'What did you say? Priyanka Mehta! Right?' Sam said.

'Ha, then?'

'Is she from Andheri east?' Sam questioned.

'Yes, but how did you know?' I floored.

Sam seemed somewhat down. I don't know why but when I spoke out Priyanka's name I saw a different fire in his eyes. I really want to know what was going on. Sam suddenly got up from his seat. I followed him.

'What happen Sam?' I said.

'Rohit, I think we should leave now!' Sam said as he leaned over to leave.

I caught his right hand and pulled him back.

'Eye Contact' I said. 'Something is wrong, and you are hiding it from me'

'Nothing'

'Dude, I know you from so long, you can't lie me' I said 'What is it?'

'Do you want to listen the truth?' Sam said.

I stared at him.

'She was my first…' he stopped mid-sentence.

'Say it Sam' I said 'First…?'

'Girlfriend'

I floored.

'You guys aren't in a relationship now?' I questioned.

'We had a breakup.' Sam said.

'What? Are you serious?' I said in a little louder voice. 'How?'

'Listen, so the story was' he started.

8 Months Earlier…

I sat on my computer table playing PC games. I don't really know what the hell was going to happen with me few minutes later.

'Bhaiya, Bhaiya', Susmita screamed loud from downstairs.

Susmita was my sister to whom I loved like a hell and was very close to her. Priyanka didn't know about Susmita so much because Susmita lives with her uncle and aunt in Washington DC (USA). She had landed India for her holiday weekends. She is my real sister but my parent's fights made her fro from me.

'What?' I screamed back as I got up from my chair. I moved downstairs.

I saw Priyanka entering my house. Mine and Priyanka's families were so close that they could exchange their house between themselves. I begged Priyanka to come to my bedchamber as we both sat onto my soft bed. I had a very 'something, something' talk with Priyanka. We both soon came downstairs as there was our dinner served.

'Priyanka, sit' Mom said.

Priyanka smiled at my mother and had her seat on the dining table.

I threw my mom a loving kiss.

We all started our dinner as my mom have very joyful talk with all of us. I really don't know why had she did it but I know one thing that she wants us both to stay happy. (Love you MOM)

'Do you love each other?' Mom suddenly questioned as we were busy having our dinner.

Silence filled all over the kitchen room. Only the sound of the fan rotating was noticeable. I don't know why did mom asked this question suddenly now. Some Indian parents decide their children future plans when they are born.

'Priyanka beta, say no, do you love Sam?' Mom dropped another bomb.

'Of Course!' Priyanka said in a shy way.

'You?' Mom said looking towards me.

'More than myself' I replied.

All of them resumed their minds into the plates. 'What the pleasant day it is, I got known to my future life partner.' I told myself.

My face had a smile.

Priyanka noticed me as she too smiled at me. We both finished our dinner as we were at our backyard garden. We both stood on the grass in our garden as the wind made our mood romantic. We both stared at each other as we did not break down the eye contact. Priyanka had tears into her eyes as I held her close to me. I hugged her as the wind passed through which said '*lovers don't need any support of their minds, heart does its work*'

Present day.

'And then two days later…' Sam stopped mid-sentence.

'What after two days Sam?' I suddenly questioned.

'No, let it go Rohit!' Sam said. 'I really can't…'

'No, you have to tell me!' I blunt. 'Tell me what is it?'

2 Days Later…

We both were in my bedroom, chit chatting with each other. We had a chocolate cake which we ate with the same spoon. I had no intention of implying anything else rather eating my cake.

'Can I kiss you' Priyanka said.

'Of course, not' I replied.

She smiled at me.

She brought her mouth close to me as I pushed her back.

'Are you crazy?' I questioned. 'Our Parents are downstairs'

'What will they do?'

'No, I can't'

'Please Sam!'

'No'

She again brought her mouth close to mine as I pushed her back. This time a bit forcefully.

'What's wrong with you? Why are you behaving like you are a stranger to me. And why are you pushing me back?'

Actually, I was in some tension about my sister. She had made a mistake and that was bothering me so much. My mind was actually not at its place.

She came close to me again.

Slap!

I treated her with a slap.

'Sam what's wrong with you? How could you even dare to slap me?' she said as I had already done a mistake.

'I had just asked you to kiss me not killing yourself or something' she said.

'I'm sorr…' I said as she interrupted me.

'This shows your love! That is how much you love me?'

'No, Priyanka you are getting me wrong!' I said. 'Let me explain'

'There is nothing to explain now Sam. It's over!!!'

'I did not mean that Priyanka, listen to me…' I said as she had already left my bedchamber.

Present Day…

'So, that's the truth ha?' I said as I noticed tears into Sam's eyes.

'From that day, we haven't meet each other and not even talked' Sam said in a crying voice.

I had a belly laugh.

'I'm sorry...' I said.

'You think that's the joke?' Sam questioned.

I was ashamed with myself. Sam and I kept silent for few minutes. I was totally puzzled with what Sam had told me. But I understood somewhat and I was in a condition which can fully fuck off my story.

'Then, why Priyanka proposed me that day?' I questioned.

Sam kept quiet.

I really don't understand that why this girl has to propose me. She already had a happy love life and left her love for only just a kiss? What's the big deal with the kiss? If I would be there I would definitely have kissed Priyanka first. I know that Sam is a shy kind of boy. He must have felt ashamed of all that, but Priyanka would not be so rude. For a single kiss, she is ready to let go her future love-life.

I brought out my cell-phone from my right jeans pocket as I opened my contact list. I typed 'P' in the search box as it flashed 'Priyanka' first. I then pressed the call button as Sam peeped into my cell phone and took it off my hands.

'Don't call her, it's of no use!' Sam said.

'Sam, don't be silly, I want to ask her that why she did so. And after all it's your life. I have to do it' I said.

'Please don't!' Sam begged.

'I will'

'Please, listen to me, this is not going to be solved on the cell-phone. When you will meet her the next time, then talk to her' Sam said.

I stared at Sam for few minutes.

'You still love her?' I said.

'More than myself' Sam replied.

I really felt romantic at this stage. When the girl already left, the boy still loves her. That called true love.

I kept the cell-phone down at its original place and sniffed in. I was really proud of my friend and proud of myself too for having such a nice friend.

'So, what about Priya? How is she?' Sam inquired.

'Fine, but I think I have to give her more time, spend some time with her'

Sam gave me an understanding nod.

'Finally, I got rid of my problem, I'll say no to Priyanka as she is yours and forever will be yours' I said.

Sam finally smiled. I was waiting for this smile from a long time.

I heard Sam's cell-phone ringing into his pocket as he took it out. It flashed 'MOM' on the screen. Sam accepted the call.

'What…I will… Yes…'

I saw Sam talking to his mom as if she was his girlfriend.

'No, No…. I'll definitely reach there… yeah… sure…'

Sam kept his cell-phone down.

'What happen?' I questioned.

'I have to go now'

'Why?'

'Mom has some work in her office, and just I have to help her out' Sam said.

'Sure then, you can' I said as Sam got up from his seat. 'So, when we meeting again?'

'Soon! You have to talk to Priyanka now!'

I smiled at him.

I had received a letter from Radhika. Radhika was my elder sister 'Radhika Didi' I should say but I call her by her name. She had send me the letter one year later after she had left us for her work. Why she had written me a letter now. I got floored.

Dear Rohit,

I could not call you because of these all things are not told on the mobile phones. I want to express my feeling about you and Priya. I know you love Priya and Priya too loves you like a hell and I totally agree with it. I have just written you today because I want to tell you something really important. I know you will feel a bit low, but I have to tell you all this stuff. But before that tell me how you are? And how is your health and how is Priya there? I know she had returned from Delhi. We met on the station that day.

I know you are in love and all that, and that too in this age. I totally agree with it, this is the age to fall in love. But I want to warn you about something. Look don't have sex so early, because it affects later. As I told you, that I met Priya on the station. We had a talk about her family liking you. She said they do like you but... but what about our parents Rohit? What will they say? You don't know all this but I do. I had a phone call from mom, days ago in which she had told you to stay off Priya. She warned me to tell you and bring you on the right path. I do know and understand that you are feeling bad at this stage. I have told all this to Priya but, I don't know that she had told you or not. And please, please don't discuss this with mom and dad, till I come. Just keep quiet. I'm returning a year later to

Mumbai, so not more days. Will sit and solve the mess. Love you a lot my dear brother.

Regards and love to Priya too. Love you!!!

Lovingly sister,

Radhika

I refolded the letter as I kept it down of my pillow. I was thinking why Priya had not told me about all this stuff? I was confused, what was the big fuss of our parents to interfere in our life. I laid down onto my bed as I closed my eyes. My eyes brought two things in front of me at this stage. Firstly, I and Priya were alone in our bedroom as no one else was in our house. I went close to her as I kissed her lips. My hand slowly touched her as we kissed. And secondly, Priya hiding a thing from me as it can change and destroy our whole life. So, which one should I take as real? The first one in which Priya is with me. Or the Second in which Priya is not with me. I prefer to select the first one as I know Priya would never break my trust. She will never.

I sniffed in as I opened my eyes. Only I could see was a rotating fan and the silence filled my room with all the emotions. I know Priya has loads faith in me rather than my friends, relatives, mom and dad.

'But, why not Priya told me about this?' I questioned myself. 'Does she really don't care about me?' 'Or she does?' Many questions popped into my mind.

I kept quiet for few minutes thinking all the way about Priya. I heard a knock onto my door as I got up to open it.

'Mom?' I said. It was my Mom on the door.

She kept quiet for few seconds.

'Rohit, we are going for a birthday party' she said entering my room.

I gave her an understanding nod.

'Get ready fast, we are leaving now' she said.

I didn't say anything as I didn't want to talk to her at all.

She mom left my room saying 'Get ready fast' as I did not pay more attention. I laid down on my bed thinking 'When will I talk to Priya about this?'

6

'What the fuck is this?' Is this an exercise or a whole da'am book to write down?' I said to myself. I sat completing my science and technology notes in my classroom. I had borrowed Chetan's notes as he had to visit Varanasi, because of some of his family problems. I had just begged him that tell me what the hell had happen, but he had only one single fucking answer 'Nothing, it's just a family problem' as if he didn't have any other answer to tell me. I noticed professor Pradhan entering the classroom. He had his tablet into his right hand and the laptop bag hung around his neck. I thought as if he was going to show us some educational programs, which I really hate a lot. He placed his all the belonging on the table and sat down into his chair. I didn't pay more attention towards him and started doing my work.

I soon remembered the 'out-of-box' policy discussed between me and professor Pradhan.

'Rohit, where were you yesterday?' professor said in a husky voice.

I really had no answer to answer professor Pradhan. What will I tell him? 'I'll tell him that I had spent my whole day with my girlfriend?' I questioned myself.

'I was sick sir' I lied.

'How are you feeling today?' Professor said.

'Fine, Professor'

As soon as I said 'Fine, professor' he buried his face into his tablet as if he was burring a dead body into ground. As he buried his face into his tablet I could see the full moon day. I thought if there was a *Pornima* today! I grinned at my own joke. I saw Priyanka entering the class as she had some of the notebook into her hand. She noticed me as I paid my full attention towards her. I really had no interest into her. I noticed her only because I had to help my friend, Sam. She moved towards her place as she dropped down her notebooks on her bench. She signed me to come out of the class as she moved out. I followed her outside the classroom. I thought she was…. She stood before me.

She smiled at me.

'Where were you yesterday?' Priyanka questioned as she caught my hand. I hate it when she does that.

'I was sick'

'What? How are you now?'

'Fine'

I saw a girl coming towards Priyanka. She had biology notebook into her hand.

'Priyanka, how did you did this concept...' the girl said pointing on the pages of the notebook.

'Simple…' Priyanka started explaining.

I heard their *Ramayana* few more minutes as I learned over to move towards my classroom.

'Wait… Where are you going?' Priyanka said.

'Class'

'Why?'

'I have some notes to complete, and I have to complete them today itself' I lied. I had no interest talking to Priyanka.

'I'll talk to you later' Priyanka signed that girl as she left.

I stared at her eyes. One, two, three, four, five, six seconds passed as I was still staring into her eyes. I don't know what made me look into hers. I suddenly broke down the eye contact as I looked down at my watch.

'Priyanka, if you don't mind can I go to the class now?' I said. 'I have some work. I'll catch you later'

'Sure, you are coming to Shivaji Park at 6:30 PM today, we will have fun' Priyanka said.

I didn't say anything as I moved into the classroom. I had no courage to look back at Priyanka as I had already broken down her heart into millions pieces. A droplet rolled down my eyes. I closed down my eyes.

Priyanka threw me a puzzled look.

I took my seat back as I started doing my work. I kept thinking about Priyanka for about five minutes. The first two minutes were for, what if Priyanka doesn't talk to me henceforth because of my behavior today? What if our friendship become hell? Yes, I have to be friends with Priyanka and I have to maintain it for my lifetime. But not the close one. And the rest three minutes went thinking, if I became closest friends with Priyanka, the matter has already reached to kiss. She always protests to kiss me but I always refuse her. And what if this takes us to sex and then marriage? And what if Priya comes across this, I have to definitely quit my life.

♦

Needless to say, I sat pointless on my bench with my eyes closed. I was encouraging myself to talk to Priyanka about this hell. Not only about being best friends but about Sam too. 'How this girl can break up with Sam for this simple reason?' I thought. I really had two lives into my hand now. The first one was of Sam and Priyanka and the second one was myself. I buried these thoughts into my mind as I brought up my pen into my hand. A plain white color paper fell down from professor Pradhan's table. I protested to pick it up as I saw 'SDIH dooms Program' printed over it. I handed it over to professor Pradhan as I sniffed in. I was confused over the policy of 'dooms program'. I learned over to ask professor Pradhan itself.

'Professor what's this dooms program?' I said.

'Oh this!' Professor said looking at those bloody papers. 'We all the staff members the management and the principle had decided to start the hostel facility too'

I really hate the word 'hostel'.

'Oh, that's good' I faked.

'But that's not for the college students, that's only for the external purposes only. Mumbai is the metropolitan city. Many students come her for their education, then where will they live? So this...'

I gave him an understanding nod.

'I'll see you later professor. I have some work' I lied as I moved out of the classroom.

♦

I was surprised watching Priya's mom and dad sitting on the sofas. I was really surprised that what Mr. and Mrs. Sharma were doing at my place. I moved towards my room upstairs. I breaking down my eye contact with all the members in the hall. I pushed the door and stepped into my room. I noticed Priya packing her bag as if she was going to a world tour. I moved forward towards her placing my right hand onto hers. Priya looked up at me.

'What's all this?' What is this madness?' I said.

She stared at my eyes like she had never before.

'I'm going back to my home' Priya said.

I felt anxious. I couldn't believe my ears. It was hardly two or three day passed Priya had visited us and she was now here to go back?

'Why? You are not comfortable here?' I questioned.

'No! That's not like that Rohit. My grandmother has expired. So we are going for the condolence' Priya replied.

'Oh!' I said as I relaxed myself. I noticed tears into her eyes. One droplet rolled down form her right eye. I looked at it gingerly. It said 'I Love You'. I hugged her as I heard crying voice. I hugged her for about two minutes all the way thinking about our future. Should I talk to my parents about Priya's place into my life? Should Priya talk to her parents about me? 'What about you, idiot?' I told myself. Yes, I really had no courage to discuss these things with my parents. I patted her back regarding 'its ok'. I released her as I made her sit down onto the bed. My hand reached to the glass full of water. I passed the glass to Priya. I placed my hand onto hers and continuously stared at her eyes.

'So when are you returning?' I inquired.

'No idea, but I think in two to three days' Priya replied.

I just could not understand how could I live two to three days without her? This three days' gap was a three years gap for me. 'Priya it's getting late we should leave now' Mr. Sharma shouted for downstairs. Priya looked at me as her eyes said 'Shall I go?' I smiled at her as we moved downstairs and I stood right beside of Priya. 'Err... idiot at least touch the feet of your in-laws' I told myself. I learned over and touched the feet's first Priya's mom followed by her dad.

'Shall we leave?' Mr. Sharma said to Priya.

Priya gave him an understanding nod as they moved towards the entrance door. I waved a good bye to all of those (especially Priya) as they disappeared from my eyes. The joy, the happiness I could never get, my life, was disappeared a few seconds ago from my eyes. We all reached to our kitchen for our lunch. We sat on the dining table as mom served us. 'Good the girl has gone; my hands are relaxed now' Mom whispered to herself.

'What?' I said.

'What?'

'Your hands are relaxed now?' I inquired.

'Yeah, I don't really like that family. Such an old fashioned people.'

The volcano of anger filled my eyes. I could not understand how could I talk to my parents about my life, about Priya?

'Mom, pass me the rice' I said trying to change down the topic.

I couldn't really understand that why parents take part into our life? Don't they have their own to da'am fuck with it? They take part because 1. They have given us birth 2. They care for us too much 3. They have no other work to do rather than interfere into our lives.

I sniffed in.

'So, Rohit how is your college doing?' Dad said.

'Simply better' I said.

'Fuck the college' I whispered to myself.

'Did you say something?' Dad said as I shook my head and focused on my meal.

I heard my last Christmas ringtone as I ran upstairs to my room leaving my food. My cell phone flashed 'Priyanka' in bold letters. I had no idea that why Priyanka was calling me at this stage. Yes, we had talked in college but she never calls me before six after college.

I got floored.

'We are meeting today' Priyanka said.

I kept quiet for few seconds thinking this is the best chance for me to talk to Priyanka about Sam. I should not tell Sam about me meeting Priyanka today and talking about him. 'I have to give him a surprise' I told myself.

'Are you there?' Priyanka said.

'Yeah'

'So where are we meeting?'

'Same, at Shivaji Park'

'Fine then. At 6:00 PM sharp. Okay?' Priyanka said.

'6:00 PM. Done.' I said.

I brought my cell phone down as I closed down my eyes and sniffed it. I thought of me bringing two lives together.

♦

I stood pointlessly looking into Priyanka's eyes. I broke down the eye contact as I learned over to sit down on the bench. We had reached the Shivaji Park at 6:07 PM. She had worn a blue T-Shirt and some black denims. I felt a bit comfortable sitting with Priyanka for the first time.

I shrugged my shoulders.

I saw Priyanka tugging her hairs behind her ears. She looked up at me. Our eyes met. I thought of our college matter. 'Has she called me for telling the same thing again?' I thought.

'So, why had you called me here?' I said. 'Speak'

'You were too busy with your work, your studies that you had no time to say at lease good bye to me after college' Priyanka said.

I sniffed in.

'No, I was just completing my notes and in that…' I lied.

Priyanka gave me an understanding nod as she placed her right hand on mine. I closed down my eyes as I thought over to talk to Priyanka about Sam.

'Sam is nice!' I said.

'What?'

'Samsung Smartphones are good. Don't you think?' I said. I had lost my all the courage to tell Priyanka about Sam. But this time I protested myself to ask her.

'Priyanka do you know Sam?' I questioned.

'Sam?'

'Yeah! Sam, your boyfriend'

Priyanka looked up at me, floored.

'I'm leaving' she said as she got up from her seat.

'Why? That's not too late now' I said.

'I have some family work; I have to go' Priyanka lied as she started walking.

I caught her left hand as I pulled her back. Her black silky hair was almost on my face. She tugged them behind her ears. I noticed her eyes were wet. A droplet rolled down from her right eye.

'Rohit, I was about to tell you all this but…' she stopped.

'Do you know something? I really don't love you. And I started hating you from the day Sam had told me about you. He explained me everything that why you and Sam had a break-up. Silly things, you should not be that silly Priyanka that you should fight on so small things.' I started. 'And this silly small thing leads you for the break-up? How silly!'

She released her hand from mine and stood fro from me turning her back towards me. Her crying voice still smashed my ears.

'And what do you really think? Don't Sam love you?' I said. 'He still loves you like hell. He is always ready to sacrifice his life for you and you…'

I shook my head.

Priyanka turned around facing her face towards me. I think I had spoken more before her. 'Speak, speak idiot, if you have haven't spoken today you have been eating chicken rolls at home' A voice inside me said. I slowly moved forward towards her and held her.

'See, go to him and talk to him and sort things out' I said. 'He is like dying to listen from you'

'Where is he now? I want to see him' Priyanka said.

I can't make these both meet at this stage. I have to first talk to Sam about this meet. And first of all I have to control the atmosphere and let Priyanka and Sam meet. I thought. By the way Sam has is birthday in coming two days. He has also planed the birthday party. I think I should give him a surprise.

'No, not now' I said.

'Why?'

'He is in Chennai now for some of his family work. He will be back in two days. You can meet him then. I'll directly take you to the party.' I said.

'Party?' Priyanka puzzled.

'I mean; I'll directly take you to the part of his heart'

I sniffed after controlling the situation.

Priyanka hugged me as I accepted that hug for the first time. I released her as she smiled at me.

'Thank you' Priyanka whispered.

I gave her 'its-ok' glance, smiling.

I heard my cell phone ringing to its last Christmas ringtone. I did not paid attention towards it and kept chatting about Sam with Priyanka. She asked me for Sam's cell number as I gave it to her. Her aroma filled my nose as I heard the same last Christmas ringtone. I tugged my hand into my jeans pocket and brought out the bloody cell-phone. It flashed an unknown mobile number.

'Hello' I said.

'Hello Jaan' the voice said.

'Who's this?'

'It's me, Priya' Priya said.

I really didn't recognize her voice and after all why she was calling me from an unknown mobile number she already had her own cell-phone. I got floored.

'I had forgotten my cell phone in your room. Please do me a favor, keep it safe from others. I don't need it now. But you know why…' Priya said.

There was only reason that we had text messaging every day, and we don't want that anybody should read our private messages. I smiled. Mom will not let me be friends with Priya because she herself don't have any respect for Priya, and the way she has talked to me at the lunch time was also rude. I thought.

'Don't worry, I'll keep it safe'

'Just one day, I'm returning Mumbai tomorrow'

'I'm waiting. I want to tell you something really really important'

'Bye then'

'Bye'

I placed my cell phone at its original place as I relaxed myself. Priyanka and I sat on the benches as we smiled at each other.

'Who was it? Your father?' Priyanka asked.

'No' I said as I kept quiet.

I thought it was the time to tell Priyanka about Priya. I was about to tell her but she interrupted me.

'A girl?' She guessed.

'What? How did you know?'

'Your eyes and the silence now, made me guess that that's definitely a girl' Priyanka said. 'Who is she?'

'The girl I loved' I replied.

'Oh, so she is the lucky girl to have the guy like you?'

I heard the last Christmas ringtone again. I didn't bother to answer it this time. I could see only one thing, to bring Priyanka and Sam together and to talk to my mom about my future. I smiled mentally.

'Yeah' I said looking up at Priyanka.

'Miss had a name or not? Or she is without name?'

'Her name is Priya'

My cell-phone rang again as I didn't paid attention towards it and continued with Priyanka.

'Pick it up, your miss would be calling you once again' Priyanka said.

I brought out my cell phone from my jeans pocket as it flashed 'MOM' on its screen.

'It's my Mom' I announced picking up the call.

'Are you free now?' Mom asked.

I looked up at Priyanka. What should I answer my mom? A 'yes' or a 'no'? I had two priorities before me. But Mom's was important. I chose to select the Mom's one.

'Yes, Mom?' I said.

'Beta, we are going for some important work. Will you be at home?' Mom said. 'Your aunty is going to arrive so…'

'Yeah Mom sure, I'll be there in half hour.' I said as I hung up.

I placed my cell-phone at its original place. Priyanka looked up at me puzzled.

'What happen? Any problem?' Priyanka said.

'Priyanka if you don't mind, can I leave you alone with this park? Actually I have to leave for some important work at home…' I said.

'Yeah, sure'

'I'll catch you up later'

I moved from my place as I was about to reach the Park's exit. I turned back at Priyanka as she waved me a good bye.

♦

Needless to say, but I sat pointlessly watching television channel 'Discovery' the show 'Man v/s Wild' which bored me a lot. I was already bored sitting in my home alone. And these discovery people do every time the same, catching the snakes, inquiring about them and let them go as if they really didn't have any other work to do. I switched off the television as I rested my head on the sofa. I closed my eyes and sniffed in. I thought about my future, will I really be able to have the girl like Priya into my life? Lots of questions popped into my mind as I had only one answer for all of them 'I can do it all' my mind changed the topic from 'my future' to 'Sam and Priyanka' like a racing car changing its track. I'm trying my best for bringing them both closer. I concentrated my mind on their ages. Priyanka is one year elder then that of Sam. But do ages really matter in love? 'Love is not counted in ages, but in love itself' I told myself.

They will be happy with each other and they will have a fantastic life together.

I smiled at myself.

I heard a door knock as I suddenly opened my eyes. I got up from my sofa and moved towards the door. I was happy that someone had arrived after a long time. I opened the door. 'SAM' I surprised.

'Sam!' I exclaimed. 'How come you are here today?'

'Just want to discuss something with you so... I came' Sam said.

I shrugged my shoulders.

I brought Sam in as I locked the door from inside. We both moved towards my bedroom. 'If Sam had to discuss something with me, then this something is really important' I thought. We both sat up on my bed as I kept my cell-phone on my bed as I paid my full attention towards Sam.

'Yeah, so what do you want to discuss?' I said.

Sam stared at me as I was offering him a girl for Entertainment. I smiled at my own jest. I tapped Sam's shoulder as he started to speak.

'Have you talked to Priyanka?' Sam said in an excited voice.

'Hmm'

'She had called me!'

'What?'

I got surprised that Priyanka called Sam the first time (of course after their break-up)

My heart beats started beating as fast as it could. I placed my right hand on my chest and relaxed.

'Really, she had called you?' I questioned.

'But I disconnected the call immediately' Sam said.

'Why?'

'I just don't know what made me do that but I suddenly felt that I should disconnect the call' Sam said. 'I want to meet her now. Please take...'

'No! You will not at least call her once again'

'But…'

'No, I have planned something for you' I said. 'I'll let you both meet after two days from now'

Sam's face lit up. I saw a different gladness onto his face. I was too happy to see it too. I had already told Priyanka about I don't love her and love someone else, but Sam was unknown about this. I really don't want to disturb Sam by publishing this after him now. 'I will not tell him' I told myself. I passed him a glassful of water and sat up straight. I heard a SMS beeping sound. I reached my cell-phone and opened the inbox as it flashed the same unknown number that I had on that that in park. I opened the message.

XOXO

I had no idea what was this message about. I buried the message into my mind as I kept my cell-phone down.

'Promise me you will let us meet after two days' Sam said.

'Yeah, I promise' I said.

'By the way why after two days? Is something special?' Sam said.

This fool had forgotten his own birthday as if he has to take sexology lectures in colleges.

'I think you are forgetting your own birthday!' I said.

'Oh…! I remember'

Sam stared at my eyes as he did not break the eye-contact. His eyes filled up. A droplet rolled down from his left eye. He hugged me. I felt proud that I was helping my best friend.

I shrugged my shoulders as he released me.

I thought I should talk to Sam what I had talk to Priyanka about, that I don't love her and love someone else. I looked at Sam as he looked glad. I thought over to make him even happier.

'Sam… I have…' I said.

'By the way have you talked to Priyanka about you not loving her and loving someone else?' Sam interrupted.

I looked up at him as I felt shy to talk to him the first time.

'Yeah, I have and she had accepted it too'

'What did she said'

'She said… nothing. I told her about how much you love her and all, but she accepted the truth.'

'Really?'

'Yeah'

I smiled as he smiled back.

'So, when are you getting married?'

'Not now. Come on'

'Then when?'

'Rohit Stop!'

'When can I meet my *Bhabi*?' I said playfully. 'I am just dying to meet her'

Sam threw a pillow at me. Life would be too easy if we trust each other that same way as now life-long.

♦

I sat straight on my bench watching professor Patil writing 'HUMAN AND SEX' on the digital board. I was really bored for the lecture but the topic was so good that I fully concentrated on the professor Patil's lecture. Professor had arranged the surprise exam on some chemistry topics. It was full of eighty marks in which professor had told us your paper should be clean and tidy, it contained full ten marks. I had done well but I was worried because I had really not maintained the cleanliness on my paper. My full ten marks were lost. The results were due today. My guess was that I could at least get eight marks out of sixty-five marks, but let's see today.

'So, students your results are due today of surprise exam no.6' the professor said.

The class felt silent. All the faces fell down. I was well known that all the class had done poor in this exam, only Priyanka would had done well and passed. Professor called out the names and handed over the papers. Pritviraj Patil, Yash Prasad, Aditya Chougule, Priyanka Mehta, Rohit Deshpande… came my paper. I had got sixty-seven and a 'B' grade in the surprise exam of chemistry. I moved back to my original place. Professor took the next name.

'Chetan Obiroi!' Professor exclaimed.

I thought Chetan had did something wrong or did poor in the surprise exam, but the thing was something else. I really hadn't seen such a funny person in my whole life. Chetan got up and moved forward towards the professor. Professor tightened up his lips controlling his laugh.

'What have you done? Wrote nothing?' Professor said as he threw the paper towards Chetan.

Professor smiled at him.

'Why have you left your paper blank? Why haven't you written nothing?' Professor said.

'Professor, you have warned us to keep the paper neat and tidy!' Chetan said.

'So?' Professor said.

All the class burst out laughing. I was too included but laughing at my friend was not good. But what else can I do? I tightened my lips and buried myself into the bench. Professor's face looked flushed.

'Quite everybody, quite I said!' Professor screamed.

The class felt silent.

Slap! Slap!

Chetan got non-stop two slaps on his right cheeks as his face turned red. If I would be in his place, I would have been totally fallen down.

'Get lost from my class' Professor said as Chetan left the class.

I looked at Priyanka as I found her adjusting her hairs. I thought over when these both, Priyanka and Sam meets what would be the reactions? How will they feel when they are finally back once again? How would I feel? Random question kept entering my mind. I kept thinking and thinking as my hand reached my face as a piece of chock smashed my face. 'What the fuck?' I said to myself.

'Where is your attention?'

'Sorry professor. I was…'

'Better pay attention towards me'

Priyanka looked at me in a foxed way. Priyanka threw me a 'what-happen' glance.

I shook my head.

Professor moved towards the digital board as he explained us the human and sex theory. I was board listening to this bloody stuff. I learned over to write a letter to Radhika didi to tell her the current atmosphere between us four of us and the stuff happen into the house during the lunch time. I tugged my hand into the desk and brought out a blank page.

Radhika Didi,

I love you as much as my own life. The first day I born and when you took me into your hands, the love you gave me was enough to live my whole life. I haven't written you this letter because I am missing you, but I want to let you know the atmosphere between us here. I am missing you a lot Radhika didi, I really can't handle our parents any more now. Please be back soon.

Didi, as you know about me and Priya being into a relationship, but there is someone who is also in love. My friends. The thing is that they loved each other a lot but because of some circumstances they both broke up. I am trying to bring them back. I hope that I am doing the right thing. Am I doing wrong by bring together two lovers? Well, I really don't want to make your mood off, let's turn to the main point. We were taking the lunch and Priya just left the house and mom started her lecture. I really didn't understand that why do mom interfere in my life? She says that Priya is a heavy luggage on her head and all that. I respect you a lot and I think that you are the right person to talk to my parents, especially mom. Didi, if mom didn't accept me and Priya being life partners then you will be having a suicide letter in your hand. If we really can't live together at least we could die off together. And promise me you will not talk anything about the suicide note to mom, that's my promise to you.

I'll end up here as I don't have time to write more. I love you a lot, Priya too loves you a lot and will be loving forever. Better keep your promise. I have sent you a rose along with this letter as my and Priya's affection to you.

Love you a loads.

Yours lovingly,

Rohit.

I was serious about the suicide. If my parents really don't agree then I have to commit the suicide. I closed my eyes and tried to vanish the thought of suicide completely from my mind. I folded the letter and placed it into my left jeans pocket. 'I should definitely send it afterwards' I told myself. Our lecture got over as I threw 'come-out' look to Priyanka. We both came out of the class. I should really invite Priyanka at my place tomorrow as Priya was going to arrive the same day. 'I can easily introduce both of them' I thought.

'So what's up tomorrow?' I asked.

'Nothing' Priyanka said.

'Can you join me tomorrow at my place?'

'Something Special?'

'Something but very important'

'Sure. I'll be there tomorrow'

I heard my cell-phone ringing. I brought it from my left jeans pocket as the iPhone screen flashed 'SAM' onto it. I rotated the cell-phone to Priyanka as I saw her face lit up, but this was not the right time that Priyanka should get in contact with Sam. I re-rotated the cell-phone towards me. Priyanka gave me a 'Please' glance.

I shook my head.

'Rohit, I am coming at your place tomorrow at 10 'O' Clock sharp' Sam said. 'My parents are hanging out for Pune tomorrow, I thought sitting in home pointlessly is a waste of time'

'Sure'

I hung up. 'What a coincidence? Everybody under one roof, but what if Priyanka meets Sam tomorrow? What about the birthday surprise? Think about it idiot!' I told myself. I really have to handle tomorrow's situation very gingerly.

♦

It was imminent that I was going to enter a bathroom in which a women was bathing for the very first time but my cell-phone stopped me. I stepped back at my cell-phone as the call was already disconnected. I sat up on my bed as I thought over today's jobs. 'What I have to do today?' I asked myself. 1.) I have to introduce two women's. 2.) I have to handle today's situation very gingerly. 3.) I really have to make this meet memorable. I laid down on my bed as I closed my eyes. My nose filled with a great aroma. Girls really have a great fragrance after bath. Priya moved towards me. She has none of the single cloth rather than a red towel onto her body. The towel was too filed with great aroma.

'Sit' I said.

'No, I'll get dressed' Priya said.

'Well, no one is in home. You can…'

'Don't be silly, I'll dress up and we will talk'

Priya moved towards the changing room as I sat up. I took a pillow and sat on the bed. 'It would be too easy without problems' I thought. Priya came out wearing a black T-Shirt and black jeans in which she looked very pretty and beddable. She sat next to me as I passed her the pillow. We both were alone into my house as my parents were been to their respective works.

'Priya, you are going to meet someone today to whom you should really know' I said.

'Who?'

'Not now, have patients' I said as it was too innocent.

My cell-phone rang it was right side to Priya. She picked it up into her hand as it flashed 'PRIYANKA' on the screen.

She looked up at me.my stomach roused up a ball. 'This was the right time idiot, tell Priya about Priyanka and Sam' I told myself.

I sniffed in as I gathered some courage to speak to Priya about this.

I looked up at Priya as her eyes filled up. She threw my iPhone on the bed and got up. She moved back looking at me. 'Priya I can explain' I wanted to say but I had lost Priya's faith on me.

'Who is this girl? Priyanka?' Priya said with wry face. 'You broke you promise Rohit.'

'Priya please don't get tensed. I can explain'

I thought of 'I can explain' on her to keep her quiet and explain her the whole story.

'What will you explain? The first date with her?'

'Priya please' I said as a droplet rolled down from her left eye.

I moved forward towards her as I held her. She shrugged her shoulders in an angry mood.

'I am leaving. It's over Rohit' Priya said as she moved towards the door.

I moved forward towards her as I caught her right hand and pulled her towards her.

'Will you listen to me? I can explain you that who this girl is. What relations do I have with her and why she had called me now? Everything' I said as Priya looked into my eyes.

I told her everything what was between me Priyanka and Sam. I told her that how was I helping them to sort out their problem. I told her about the birthday party tomorrow. I looked at Priya's eyes as she was still crying almost red. I moved close to her as I touched her eyes. I held her.

'Please don't cry, it makes me cry too' I said.

'Only because you love me a lot right?' Priya said.

'Right'

She hugged me as I hugged her harder. I was really happy to bring back my faith. I released her as I kissed her forehead. I looked into her eyes as she too stared at mine. We maintained our eye-contact. My cell-phone rang again as it broke down our romantic mood. I moved at my iPhone which was some minutes ago thrown onto the bed.

'Rohit, if you don't mind can I leave you and your home alone?' Priyanka said.

'What?' I was floored.

'I really can't come today' Priyanka said.

'Why?'

'Mom is sick and we have to move her to the hospital so…'

'Oh… I understand. That's not that important to come' I said.

'Thanks Rohit' she said as she hung up.

I threw the iPhone back onto the bed as I moved towards Priya. Closer and closer. I brought my mouth close to hers. I really had no idea that was this myself who was doing this or the gladness inside me.

'What are you doing?' Priya said.

'Nothing' I said.

'By the way, whose call was it?' Priya questioned.

'Oh… Priyanka's. She will not come today. She has some personal problems.'

I brought my face close to hers as she did the same. We were just going to kiss as the doorbell resonated. I thought this was Sam, but he had not told me that he would arrive this early. I moved towards my bedroom door. I turned back.

'Can I suggest you something?' I said.

'Sure' Priya said.

'Wash your face. You really don't look nice when you don't wash your face sometimes' I said.

She smiled at me.

I turned to the door and soon reached the main door. As I opened the door I noticed hot-shot Sam in front of me. I thought if there was a festival or something as Sam had worn such good togs.

'How come you are too early?' I said.

'The Flight was early so…'

'So, come in. Why are you there?' I said as I made Sam come in.

We both moved up towards my bedchamber. I stepped inside the room as Sam was unable to as he was seeing Priya for the first time in my room. I threw him a 'please-come-inside' glance. He stepped in as he took his place onto my bed. Priya passed him a glass full of water.

'Priya this is Sam; about whom I had talked to you' I told Priya.

'Sam, that's Priya' I introduced.

They both shook their heads. I sat in the middle of both of them. I felt like a *Pandit* has sat between a bride and a groom during the period of marriage. Tomorrow was Sam's birthday as the greatest gift from me was Priyanka. 'Why did Sam had not invited us for his birthday?' I thought. He slide his hand into his right shirt pocket. 'Was he showing us the love letter which he was going to give Priyanka tomorrow?' I thought. He brought out two cards as passed one to me and another one to Priya.

'There's my birthday tomorrow, all you have to come' Sam said as me and Priya buried our faces into the cards.

We both greeted him with a smile.

'Ok, I have to leave now. I have to distribute rest of the cards.' Sam said.

Sam got up to leave. He turned to Priya.

'Priya, can I share something?' Sam said.

Priya nodded.

'You have got a good, the best life-partner ever. You are really lucky to have Rohit.' Sam said.

She gave him an understanding nod.

We both stood up as we both of us moved downstairs' to wave a good-bye to Sam. Sam was disappeared but his words still sounded Priya's ears.

She looked up at me in excitement.

I shrugged my shoulders.

♦

We reached Sam's birthday venue at sharp 7:00 PM in Andheri (East). I Priya and my family (of course including Priyanka) had reached the venue. There was a musical welcome outside the gate. I reached the party hall as I saw 'HAPPY BIRTHDAY' proclaimed on the walls. I was in search in Sam and his family. I wanted to meet Sam and hand over his gift to him. I had already asked Priyanka to wait outside into the Scorpio. Our parents were mixed up in the stuff of those hosts. I and Priya was on the party stage. I learned over of asking someone about Sam. Priya tapped on my shoulder as she pointed towards the door which proclaimed 'Change Here' onto it. I saw Sam inside as we both moved towards the room. We entered as we heard a romantic song played on. I was floored. I saw a piece of chocolate cake on the table. I took out one piece and tugged it into Sam's mouth.

'Happy Birthday Brother' I said.

I could notice Sam but not his Parents. 'They would be busy with some of their hosts' I thought. Priya too picked a piece and put it in Sam's mouth.

'Happy Birthday Sam' Priya wished.

'Thanks. Where is Priyanka? Has she arrived? When are you going to make us both meet?' Sam questioned.

'Wait, wait… Priyanka had arrived and is waiting for you.' I said. 'But before that, where are your parents? I hadn't meet them before'

'Come on, I will take you to them'

We moved outside the room as whole aroma filled my nose. I noticed many togs, some wore Kurta and Kurtis's, some worn jeans, some worn party togs and some in formal. While moving through this traffic I noticed all the people here were from a good family. That means Sam had a good reputation among these all. I held Priya's hand as if she was a five-year-old girl and will get lost here somewhere. Sam took us to his parents, Mr. and Mrs. Obiroi. Sam tapped his dad's shoulder as he looked back.

'Dad, I want you to meet Rohit' Sam said.

'Sam, these are my Parents' Sam introduced. 'Dad, this is Rohit about whom I had talked to you before.'

'Ho! Hello Uncle!' I said as I put my hand before for a hand-shake.

We shook our hands.

'Uncle, if you don't mind, can I borrow Sam for a second?' I said as I put my hand into my pocket as I brought out my cell-phone.

Mr. Obiroi smiled at me.

I typed a message to Priyanka.

BE READY WE ARE SOON
COMING WITH SAM

We all moved towards the gate and then towards the Scorpio. Priyanka stood there, her back towards us. I protested her to call her at once.

'Priyanka' I called her.

She turned towards us. When she noticed Sam, her eyes lit up. I noticed her eyes. I looked at Sam as he couldn't believe his own eyes. Priyanka ran towards Sam as she hugged him. Sam got a backward jerk. I moved aside.

'I'm sorry' Priyanka cried.

'No, I'm sorry. It was my mistake' Sam said.

They both were meeting after such a long period. The meeting back scene was an emotional scene. The scene which filled my eyes.

'Priyanka, I'm really sorry. I made you stay away from me for such a long time' Sam said.

Priyanka kissed Sam's face as she cried. She buried her face into Sam's chest. Priya came forward towards me. I looked up at her. She held my right hand.

I smiled at her.

I thought that we should leave them alone for some time. Priya and I moved towards the gate. I had done my job and I was really happy to be successful into it.

'Wait, where are you both going?' Sam screamed.

I didn't say anything as Sam and Priyanka came forward to us. Sam held my hand.

'No friend does this much for any other friend, but you… Thank you' Sam said as he hugged me.

'Have you both meet earlier?' I said to Priyanka pointing towards Priya.

'No, but I guess that's Priya' Priyanka said.

'How do you know?' Priya questioned.

'Rohit had talked to me about you earlier so…' Priyanka said. 'Well nice meeting you'

At this stage the wind felt romantic. We are in love. The people, the music, the light, all the things around us felt romantic at this stage.

7 Years Later

7

'Home Electronics, let's go there' my mom said pointing towards the electronics section. We had arrived at the mall for shopping. I always liked shopping. 'Why can't the mall owner gift us the entire mall right now?' I thought in a childish kind of way. I moved towards the medical section. I wanted to buy some health supplementary products. I flipped through some as I found one prominent 'Amway'. I grabbed it and threw it into my shopping cart as I moved back. My eyes flipped through the condom packets kept on the rack. I was thinking to buy one or other. 'Beta it's not Priya with whom you are here for shopping, it's your mom idiot' I told myself. I dropped the idea as I walked straight towards the electronics section.

'Where were you Rohit?' Mom questioned.

'Just looking for some health supplementary products.' I said.

Mom gave me an understanding nod.

Mom was busy staring at the oven's, which will really help her to be lazy at home. I thought over to take a look through some tablet PC's (which will definitely help me watch blue film's at night) I smiled at my own joke. It seemed that an IPad would be a good option. I added it to my cart which priced at twenty four thousand bucks.

'Look at this, shall we buy this?' Mom said pointing towards the red colour oven as I looked back at her.

'Sure, we shall'

I heard my IPhone ringing to its Last Christmas ringtone. I slide my hand into my right jeans pocket as I brought it out. As I read the work on my IPhone screen it brought a smile on my face. It was Priya.

'Where are you?' She questioned.

'Electronics section' I replied.

'What?'

'I mean, I am in Mall. Out for some shopping with mom'

'Oh! I have some news'

'What?'

'We have planned a party. You are too invited.'

'We?'

'Actually Priyanka and Sam had planned this but…'

'Oh! So when are we meeting?' I interrupted.

'Tomorrow at 8PM Sharp at Hotel Tiny'

Why this people had planned this party at such an odd time. I got floored. I was going to ask Priya about this, but I let it go. I thought if there must be a surprise. I was too excited as if 'Salman Khan' was going to attend the party himself.

'Hehe, I'll be there darling' I said in a romantic way.

'Grow up' She said playfully. 'Ok, I'll hung up now'

'Hmm'

'Bye' She said as she hung up.

I placed my cell phone at its original place. I looked up at my mom straight as she looked muddled. The lines on her forehead were almost visible. I was too confused by looking at her. I acted as innocent as I could in her presence as if nothing had happen. Expounding you parents about your love is very difficult thing in one's life.

'Who's call?' Mom questioned.

'Priya' I replied.

'I have warned you earlier, don't get involved with that girl, but you are like gone really mad with her.' Mom said catching her breadth. 'Enough is enough, I am going to see a good girl for you next week. And once you get married my all the duties are terminated.'

What's really wrong with mom? I had told her earlier that don't get busy in searching a good girl for me as I already found one for myself. But who will expound her the thing? She is like Fevicol type minded. Once get stuck to a topic means permanently stuck. When will this parents really understand their children, their heart and their choice? I thought. I know this was not the right time to think all this.

'Can we leave now?' I said in a heavy voice.

We moved towards the billing counter as I paid the bill by my Credit Card. We moved out as I waved our driver to come near by us.

'Mom, what problem do you have with Priya?' I said.

'I don't want any relations with that middle-class family' Mom said.

'Are they not human-beings?' I said.

'Buy, try to…' Mom said as I interrupted her.

'Can we be quite for few minutes?' I made my mom quite from such a boring but serious topic so I can only dream about Priya.

♦

It took me half an hour to move to all of their houses as to pick them up. I finally reached hotel tiny as I moved out of the car to make myself comfortable. I sniffed in which made my laziness go down. All of the rest gather around me as if I was a film star. I looked up at Sam as I threw him a 'shall-we-go-in' glance as we both moved in. Priyanka and Priya following us, like all Indian families do. As we moved in the waiter welcomed us with a welcome juice. We had already booked the table. Table number six. We all took our seats on the table. The waiter passed us the water glass. Veg was in our daily routine, we all learned over to order some Non-Veg food. Now if the Non-veg had decided to be ordered what's better than chicken?

'What shall we order?' I said.

'Chicken, Non-Veg, and Something Spicy' I got three non-stop answers like I was on the 3G network.

'Yeah, two full Chicken Handi' I ordered.

'Sure sir' The waiter said as he left.

Why each and every waiter has the same type of togs? These black and white crows always appear before me and I get bored. Why can't they change it? I wondered. We sat comfortably, Priya besides me, Sam before me and Priyanka besides Sam. I wanted to start a conversation.

'So, Priyanka what up?' I said.

'Nothing, it's quite fine' She answered.

I gave her an understanding nod.

'By the way Priya, your future husband wants to be a Software Engineer. Do you agree with it?' Sam said looked at Priya.

Priya looked up at me. She smiled at me. Her smile gave me the answer that she didn't had any problem by me being a Software Engineer.

'Look, I do agree with it and I really could say that he is good at it' Priya replied.

'Do you support him then?' Sam said.

'Of course, I am here to support him his entire life' Priya said looking straight into my eyes which said, 'I Love You'

'How romantic' Priyanka whispered to herself as I heard it. I noticed Sam, he was in the mood of asking me something.

Priya put her right hand on my shoulder as it made a warm feeling in my heart. I placed my hand on hers beneath the table. I really like to make dates with her. I thought of when will we go next? I could smell the chicken as the waiter was already around us with our order. He kept the food on the table, ongoing serving us. Noticing Sam from passed few minutes his face showed something was wrong. It seemed he was hiding something from me. He never looked that nervous at all first. The food was served as we started. I could feel the mobile vibration in my right jeans pocket. I brought my iPhone out as it had a text message from Sam. I opened my Inbox.

ROHIT, PLEASE GO TO WASHROOM,
I'LL MEET YOU THERE, NOW!

I looked up at Sam, fully floored. He threw me a 'go' glance.

'Sorry guys, I'll be back, just five minutes' I said as I got up from my chair.

Priya held my hand as she looked up at me.

'Where?' She whispered.

'Washroom' I replied.

I moved towards the washroom and stood at the door. I was really floored that why Sam had called me here? One, Two, three minutes passed as there was no sign of Sam coming. At the fourth minute I saw Sam walking towards me.

I shrugged my shoulders.

Sam held my arm as he brought me inside the washroom. The washroom contained no people excluding us both. It was fully empty. He put his hand into his pockets.

'Why have you called…'

'Wait, just look at this' Sam interrupted as he brought out a gold ring from his left jeans pocket.

'It's nice, for your mother?' I inquired.

'No, that's for Priyanka' Sam said.

I got floored.

'I'm going to propose her now' He said. 'I didn't had courage to tell this to you in presence of them. I needed to share this to someone, so I found you who can understand my feelings.

'Again?' I said.

'That's called Romance' Sam replied pointlessly.

I smiled at him as I place my right hand on his.

'I hope it goes nice, I support you!' I said.

'So shall we move?'

'Yeah'

We both moved back to our plates. I sat on my seat as Sam on his. I picked up chicken's leg next. I took my first bite looking at Sam. I threw him a 'talk-to-her' glance. Sam sniffed in as he stared at Priyanka. I looked down into my plate.

'Priyanka, I want to tell you something' Sam said.

'What?'

Sam brought the ring out of his pocket putting it in his palm and covered it by his fingers.

'Will you marry me?' He said.

I looked at Priya. We both look up at them. Our table felt quite as we could hear only the public around us.

Priyanka looked up at Sam, Surprised.

'Are you serious?' Priyanka said.

'Yeah, I am serious Priyanka'

Priyanka smiled at Sam.

'What about our parents?' Priyanka said next.

'We will talk to them too. I'll talk to mine, you talk to yours'

The droplets rolled down Priyanka's eyes. I looked at Priya as she rested her head on my shoulders.

'Life is what you enjoy, but by your own way, not by your parents' I wanted to say.

♦

I sat crossed-leg on my computer chair watching some funny videos. I was doing so only because I was bored. I took our 'Mr Beans' DVD next. I heard some footsteps from downstairs as I thought someone was coming up. I looked back at the door as I saw Radhika di entering my room. I got up as if I was seeing Katrina entering the room. She moved towards me as she caught my right hand and brought me towards the bed. I looked up at her.

I baffled.

'You must be curious about why I am here?' Di said.

'Why?' I asked.

She sniffed in as tugged her hairs behind her hairs.

'See, I heard that mom is seeing a girl for you' She said.

'I'm going to tell her that I'm not going to fall in this right now' I said. 'And have she asked my choice ever?'

Radhika di shook her head.

'I accept that what's going is wrong but…'

'But what?' I interrupted.

'I'll talk to her' Di said.

Talking to mom is of no use, its waste of time. She would not listen to anyone, if even God comes and tells her, her decision would never change. And I think I will not get married to Priya if her mind will be stuck on the same thing like a bubble gum. Needless to say buy Mom's always have ego in their mind fixed. I really don't understand that why parents have to interfere into their children love-life. It's ok to interfere into the personal life because they are our parents. I had only one family member who supports me through this. Radhika di.

'Will you? Really?' I asked.

'See Rohit, you are now in adult age and you have your own choice, your own freedom. You can talk to mom directly and after all I'm supporting you to get through this. Be courageous brother' Radhika di said.

I rested my head on her lap as I closed down my eyes.

'Don't sleep on my lap you are not small'

'I'm, I am still younger then you and will be ever'

'By the way you had been to a tour last year with Sam and Priyanka, so how was it?' She asked.

'Good and enjoyable' I said. 'We had fun'

'Where were you been?'

I moved towards the side table as I brought my laptop. I switched it on. I brought out the camera from the same drawer and connected it to my laptop. I opened the pics and passed the laptop to Radhika di. I moved aside from her. I had no interest seeing those pics all over again. But the thing was the pics contained my pics with Priya too. I moved back and back.

'My cell-phone is downside, I'll just get it' I lied

'But it's here' Di said showing it to me.

I freeze at my place wondering what to say next.

'Why did you lie me? What's the matter?' Di inquired.

'I'll try to talk to mom now, dad first. If he goes with a yes, then I think expounding mom will be easy.

'Then can't you tell this earlier?'

I didn't said a word. I sniffed in.

Radhika di smiled at me.

I moved downstairs towards my parent's room as I entered, I found both of them sat crossed-leg on the bed. They looked surprised looking at me as if I had born just now. Dad threw me a puzzled look.

'Mom, can I borrow Dad for a minute?' I said.

'Why?'

'I just want to marry him in a historical way' I wanted to say. I don't understand why she asked me a question every time I appear before her?

'Just some work!' I said.

'Sure' She said as we moved outside the room.

We reached the balcony. Dad tapped my shoulder as she made me sit on the rest chair and took his seat right before me.

'Dad what have you planned?' I asked

'About what?'

'My life?'

He sniffed in.

'Well, we are thinking about your marriage soon. And we will be free.' He said 'We have started to find a good girl for you. I hope the matrimonial ads will do well'

Yeah, here is something well. Find a girl and tell her to marry me and you guys get free as if you had got independence from me. And if all parents were independent why they give us birth and wait for getting independence? The same thought burned into my mind as I put a glass of water on it. Why parents don't ask for our choice, if the parents have to live their life with our life partner the thing was different but here we have to live it. At least ask for our opinion.

'I hope me calling you a lazy?' I said.

'Sorry'

'Here, dad you only think about yourselves and not about their children's. I and the children in this nation have a different choice. You want your daughter-in-law to cook, as a home maintainer, as a plate washer, as a maid. But we want a wife who trust their husbands and nothing else' I said. 'You too had a love marriage Dad!'

He smiled at me.

'Why did you chose mom? Because it was your choice' I said.

'Yeah'

'The same thing is with us dad, I too love someone and I too have a choice, we also have heart, why don't you all understand me?' I said.

Dad sniffed in.

'Beta, after all it's your choice, it's your own life, and it's your choice. You have to live it.' Dad said. 'Who is the lucky girl?'

'Priya' I said.

As I called out her name dad's face turned low.

'What happen dad?'

'Your mom, she is against her beta'

'So, you have to help me out with this dad' I said.

He smiled at me.

I hugged him. He tapped my back as he threw me a 'go-live-your-life' glance. This stage makes every child happy. I suddenly thought about mom, who would expound this to mom? Will she accept me? I think, no! But I really have to keep self-confidence and courage in me as Radhika di told me. I had read it somewhere that 'Love is the only power, it can break the strongest rock'. I learned over to go and see Radhika di. I wanted to talk to her.

'Thanks dad, love you' I said.

I moved upstairs to Radhika di as she was busy flipping through the same photographs. I went towards her as she looked up at me. I smiled at her.

'Why are you smiling?' She questioned.

'You know what...?'

'What?'

'Dad had a green signal with my point'

'Really?' She said putting the laptop down from her lap.

'Yes, he also said he would help me out of this'

She got up as I moved towards her. She moved towards the door.

'Where?'

'Down, towards Dad. I'll talk to Dad about something' She said.

'What will I do here alone?'

'Just think about your past dates with Priya'

I smiled at her.

I moved towards my bed as I lay down. I closed my eyes as my mind took me to the reminiscences of Priya.

8: A Date

Needless to say, but my tooth-paste was magically indiscernible today. It was almost 7:45 am and I was getting late for my date with Priya. I had already booked a room in hotel tiny. Room number 24. I could not understand where the fuck was my toothpaste. Did this bloody toothpaste has got this day to get fucked-up?

'Mom, where is my toothpaste, it's not in my room' I screamed.

'Well, where are you going today in so hurry?' Mom said.

'There is my friend's birthday party' I lied.

I think I should not lie at this stage because I was going for a date with Priya and I have to marry her soon, and after all why should I hide things out? But what can I really do? I really had no pluck to tell mom about Priya.

I sniffed in.

'Mom, I'm going for a date with Priya' I said.

'But just now you said that you are going for a birthday party?'

'I lied'

The expressions form my mom's face changed. It said like 'what's-wrong-with-this-boy?'

'Very good, lie for that girl now!' She said. 'And if possible kill us for her'

Mom moved towards her bedroom as I threw her a dirty look. I was deeply thinking 'When will the parents comprehend their children?' I was floored. 'Mom your child also have a choice and you have to accept it. You really can't go against your child's love-life because I and my life-partner have to live the life together and not you.' I wanted to say. I went towards the bathroom as I got ready. I wore modish togs as Priya like me wearing more fancy western cloths. I grabbed the car keys from the key holder hung on my wall and moved out of the house.

'You have to accept it' I said.

I sat into the Fortuner as I drove it towards Priya's house. I think falling in love is not a crime. But of what crime I'm getting this chastisement? And what if Priya's parents asks me for their daughter's place in my life? What will I really say?

I shrugged my shoulders.

This was the first time I drove the Fortuner to Priya's home. I was a bit freaked at this stage. I often go to her place but sometimes I feel 'lose your nerve' and sometimes I feel like I am going to my own house. I slide the window down. The cold wind crashed my body as it really felt good and created a romantic mood. Reaching Priya's home was fun but talking to her parents was a double fun. There was only one member in my family who was against my choice and that was mom. If dad and Radhika di accepted this, why couldn't mom? I thought. And if parents are in contradiction of their child the child have to fight against them for their freedom.

I soon reached Priya's home as I stopped my car right in front of her gate. I blew the horn, I blew it the second time.

No reply!

I blew it the third time, this time in an angry mood as I called Priya out.

'Hey, come in, I'm not ready yet' Priya said coming out in her balcony.

I looked up at her in her balcony. She was busy adjusting her hairs. 'Has this girl gone mad? We are already getting late and this girl is not ready yet' I told myself.

'Why in? You are not ready still? We are getting late baby' I said.

'Wait, I'll come down' She said.

Priya came down as she stirred towards my car. She brought her head in from the car window as her hair's aroma filled the Fortuner. 'Why should I really buy the car fresheners? I should request Priya to loan me few of her hairs so that I could place them into my car as they had good smell then of the car fresheners.' I thought

I shrugged my shoulders.

'Come in, I need some more time to get ready!' Priya said.

'Priya, what's this? We are getting late!'

'Yeah, I know baby, some more time' Priya said in a childish way. 'Please'

I stepped out of the car as we both stepped in Priya's house hand-in-hand as if we were a 'just-married-couple' I noticed Priya's dad watching television with some of the mind-numbing channels put on. Priya threw me a 'sit' look as I sat down on the sofa.

'I'll be back soon' Priya said as she moved towards her bedroom upstairs.

Uncle switched off the television as he placed the remote on the table side to him. The hall felt silent as if it was a meditation hall. Priya's mom brought a glass full of water in a pink tray. 'This must be vodka!' I thought. She passed it to me as I took two big sips. I placed the glass on the same table on which uncle had placed the remote earlier.

'So, beta what's up?' Priya's mom questioned.

'Nothing aunty, it's quite good' I replied.

'Where are you going today? This early?' Uncle said.

I sniffed in thinking what to say next.

'For a birthday party' I lied.

Why do each and every parent have a horde of questions in their mind? This concept is not clear to me yet. My future *in-laws* stared at me as if I was offering them some of the blue-films.

'How is it? I mean between you and my daughter?' Priya's dad asked.

'Good!' I said in a no-option way. 'Why?'

Both of them looked at each other. I was floored. Why had they asked me this question? Does this question mean something else? I buried this thought in my mind as I thought of, if these people as so welcoming to me then why not my own parents?

I twisted my neck.

'No, what about your future planning?' Priya's dad said.

This question clicked my mind a little. These people has not asked me about my line of business, this was something different.

'I want to work for Microsoft' I replied.

'Being that will fulfil your life? What about your personal life? Have you thought about your soul-mate?' He said.

'Yeah, I'll marry a girl. Mom is in the search of the same.' I said.

The expressions on the both faces transformed. I thought if I had said something wrong.

'So, why don't you both get married?' Priya's mom said.

'Both, who?'

'You and my daughter?' She blunt.

I felt silent as I hung my head low. What will I tell them that my mom is against it? Or   I love your daughter but my parents junk this relation?

'What?'

'Mom, stop. I'm not going to fall in this marriage-*varriage* this early. And how could you at lease think to ask Rohit?' Priya said coming down.

We all stood up as I saw Priya before me.

'But beta…'

'Mom please, stop' Priya interrupted. I noticed tears in her eyes.

We both moved towards the Fortuner as we stepped in. I drove the car direct towards hotel tiny. I had booked beach side room to enjoy the beauty of sea. I moved towards the reception.

'Excuse me, I have booked a room here. Can I have the keys please?' I said.

'By what name sir?' The receptionist asked.

'Mr and Ms Deshpande' I blunt out.

I had booked the room by Mr and Ms Deshpande because hotel tiny offers rooms for only married couples.

'Here are the keys sir' The receptionist said passing me the keys.

I grasped the keys as we moved towards the sea. I felt the sea waves. We both moved to room number 24. I opened the door with the keys as we stepped in. Priya jumped on the bed as I moved towards the side table to place the keys. I sat next to Priya as we were relaxed now. 'Priya had tears in her eyes, why had she did so?' I thought.

'Why you were crying? I said.

'When?'

'In home, when your parents asked me for the marriage?'

She looked up at me suddenly.

'I love you a lot Rohit, but…'

'But what?'

'I feel freaked to tell my parents that I really love you a lot'

I closed my eyes and sniffed in.

'So they say that adults are coward?' I teased.

'Rohit, Stop!' She said tapping my hand. 'Take it seriously'

I think one should not get anxious of their parents to share their opinion. They should speak out their feelings. We think 'this is not the right time to tell them' we say the same and the time gets on hold.

I looked up at Priya as her face looked tired. I think this was because I had spoken to her about this matter. When I had proverb her in the car she seemed glad because she was with me. I should say her sorry for this.

'I'm sorry, I made your mood off' I apologized.

'No, but…'

'I should not ask you this at this time, we are on date and I should not spoil our time' I interrupted.

Priya placed her hand on mine as I found a droplet rolling down from her cheeks on her hand. I made her look up at me. I blamed myself for all this. 'You are responsible for all this idiot' I told myself.

'This are not the tears because you hurt me, these are of you having faith on me so much' She said. 'Thank you'

'Oh, ma'am don't you want launch?' I asked.

'Of course!' She said.

'Then get ready'

She got up from her seat as she passed me her mobile phone and her purse. She moved towards the washroom as I placed aside her things. I removed my shoes and strapped them under the bed. 'Life would be too easy without these bloody shoes. No tension of washing those bloody stinking socks' I thought. I brought my cell-phone out as I opened the web. I thought over to search some of the 'date information'. '*Your inbox has a new message*' the cell-phone screen flashed. I turned to my inbox.

HI, I THINK WE SHOULD,
HUNG OUT FOR LUNCH,
I'M IN HOTEL TINY, SO,
HEAD ON SOON!

I was surprised seeing those texts. I checked the sender's name. It was Sam. I closed down all the applications as I dialled out Sam's number. There was some silent music as a caller-tune. The music felt nice I thought it could do well for a candle light dinner.

'Got my text?' Sam said.

'Yeah'

'So, soon meeting at tiny?'

'What a coincidence?'

'What?'

'I'm in hotel tiny!'

'What are you doing here?'

'Date!'

'Where precisely are you now?'

'Room No. 24'

I sniffed in.

'Listen, I had reserve a table, its Table No. 16, so better be there in twenty minutes'

'Yeah, sure' I said as Priya came out from washroom with a pink towel in her hand. She threw the towel on the bed as the aroma from the towel filled my nose.

'You're Parents?' Priya said mortaring towards my cell-phone.

'No, that's Sam' I said.

'What did he say?'

'He asked us for a lunch'

'Have you told him that we are on a date?'

'Yeah, but the coincidence is he is in the same hotel and had previously booked the table for us'

She sat next to me as she took her cell-phone.

'What are you doing?' I said

'If Priyanka is also coming?' Priya said.

'If Sam is coming means Priyanka would obviously come' I said as I grabbed the cell-phone from her hand and I kept it aside. I brought my mouth close to hers.

'No, not now, you get ready we will go for lunch' Priya said as she got up from her seat. I caught her hand and got up too. I yet again brought my mouth close to hers saying…

'Okay ma'am, I'll get ready you wait!' I said as she smiled at me.

I moved towards the washroom. I got ready in next few minutes. We stepped out of the room. I locked the room and placed the keys in my left jeans pocket.

We often go on dinner (especially on candle light dinners) when we are on date. Regularly a girl likes to go out for a dinner because the night wind blow with a romantic mood. It's true that hanging out with parents is different and with friends is different. I often had hang on with my friends, and never with my family. I remember going out with my family for a dinner when I had passed out 12th HSC.

I had ordered two bottles of alcohol from which I had put one in my pocket thinking it would be useful further. I passed one to Sam, the two girls stared at us as if we were a terrorist. Priya was busy cutting an apple as she had only ordered some fruits for herself. She had put on a fast today so I had suggested her to have at least fruits. The knife had cut her soft index-finger, the blood popped out. She jerked her hand in air as it hit the alcohol bottle kept on the table. Gravity had done its work. I suddenly looked up at her then at her finger. I grabbed it as I sucked it off. God had done a good thing, our blood groups were same.

'Waiter' I called out.

'Yes, Sir!'

'Just clean this off' I said pointing towards the alcohol bottle.

He gave me an understanding nod.

I told Priya to roll around her hanky on her index-finger which was cut by the fucking knife which could stop the blood flow. The waiter must be thinking that 'these people are wasting the precious alcohol by dwindling it down and telling us to clean, at least contribute us so that we could enjoy.'

'Did you get it?' Priyanka said.

'Yeah, it's paining' Priya said.

I threw Priyanka a dirty look.

'Shall we order something else?' Sam said.

'No, I think we are getting late' I suddenly poked.

Sam gave me a smile which said 'you enjoy'. I had no idea what to do next because it was my first date. It was like being in bathroom and not having bath. I thought I should really go and rest in room and then hung out somewhere. It was becoming too good to spend my day with Priya. 'Beta it's only a day, you have to spend your entire life together' I told myself. Yeah, it was right that the joy was not ending here because I have to enjoy my rest of the life. 'Will my parents be with me?' I asked myself.

♦

It was 6:37 pm as we were on the beach. Our rooms were also on the beach side so it got easy to get us on the beach. I thought over to take Priya to the disco. I diverted my mind towards beach. The sea could make our date dreamy not the disco lights and sound. We placed our shoes aside and sat down on the cold sand. Priya placed her head on my shoulder as I gave her body support. I leaned over to ask Priya about our relationship. Days were passing by and we had to talk to our parents.

'Priya, why don't you talk to your parents?' I said.

'About?' Priya said politely.

'Our marriage!' I said.

'Yeah, I will but you have to wait'

'Why?'

'I'm thinking ask them my way. So…'

Priya will talk to her parents but what about me? There is something inimitable thing about me that I have to give my parents an exposition. Dad had accepted, Radhika di accepted but what about mom? Will she be ready for this? I really didn't understand that what sin I had committed.

'Take your time' I said.

'By the way, have you talked to your parents?' Priya asked.

'Yeah'

'So, what did they say?'

'They said they will think over it!'

I should not lie Priya, but now I have to do it. 'Let the time come I'll tell all this to Priya too' lying to your girlfriend could bring misunderstandings and led to breakups. But I know Priya could understand me. I have to find veracious way to reach my destination, and I have to get successful in it as well.

We both got up from our seats as we put on our shoes. As we walked through our legs felt too heavy. Priya held my left hand in her right and started walking. I should really pick her in my arms and walk, the public around made me control myself. I placed my hand on her shoulder as we had reached the sea water. An eight year's old little girl rushed towards Priya and buried her face in her stomach. Priya looked up at me as I gave her a smile.

The mother of that girl ran towards us as she stopped before us to catch her breath.

'I'm sorry' The mother said looking at Priya. 'Come, beta we are getting late. Let's go!'

'It's Okay. By the way what's your name?' Priya asked bending down to match the girl's height.

'My name is Neha' the girl said in a childish way.

When I heard the first three words 'My Name is' I remembered Sharuk Khan's 'MY NAME IS KHAN'. Both of them disappeared from our eyes. The girl's face still flashed before my eyes. She was cute.

'Priya, you know I should have the same girl as my daughter' I said.

Priya smiled at me. The smile she gave meant whole world to me.

'Good Choice' she teased.

◆

I sensed that Priya was hiding something from me. When I had asked her that why she had cried in house she had given me a unique reason that she is feared of telling her parents. But I don't think so because the way she talked to her parents was not seemed that she was afraid or anything else. 'You should find it out' I told myself.

We moved into the cold sea water as Priya liked to wet her legs. I made my hands wet.

I wriggled.

We both moved back to our room. We moved in as I locked the door. I threw my shoes in a corner as I rested myself on the bed.

'Priya, are you hiding something from me?' I probed.

'No' she replied.

I sniffed in.

'But I think you are hiding something' I said as she sat next to me and placed her hand on mine.

'You don't trust me?' She said.

'I do'

How can I really find that what Priya was hiding from me actually? My mind landed on the alcohol bottle which I had brought. I leaned over to give Priya a little as it is said that alcohol makes people speak truth when they don't want to. I really don't know what madness I was doing but I have to do so.

'Let's try mango juice' I said.

'Sure'

I poured mango juice in a glass as Priya went into the washroom. This was the good chance to mix the alcohol with the mango juice. I unsealed the alcohol bottle and poured a little into the mango juice warily.

'I'm sorry Priya for what I have done. But serious baby I have to do it' I said in a low voice.

Priya came out of the washroom as she sat on the bed next to me. I passed her the glass as she took three big sips. She passed me the glass back as I placed it on the table besides me.

'I'll get back from washroom' I said as I want Priya to be alone for some minutes.

I stared at her from the bathroom window gap. I found her eyes half-squinted.

I sniffed in.

I suddenly ran towards her as I sat on the bed. I really don't know that what made her do the thing that she had never done before.

'Priya, are you…'

Priya done a thing that she had never done before interrupting me. She held my right hand and placed it on her stomach. Was this Priya herself who was doing this or the alcohol made her do so? She slide her right hand into my T-Shirt. Her hand felt too soft. What had happen to this girl? What was this madness she was doing? I lost my mind too as I slide my hand into her Kurti. My hands were now almost on my breast. I took off her Kurti and then reached for her bra. I took off the bra next. She took off my shirt and hugged me tight. She released me from her hug as her hands reached for my jeans next. She unhooked my jeans and lay down on the bed.

She sniffed in.

I continued. I hand completely lost my mind. We really feel too good after having sex. I looked up at her as it showed that she adored it.

'How do you feel?' I said.

'Good' She said in a childish way. The alcohol still acted on her.

I sat up to dress up. My eyes turned towards the alcohol bottle as I felt that drinking alcohol is good after sex. I poured some for me and another one glass.

'Wear your cloths before someone comes' I said as she sat up. She wore her cloths as I passed her the glass.

We both got up as we packed up our things as it was getting too late for us.

'Pack your things Priya, its 8:30 pm' I said.

'So?'

'Don't you want to go home?'

'No, I want to stay here with you'

I nodded.

'Don't be silly and hurry up'

We both moved out at sharp 9:00 pm. I placed the bags into the Fortuner as stepped into the car. But I had not got my answer yet. Was Priya lying me? I really didn't know this. But what I had done today was right? Maybe it be wrong but this will have a strong and romantic effect on us both. This special time we had spent together today will make our bond strong.

9

We were in Sam's home. I, Priya, Priyanka and Sam sat on the sofa as Sam's father had his drinks. 'You idiot, you know for what we are here?' I told myself. 'Stop drinking and listen to us' I wanted to say. Sam's mom passed a cup full of tea to all of us present in the hall. She took one for herself and took her seat next to her husband. 'Sam's mom, I know you love your husband a lot but you should control before us' I told myself as I smiled. I was about to laugh but tightened my lips. How could Sam do an inception? We were her to talk to Sam's parents about Sam and Priyanka being together. Sam wants to turn his love-life into a couple, a marriage! 'Why should we talk to our parents about our love-life? We should only tell them. No need for taking any permission and whatever…' I thought. Sam's dad had a phone call.

'Yeah. Now… I'll be there' He spoke.

He placed the cell-phone down and looked up at her wife.

'Sunita, CA wants us to see him urgently. We have to go' He said.

Sam's mom gave him an understanding nod.

I heard their conversation, it seemed like they were going out somewhere. I stared at both of them.

'Beta, we have some work at CA's office and we have to go' Sam's mom told him.

'Mom I have to tell you something very important' Sam said.

'But the work is also important beta' She said. 'Just half an hour, we will be back soon'

Sam's face fell down as both of them were going out. 'Can we have sex now, there is no one in the house' I wanted to ask Priya.

When we are about to tell something important to our parents they neglect it, they find their priorities important and not ours. We are here to tell them something important about our life and they are busy into their own work. It's true that having control over parents is so important, but parents have control on us, very simple.

'I'm panicked' Sam said.

'Why?' Priyanka asked.

I tapped Sam's shoulder as he looked up at us. His fallen face was limpid before us all. I felt low looking at his fallen face. I want him to tell his parents about his marriage by being courageous. I could see clearly on his face that he had lost all his courage.

'See, don't be so tensed, after all we are all there for you, Priya said as Sam gave her a smile.

'I think siting in this bloody hall is a waste of time, let's go to the terrace garden upstairs' I said. 'It's too hot here too'

Sam didn't said anything, he moved upstairs without noticing us. I checked my watch it said 6:38 pm, it was a simply Tuesday evening. I looked up at everyone as I threw them all 'we-shall-go-up' look. We all got up to go upstairs. I held Priya's hand as I told her to walk slowly. Let Priyanka go up first and be with Sam. Priyanka moved faster as we were still on the stairs. Priya hit me playfully with her hairs and she moved upstairs. The aroma felt good. Why don't she pack it in a bottle and sell it as a ladies deodorant? I thought. I ran up to catch her. We reached the roof. Priya stood there quietly as I stopped suddenly. We found Sam and Priyanka hugging each other.

'How nice of them. Really a romantic couple' Priya said holding my arms.

'Yeah' I whispered to her.

We both moved close towards them. I was speechless.

'Can we have your attention please?' I said cleaning my throat as Sam released Priyanka from his hug.

We noticed Priyanka had tears in her eyes. Priya moved close to her and held her. I moved towards Sam.

'Why are you crying? Did anything happen between you and Sam?' Priya questioned.

Priyanka shook her head.

'They why?'

'I don't think Sam's parents will ever accept me' Priyanka said pointlessly.

Priya tapped her shoulder.

'Mad girl, why are you stressed? You should not lose your confidence' Priya explained. 'Don't cry now'

'Yeah' Priyanka said cleaning her eyes.

'And Sam we all know that you love each other like a hell and you will not let her down' I said.

Sam rotated his eyes on me.

'And if your parents don't accept it, we will sort out things, and will make most of it' I explained.

Sam gave us all a understanding nod. The nod which Sam gave us was not seemed to be a little powerful. I think Sam has made his mind to talk to his parents. I signed Priya to take Priyanka down with her as I want to ask Sam something very important.

Priya gave me an understanding nod.

'We will get water for you' Priya made a reason and took Priyanka along with her.

I sighed.

Oodles of questions popped into my mind. Why are Sam's parents angry on Priyanka? Did they learn about their break-up earlier? And if they are not really erudite about it then why are they avoiding us? I really can't say that they are behaving low with us but I feel the same.

'Does your parents learned about the break-up?' I asked as Sam turned to me.

'No' He replied.

'Then why they behave like this?'

'Like what?'

'Anything!'

The expressions on Sam's face changed. Soon he has frown's on his forehead.

'They are friendly with Priyanka and her family too' Sam said.

'And when you had a break-up, haven't your parents learned about it?' I said.

'We never let them get known to this one'

I gave him an understanding nod.

If these two families have a good relation between them then there's no problem. 'And then why should Sam panic to ask his parents?' I thought. I still remember the days, the childhood days when we played together, and now are at a marriageable age. Sam's parents will be back at any time now. I checked my watch it was quarter to seven now.

'Dude you have to talk to them now. They will be back at any movement now' I told him.

Sam sniffed in.

'I will' Sam said 'I will talk to them now, for Priyanka'

Yeah, you will be able to ask them this time, Right? 'Idiot' I said mentally. I think Sam would never be able to ask his parents about this (of course including today) because his eyes showed me that he'll not be able to do so. I really don't understand that why these fucking children be afraid of their parents? Don't they really have guts? And if they really don't have those daam guts I could say that they are really a… I heard my cell-phone ringing, but the people around me can't really hear it. I neglected it as I paid my full attention towards Sam. I heard the same tune again. I have heard this once. Yeah, it was Sam's ringtone.

'Sam, I think your cell-phone is ringing' I said.

'Cell-phone?'

Sam put his hand on his pocket as he brought out his cell-phone. He stared at his cell-phone like he had never before.

'Hello mom!' Sam said.

'Beta, we are coming. Do you need anything from here?'

'No, just come fast'

'Why Sam? Before, you were not so eager to see us' She said. 'What's up today?'

'Mom that… nothing… just come fast' Sam said as he hung up.

We looked at each other as if we were a married couple. We moved downstairs as we had our seats on the dusty sofas. I sighed Priyanka to get a glass full of water for Sam from kitchen as Sam's face looked almost low and had frown's on his forehead. Priya sat beside me as she put her hand on mine. I think, it somewhat went into romance. It was not a romantic mood, it was the important time which could bring two lives together.

I shrugged my shoulders.

'Sam, Relax' I said placing my hand on his shoulders.

'Sam I think you are Rohit's closest friend and now mine too. We all think that you will definitely make it today' Priya said. 'And be free to talk to them. They won't eat you!'

Priyanka passed Sam the glass as Sam took one big sip.

'And see…' a car horn interrupted me in my conversation.

Sam's parents are back. I sniffed in.

'Sam your parents are here'

I found Sam's face as like a haunted film's villain. Same as it was. I placed my hand on his shoulders and exchanged 'you-can-do-it' glances. Sam stood up. I had something horrible pain into my stomach. I didn't knew, what the fuck was the thing. I just neglected it and fully focused my eyes on Sam.

'Where are my fucking parents? So lazy, so late' Sam said Priya, Priyanka and my eyes turned towards Sam. I heard the f-word for the first time from Sam. (Of course in his own house, else he uses it more often) Priyanka moved forward. 'Is she going to ask Sam for sex?' I thought.

'Sam, language. Mind your language' Priyanka said with her eyes extra wide.

'Daam! They are entering in. Get ready Sam' I said.

I signed all to sit on the sofa. I took my seat. My hand reached the television remote as I switched it to Discovery channel. We all pretended to be in a waiting list. I saw two human beings entering in. They both looked at us as if we were the robbers in their house. I threw them a '*don't-look-at-us-like-that-we-are-Sam's-friends*' look as I didn't noticed it at all. Sam's mom placed down the bag from her hand on the floor as his dad shut the door behind him.

'So? What's up?' Sam's mom said as her eyes slowly turned at Priyanka as she noticed her.

Priyanka stared at all of us one by one.

'And where were you Priyanka beta? For so long, I should say years' She said next.

'Aunty, I was out for studies!' Priyanka made an excuse.

I sniffed in.

'But you must have told us at lease!'

'Mom took me to Chennai' Priyanka lied the second time.

'Chennai? A quite long distance from Mumbai. Did you feel comfortable there?'

'Yeah, I did'

Priyanka didn't have any good choice other than saying 'Yeah, I did'

I signed Sam to get to the point. The main part was not mentioned in the 'Chennai-mom-education' conversation. 'What is he doing?' Priya whispered.

I grinned.

'Mom, can I say something?' Sam said finally entering the conversation.

His mom made a face regarding a 'yes'

'Mom, I love…'

'Shall we have dinner?' Sam's dad interrupted Sam.

'Sure! Come, you all will have dinner with us today' Sam' mom said as we made a face at Sam.

Sam signed us to come in to the dining room as we moved from out places. The dining room seemed a bit different. It was a triangle-shaped and it had unique things on it. We took our seats. We were six of us sitting on that fucking uncomfortable dining table. 'Why don't they change the dining table? And especially the chairs?' I wanted to ask.

Sam's mom served us the food. Sam took his first bit. 'Careless!' I wanted to say. I pushed Sam's right hand as his roti fell into his mom's plate.

'Sam, be careful with your food' His mom said.

Sam looked down at his plate. 'Sam talk to them, go!' Priya whispered.

'Mom, I want you to pay attention towards me' Sam said.

All the eyes were on him.

'I wanted to share something very important' Sam said.

This was something he could speak out like 'Very important' was average. What he said was not worth it.

'Mom, as you know Priyanka and me had a friendship from our childhood' Sam started.

'Yeah, So?' his mom said.

'So, I wanted to turn this friendship into a relationship, a couple' Sam said as both husband and wife suddenly stopped from their work and looked up at Sam.

Priyanka hung her head low, blushing. They didn't said anything. This led us to have our dinner silently for next few minutes. We stepped down into the garden talking rounds. I checked my watch. It said 9:10 PM.

I sniffed in before I could say something.

'Aunty, Uncle we should…'

'Priyanka, you are really a good girl and Sam had talked about being a couple before. I think you have already dreamt of your future. And you understand Sam better than me. Your eyes shows me that you both love each other' Sam's mom interrupted Priyanka.

Priya and I exchanged 'its-working' glances.

'Yeah, aunty we love each other' Priyanka said.

'Mom, dad please say yes. I have not asked you for anything so far. Please!' Sam said.

Both husband and wife looked at each other. Sam's mom almost had tears in her eyes.

'Sam, we had also planned something same for you. We soon were going to talk to Priyanka's parents about this. But now as you guys have asked us first, we have to say a yes!' Sam's dad said.

Sam hugged his father tight. 'Why not my parents are the same? Why don't they understand me?' I thought. Sam hugged Priyanka next. This romantic scene made my eyes fill up.

'Aunty, don't you think that it's a time of celebration?' Priya said.

'Yeah, but you know we don't get leaves these days' Sam's mom said. 'It's only a celebration. Why don't you guys enjoy?'

I was thinking expounding parents is tough so far. But, today I learnt that 'Life is very simple, you just have to find out the right way to live it'

'Guys, how about Goa?' Sam asked.

10

Pritam Deshpande – Managing Director' I read out the name plate outside my father's cabin. I had been sent to my father's office by mom. She said that dad wanted to talk to me about something. 'Does she think me a tiffin box or an important file which can be sent anytime to my father's office?' I thought. We live in same house. He could talk to me at evening. There will be two possibilities of dad calling to his office. One, there must be many other works which he alone couldn't handle himself and had called me to help him out of it. He sometimes asks me to get some documents typed and get him a printout. Second, my father whenever wants to talk to me about mine or his personal life, he always calls me at his office. He asks me to get some privacy and his office and his cabin was the best place voted for it, far away from mom. When he starts talking before my mom she starts doubting him. She always doubts! Doubt! And doubt! I heard a unique sound from a long distance which interrupted me from staring the name plate. I turned around as found an employ with his cell-phone ringing. 'What a rare ringtone he has?' I thought.

I sniffed in as I turned back. I knocked the door.

The door pretended as if it was dead. Nobody answered. I made a face. I moved close and knocked it approximately three times again. It worked this time.

'Come in' the voice came from inside. It was dad.

I opened the door as stepped in. the air-conditioned air dashed my body. I looked at my father as he signed me to sit on the chair kept in front of him. I turned my eyes around.

My eyes stuck on the cup-board. It contained some books, some of dad's material and his official files. I found a blue colour Gold necklace rectangular box proclaimed '*Swarg –* Dadar' on it. My expressions changed to its baffled stage. There wasn't mom's birthday or something. 'Why had dad got this one?' I thought.

My father offered me a glass of water from his table. I stared at his eyes. He smiled at me. He swapped out pen from his blazer. He pushed file towards me and opened it for me. I saw the pictures of the buildings which read '2BHK, 3BHK, 4BHK' on right bottom corner. I threw my dad a puzzled look. 'Are we going to ship to a new house?' I thought.

I shrugged my shoulders.

'What's this dad? Buildings, apartments?' I said, baffled.

'Guess' he put on the puzzle.

I hate the word 'Guess'. I mean we ask them a question and none for other, they give us a unpretentious answer, a simple word 'Guess'.it means ask questions yourselves, and answer them yourselves. If we have the answers ourselves then why should we ask the question? I came out of this 'Guess' theory.

'Dad, are we going to shift?' I asked.

'Not we! You both' he replied.

I was really stumped with this 'you-both' concept.

'You both?' I flabbergasted.

My father closed down the file and placed it on its original place. Life would be so easy without confusions. He picked up the glass and took a small sip.

'Rohit, is your cell-phone switched off?' He inquired.

'How did you know?'

'Sam called me to tell you a 'thank you' from him' Dad said.

I frowned.

'Thank you? For what?' I said.

Questions nipped my mind for which I had no answers. I freak out because if our parents get known to…

'Rohit, life is large. He called me because you helped him out. Remember Priyanka's matter?' Dad said.

Nerve passed my stomach. Sweat popped over my forehead. I really didn't wanted that my parents should get known to it. But it broke out. I should have warned Sam about this first! I stared at the water glass as I was in real need of H_2O.

I sniffed in.

'But why did he called you? Why not me?'

'Because your cell-phone was switched off'

'Not like that way. But…'I stopped the mid-sentence.

'Is this saying thank you was really important for Sam?' I wondered. I thought over to talk to dad about this not itself.

'Then what's wrong dad? I didn't made a mistake. I just helped them out with their emotional problem' I said in one single breadth.

'When I said that you had made a mistake? You have made two lives come together. I like you helping others. Life had many priorities and we have to accept them. You are now at a marriageable age. You will soon marry Priya, and you have Priya as your life precedence henceforth'

'If mom allows and makes up her mind about Priya' I wanted to say.

I shook my head.

'By the way, have you talked to mom?' Dad said.

'About?'

'Priya!'

I gave him an understanding nod.

'What did she say?'

'Her common answer dad! 'That girl is not good for you. Why don't you listen to me? When will you change your mind about her?' I mean, she is driving me crazy' I said.

Mom thinks that we should change for her. She thinks she is always right. Some had said really true that 'Everyone thinks of changing the world, but no one thinks of changing himself' 'Can't she be common and sedate like Sam's parents?' I thought.

'Why don't you talk to mom once?' I said.

He rested back on the chair. He slide his hand into his pocket and brought out a red-colour heart shaped box. I wondered what that box was for. 'Is he going to make mom happy with it?' I thought.

He brought it close to my face. I wondered if he was showing me the colour.

'Rohit, see this. I had almost got an engagement ring for you. But... I... think...'

'No dad! I'll fight this. And nobody gives a fuck on mom taking decisions on my life' I said unable to control myself.

'Rohit language!'

'Sorry'

I soon remembered our 'Celebration' policy. Sam said about Goa. I think I should ask dad to join us. I could invite mom too as she could spend time with Priya.

'Dad, Sam had arranged the Goa trip for celebration' I blunt.

'Oh... enjoy yourselves' Dad said.

'Would you like to join us?' I asked next.

'No'

Directly a 'no' was something stupid. He could at lease tell a reason and cut off.

'Why?'

'You could see the work, as it had to be done we really have no time from this' dad explained as I heard someone knocking the door. 'Come in!' dad said. She was dad's secretary.

I gave him a fake smile.

'Sir, Dr Shukla is waiting. He had an appointment' She said.

'Yeah, I know' Dad said as he checked his watch. 'Oops! It's 4 PM'

I think I should leave dad alone with his boring clients. I jumped out of the chair.

'I think I should leave now!' I said.

Dad gave me a puzzled look.

'Sure'

I moved towards the door as I stared at the cup-board once again. I stepped out of the office. I leaned over to call Sam inquisitive about our Goa trip.

'When are we leaving?' I asked.

'Tonight'

'What? Tonight? I haven't packed yet' I said.

'Hurry up Rohit, we have to leave for Andheri station' Sam said as we hung up.

I composed a message to Priya.

HEY MISS! WE HAVE TO
LEAVE AT 9:30 PM, SHARP
ANDHERI STATION, SUT

There was a sudden reply from Priya, which said,

I KNOW IT BEFORE, AND
I THINK MR SLOW HAD
LEARNT IT NOW FROM SAM

How did Priya know that Sam had called me? Maybe it is said true 'Girls have six senses' I smiled at myself. One thing was still kicking my mind, the ring, the blue box, the engagement…

Goa

11

We reached the 'Goa Airport' at Vasco. We then reached Panaji by car within few hours. The atmosphere here was cold and cloudy. I had just visited Panaji, But it give the impression that I had lived here for years. The beauty of beaches, the goan language, the marine food, and the people here had already drove me crazy. It was just overwhelming. Million times better than Mumbai. I think Goa is one of the developed states in India. So where were me? I think we were just reached Panaji.

We were all the way searching for the taxi. The taxi here was a Suzuki Swift. In Mumbai we have a typical yellow and black taxi's. This was something I finally looked in Panaji. I had heard about the hotel Landmark, a five-star hotel. But we really couldn't afford the hotel as we ourselves don't have much money in our own pockets. Our taxi drove us to the place called 'Dona-Paula' beach which had many hotels and lodges alongside. We booked a hotel, cheap but good. We provided our identity proof as asked by the receptionist. We hired two rooms, we got room number Twenty-Four, Sam and Priyanka got room number Sixty-Seven. Ours was on the second floor and Sam's room on fifth. We had just stepped into our deluxe rooms. We stared at our clean room. We placed our bags on the bed as Priya went towards the balcony. I stood behind her as my hands slide through her stomach. She looked back, lose her nerve.

'There is no one instead of me' I said.

She smiled at me.

I got a call from Radhika di. As the names flashed on my phone's screen my face lit us. I want to tell her that we were on a Goa tour. I prepared myself.

'I think you are enjoying, Rohit' Radhika di said.

'What? We just reached. There is a long time to enjoy still' I said.

Radhika di never asked me of my tours before. She never did. I think she must be having a reason.

'Good answer' She said in a childish way.

'So, what's up? Anything special?' I asked.

'I have called you because, actually the things are good here. Mom is talking good about you' She blunt.

'Really?' I shouted enough to spoil her ears, unable to control my excitement.

This was something good about mom. She talked something good about me. But what has she really said?

'Di, what mom really…'

'No I'll not tell you. Come back home, mom will expound you herself' She interrupted me yawning. 'But I could say that's a good news though'

The words 'long time' echoed long time in my head. What exactly she wanted to tell me?

'Rohit, promise me one thing that you'll ever thing about the suicide thing' her voice almost faded.

'Di, why do you think like that? I would never do so!' I said the first word faint.

'But on what I'll trust you?'

'Because I love you more than the rest' I said as Priya stared at me as I said 'I love you'

I sniffed in.

Radhika di hung up as she said she would call me later as she had some important work to work with. I placed the cellphone at its original place as I turned to Priya. She stared at me in a horrible way.

'What?' I said looking into her eyes.

'Who was it?'

'Radhika di' I said.

'Oh… so she is in Mumbai?'

I didn't answer this question. And I don't think that each and every question of girls should be answered. I came close to her as I held her and stared into her eyes. I held her tight, her breast almost on my chest. I thought of every movement that we had spent together so far, from when we were in schools till when we were visiting discos. It felt nice.

'Rohit, long time no? We are with each other' She said.

'No, just five minutes ago, I was a stranger to you' I replied.

She banged her fest on my chest friskily. 'It's not funny' She said as I hugged her tight. I smelled her hairs, they smelled romantic. She responded.

'It's not funny really, its love' I said in a smooth voice. 'Any don't be angry, the anger on your face really doesn't look good'

'Then don't see me anymore' She said as I frozen.

I felt coldness in the atmosphere, my eyes bigger then they usually appear. I released her as I moved towards the balcony. My eyes had tears. I think she noticed that. But what's the big deal if she wants me not to look at her? It doesn't matter me. Priya walked out into the balcony and placed her hand on my shoulders.

I shrugged my shoulders as I turned towards her. The droplet from my right eye rolled down.

'I'm sorry, I was in no sense…'

I turned around as Priya stopped her mid-sentence. She made me turn towards her again.

'I'm sorry'

'Wah! First say don't look at me… and… you know how much it hurts me?' I said unable to control myself. 'You know when I don't look at you a single second it feels like the world is against me. And all you want to say is…'

She placed her palms on my cheeks. Her soft palms really felt good. I looked away from her. She hugged me tight.

'I'm sorry baby!' She said.

I closed down my eyes as I heard a sound from a distance which said.

'Rohit, where are you? It's getting late'

Daam! It was Sam into our room. I pushed Priya back as we stood innocent.

I sniffed in.

'Sorry to bother you this way' I said as Priya smiled at me.

'Almost ready' I said next as Sam and Priyanka stood before us.

'Let's go then' Priyanka said.

'Sure' Priya poked.

We locked our room as we moved towards the Swift. Girls took the back seat as we took front ones. The sound system in our car played 'Rafta-Rafta' from the movie Raaz 3.

'It's good here, the atmosphere, the people' I said.

'Yeah' all of them said in unison.

I brought my head outside the window. I felt something that I should not. I remember my childhood memories when me and Sam played truth and dare game when we were in class five. When I remember these days I really cry. I brought my head in as Sam noticed me. He threw me a 'what-happen' glance. I cleared my face and sniffed in. I looked back at girls. Priyanka leaned down picking up her anklet which had fallen down. I then looked at Priya, she was busy adjusting her earphones. Her long hairs really seemed good.

'Hey guys' I said as everybody noticed me.

I signed Priyanka to plug off those earphones from Priya's ears. I kept quiet for few seconds.

'Do you guys believe in truth?' I said next.

'Yes' there was a common answer in unison.

I gave them an understanding nod.

'Then, you must be already knowing the game of truth or dare!' I exclaimed.

'Yes' came an answer.

'Quite known to' came another answer.

I think some were not at all known to this. I leaned over to explain them the conditions. Then expounded them the terms and conditions of the game, another minute.

I sniffed in.

'That's it?' Priya said in a childish way.

'Yeah!' Sam said. 'When we were in class five, we used to play this game together' Sam placed his hand on mine as a nerve passed my body. I looked up at Sam as we smiled at each other.

We passed over the flyover. The sea water downside made me feel really energetic. On the other side was the salt farms, on which they had stored the salty sea water made me realize how they produce salt in the first place?

'Shall we try out the game after dinner?' Sam questioned.

All of them nodded as if there was a shooting going on, and as if we have to nod for a shot. My mind clicked Radhika didi's words. I have to bring my thoughts out. But to whom I should tell this? I brought up my laptop and composed a mail to Radhika didi

Radhika Didi,

Didi, today I had just stared to explore Goa city. We are driving out at the tourist destinations. I'm thinking all over back about our family. Mostly I thought about those days when we had fun in my childhood. I'm missing you. I really can't expound this to my friends as I have written to you. You are my parent and not mom and dad. You have told me a good news today, what don't really know what it is. I'm so eager to know it. Make me know it soon. I'll stop here, my friends are around. And I'll be waiting for my answer!

Yours lovingly,

Brother.

I placed my laptop at its original place and slide my hand into my pocket.

'What was it?' Sam asked.

'Just a quick Email' I said as I looked out 'Ahh! We reached the club'

We had reached 'Lovely Disco Club' in Panaji. It was not into the Panaji city exactly, few kilometres away from its border. We stepped down from the car as the security guard welcomed us pushing in the bullet proof glass door in. We stepped in as the disco played some dance numbers, I heard was 'Mahi we'. We had our seats on the tables next to the counter. I placed my phone on the table as it was uncomfortable for me in jeans.

'Shall we order a Vodka or a Bear?' I asked Sam.

'Your choice!' Sam said.

'Vodka first!'

'Sure'

I signed the waiter as he came towards us. He was not into his dress-code. Hushh…I had seen a waiter into his civil dress once in my lifetime. I was grateful.

'Get us two bottles of Vodka in a steal glass' I said. I don't want everyone around stare at us drinking alcohol.

I noticed girls. I leaned over to ask them for their orders.

'What will you have?' I said.

'Cold drinks?' Sam poked.

'Mango juice is okay!' Priya said looking at Priyanka.

I ordered their choice. I stared at Priya's nose as it looked too pretty. She looked somewhere else without noticing us as if we were thrown waste before her. I banged my fest onto the table as the entire club noticed us. I saw the waiter coming towards us with our orders into his right hand. He placed the vodka bottle in front of us and the mango juice towards the girls. I poured the vodka into my glass and took a big sip. I leaned over to play the game of truth or dare.

'Shall we play truth or dare?' I said.

I shrugged my shoulders.

'Sure' came an answer.

I thought of playing the game in privacy. 'Can we get some privacy here?' I asked myself.

'Guys, we should get some privacy here' I said.

I wanted to play it in privacy because I want that Priya to answer my questions seriously.

'Sure' Sam said

We picked up our glasses as we stood up from our places. We transferred our places away from Sam and Priyanka on Table number sixteen. We settled down as Sam and I exchanged 'okay' glances.

'Are you comfortable?' I asked.

'Yeah'

I gave her an understanding nod.

'Shall we start?' I said.

'I'm in' Priya said.

I sniffed in.

'So, will you start first or may I?' I asked.

She kept quiet. There came no answer from her side.

'Okay, the first question is, what was the best thing happen in your day today?' I asked.

'Hmm… Today? That when we were in our room' She said.

'Are you sure?' I said.

'Hey! You can't ask two question in one go!' Priya said and laughed at me.

I smiled at her.

'Proceed' I said.

'What do you think about me?' Priya asked her question.

I really had no particular answer for her question. I have so much about her to tell. I have millions of ideas about her. I would ensure with my favourite choice' I said to myself.

'I think you should be an actor' I said.

She gave me an understanding nod.

'So, do you love my family?' I asked next.

'Yeah, a lot I guess. They are friendly to me as well as my family' She said.

I smiled at myself. 'Yeah, my mom is very friendly with you. Right?' I asked myself.

'And my mom?' I said.

'Sorry, you can't ask two in one go' Priya made her way out.

'Please'

'Rohit, see I know that your mom has a problem with me and our relation and you should not feel anything for it. I know I love you and you know you love me then why worry? The rest of the life, we have to live together with each other and not your parents have to. And think off clear. Don't think that your parents will not promote our marriage. Think positive' She said placing her right hand on mine. 'My family loves you a lot and they want us to get married'

'But, my dad and Radhika didi likes you. Only mom needs some exposition medicine' I teased.

'I'm trying to change myself Rohit, I know your mom is against me for my lifestyles' Priya said.

The game of truth and dare was fully vanished in our 'dad-mom-sister-relation-marriage' conversation. I held her hand up to my face as I kissed it. I couldn't say anything; I had just flowed into the sea of emotions. All I could say was...

'Thank you!' I said.

'For what?' Her voice breaking down.

I stared at her with my half-squinted eyes. I found something unique into her eyes. She leaned down on the table. Just slept off. I got up from my chair as I moved towards her.

'Are you okay?' I said holding her up.

'Yes' She said. This time in a normal voice.

I moved back to my seat. I held up my glass as I took two sips. I finished the glass off taking up a big sip next.

'I hope I'm not disturbing you' Sam said placing his hand on my shoulder as I looked back at him.

'No, not at all' I said.

'Priya, if you don't mind, can I borrow him away for a second? Some personal work' Sam said.

She nodded. Something differently. I had a doubt that something was wrong with her. I got up as I signed Priya to sit with Priyanka. I moved out where Sam brought me. It was the parking area.

'How was the game?' Sam asked.

'Quite good' I said. 'Yours?'

'Romantic'

I think Sam had not called me her to ask about the game! There was something protuberant.

'I recently had a call from our college Dean. Remember Mr. Shukla?' Sam said.

'Who? Marcho?' I said.

We used to call him Marcho from our college times because the underwear he wore was almost visible to all of the students. He had a habit of putting his pants as down as possible.

'What did he said?'

'He need our bio data urgently' Sam said.

Asking for the bio now was something quite silly. It's have been years that we were into the college. And why Sam had called me into the parking for this? He could tell me this in.

'So, is this to be told in the parking?' I asked.

'I think you want the girls to know about the Marcho thing' Sam said.

I smiled as I gave him an understanding nod.

He held my hand as we moved in. The music was changed to Honey Singh's 'High Heels' we stepped to our table. I noticed something strange.

Both the girls leaned on the table. We smiled. 'How could these girls sleep so early?' I asked myself. I moved away to wake them up. I moved Priyanka first.

'Let me sleep, I want some more' Priyanka said in a childish tone.

What was she saying? 'I want some more?' I smelled her mouth. Sam moved towards me. I tried to recognize the smell. I looked up at Sam. Daam! It was fucking alcohol! I held up their glasses to smell them out. I was right, it contained alcohol. I moved towards Priya to check her out. The anger filled me as I stepped to the manager. I grabbed his collar and accorded him three non-stop punches. Blood rolled down his lips. I was about to hit him more as Sam held me.

'Who served them alcohol?' I screamed as the entire club noticed me and the fucking manager.

'Sir you have a…'

'Who served, he asked' Sam interrupted.

'What kind of rubbish are you…'

Slap! Slap! Slap! Sam gave him three non-stop slaps. The crowd gathered before us. The music was put down. Sam held his collar as one of the waiter came forward.

'Sir, actually I had' He said as I turned towards him.

'Why?' I screamed.

'By mistake!' was his silly answer. 'Sir they had ordered mango juice; I had got a wrong order. I had served them mango flavoured alcohol'

I moved forward to kick him as the security guards held me. Sam was busy solving the matter.

'Rohit, be calm' He said. I was a bit calm now. The security tigers released me as I stepped towards the table to look at the girls.

'We are not paying the bill' Sam announced.

We held the girls as we stepped outside the club. They were a little conscious now. I brought the water bottle from the car. Sam inquired the girls about their ailment. I held Priyanka who didn't responded yet. I rubbed her back then her palms. We sat into the car as we drove it towards the gate

Daam! What the Fuck!

The Swift got a puncher mid-way. I stood down.

'Daam!' I said kicking the puncher wheel.

I pushed the car as it had stopped the mid-road. We brought it to a corner. Sam stepped down. The day today was bad for us. Fuck the day! And overall we didn't have a spare tire which could be replaced with the puncher one. It was a desolate road as not even a dog was around. The darkness made us feel even terrified.

I sniffed in.

I looked around. Sam elbowed me saying 'Rohit, look at that'

There were two Autos coming on the road and it was a good thing that they were not occupied. I raised my hand signing them to stop. Priyanka stepped out as she was fully conscious now. Sam hugged her tight. The autos stopped by us. I brought Priya out.

'I'll be with her' Priyanka said.

'No, you go with Rohit. I'll take her' Sam said.

'But…'

'Go Priyanka' Sam interrupted.

Sam looked up at me throwing me a 'you-go-I'll-take-her' glance.

Sam held Priya and stepped into the first auto. Sam made Priya sleep on his lap. Priyanka and I took the second one. The autos moved as Priyanka was busy asking me what had really happen. I explained her everything that they were drunk. I stared out. It was a one way and we were on the wrong track. Two couples of heavy trucks moved towards us. I looked that I shouldn't have seen at all in my lifetime. The truck had dashed the first auto. My Auto driver turned the handle suddenly to avoid the accident as the auto tilted and it slide over the road. The first auto had already crashed into the truck. And what, Destiny had done its work…

12

The first day at Panaji went glum. We had one after another disasters before us. I held Priya in my arm into the ambulance. My whole body was full of blood. Priyanka cried looking at Sam's condition. I felt really bad about it that, they were going to get married in few months and this destiny… if I could I have a chance I could have really fucked-off this destiny. The blood continuously flowed from her head. I protected the wound with my hand to stop the blood flow. I was crying in foolish manner. 'Priya come back, think about me' was all I was saying. I remembered the movements that we had spent together with each other. The way we shared our ice-cream, the movement when I first looked at her, the hug of ours, the way she talked to me and her cute nose. I only stared at her face thinking all this. The injections were given to her to keep her conscious. We reached the city hospital of Goa. The two ward boys bought us out of the ambulance. We made an entrance towards the ICU. The nurse signed us to stop at the ICU entrance. We stood there crying. Priyanka pushed me aside and ran towards the ICU. A ward boy stopped her getting in. 'Leave me, I want to be with my Sam. Please let me get in. Don't make Sam away from me' She cried. I held her. I made her sit on the bench. She rested her head on my shoulder, still crying. I held her. 'Don't worry, it will be all right' I said sobbing.

The red bulb glowed as the operations had been started in the ICU. My cell-phone vibrated. I slide my hand into my right jeans pocket and brought the cell phone out. It said 'MOM Calling' I got shocked for a while. I rubbed my eyes and sniffed in several times. I brought my breadth back to normal as I prepared myself to answer the call.

'Rohit, what's up? Enjoying?' Mom inquired.

I looked up at the ICU door.

'Yes mom'

'Where's Priya? I want to talk to her. Is he there?'

Why mom suddenly needs Priya? She was always angry with her before.

I baffled.

'No mom she isn't here. Actually she had been to a parlour' I lied. 'Why mom? Any important work?'

She cleared her throat.

'Radhika didn't told you?'

'What?'

I wanted to know this.

'I want Priya back. I want you two to get married as early as possible' Mom said. 'Radhika and dad gave me an exposition about this. And I think I have to also adjust somewhere, after all it's your life'

The cell-phone from my hand fell down. The expressions on my face changed. My face turned pale. The phone kept on talking, 'Hello… hello…. Hello… are… you… there….?' I looked down, Priyanka had went off to sleep. I stared at the ICU bulb for next few hours wondering when my Priya will be normal like before. Thousands of thoughts entered my mind. 'Our parents should never get known to this' I told myself. I looked at Priyanka as her face was wry as she had cried a lot. I don't know that how much time had passed now I only stared at the ICU bulb to get off. It was 5:38 am in the morning. Priyanka had got up with the sunrise. She got up from my lap suddenly and moved towards the ICU room. I followed her.

'Where's the doctor?' She asked.

'Priyanka, doctor has not come yet. Stay calm!' I said.

The expressions on her face changed. She pushed me back.

'Calm? How can I? Life is coming to an end and all you want to say is Calm down?' Priyanka shouted at me.

I held her as she hugged me. She busted out in tears. I rubbed her back. I looked up at her. The doctor came out from the ICU. I released Priyanka and ran towards the doctor. Priyanka followed me.

'Doctor what…'

'The patient whose name is Sam, is doing now. He is out of danger' The doctor said.

'And the girl, Priya?' I asked.

'We have tried our level best for her but…'

'But what doctor?' I shouted.

'Look stay calm, we have tried our level best for her, but she is not responding still. She had a huge blood loss' He said.

My face fell down. He tapped my shoulders saying 'take-care' I can't even take care of my own priorities and how can I take care of myself? Sam was shifted to a private room. I sat down on the floor holding my head and crying. I have really gone wrong to take care of my priorities. I looked at my entire life that where I had made a mistake. Our life consist of many priorities and mistakes and of course I agree that I had made a mistake here. But this big punishment was not at all accepted. Priyanka sat down to make me stand up. I stood up as we moved towards the room where Sam had been shifted. I firstly entered the room as I saw Sam laying down on his bed. Priyanka ran towards him as she held his hand. She rubbed Sam's hands as Sam slowly opened his eyes. Tears filled Priyanka's eyes.

'Hey, don't worry it's a normal injury and some fractures' Sam said.

'No, don't talk anything. You must rest now' Priyanka said as she got up and ran towards a corner to clean her face. I slowly moved towards Sam as he threw me a 'hey' glance as I smile at him. I sat down on the stool kept beside his bed.

'How is Priya? I hope she is fine!' Sam said.

I looked down as I started crying. He kept his hand on mine.

I shook my head.

'Doctor said she is not responding yet' Priyanka said as Sam's eyes turned on to Priyanka.

I rested my head on the bed, still crying. A nurse walked in the room as she asked us to leave the room as doctors were coming for check-ups. We stepped outside the room as the door shut before us. My cell-phone beeped as I brought it out. It said 'P Mom Calling' it means Priya's mom calling. 'But why could she have call me this time?' I thought. I prepared myself to talk the call.

'Rohit beta, can I talk to Priya please' She said. 'I tried to call her but her cell phone is switched off. Is she there?'

I looked up at the ICU room as I closed down my eyes.

'No Aunty, she is been for a bath' I lied to a mother who had created so cute creature.

'When she will be out, just tell her to ring me up' She said.

I frightened.

'Aunty, any message I'll tell her' I said.

'No, just want to talk to her' She said as I kept my cell-phone down. I looked up into Priyanka's eyes her eyes seemed happy as well as sad as like me. I should tell Priyanka to not tell anyone about anything happen. 'Priyanka this is a mistake by us. No one should get known that Sam and Priya had an accident and now are in ICU' I said politely. I looked down at my cell-phone. The light flashed on the screen as it said 'Call ended 3:56' Daam! I had left my cell-phone connected. 'What if she had heard everything? What if they come here?' I thought. Number of questions popped into my mind. I sat down on the bench as Priyanka inquired 'What happen?'

'I had left my cell-phone online with Priya's mom' I said. I hit my hands on my head like mad. I picked up my fucking cell-phone to throw it away as I had a call from dad. I can't really get through this anymore. I passed the cell-phone to Priyanka as I got up.

'Uncle, I'm Priyanka' Priyanka said.

'Is Rohit there?'

Priyanka looked at me throwing me a 'your-dad-is-calling-you' glance. I shook my head slowly as I moved back.

'Where are you now?' Dad inquired as Priyanka's expressions changed.

'Where… means… we are…' Priyanka stammered.

'I'll answer this, you are at the hospital' Dad interrupted.

As Priyanka heard the word hospital she moved back a little. She brought down the cell phone from her ears and stared at me with her eyes extra wide. Priyanka moved close to me as she passed me the cell-phone. 'It's finished' Priyanka said as she moved fro by me. I stared at the phone thinking what a big mistake I had done? 'But I have to face the reality' I told myself.

I brought the phone towards my ears.

'Hello'

'I have not called you to say hello and hey' the voice from other side said. It was dad. 'How can you be so careless? This is how you showed your colours? Then what after the marriage Rohit? And you say that you want to marry Priya and you love her too much. This is how much you love her?'

I cried hard.

'Dad… I… have… done… a… mistake…' I sobbed.

'You have not made a mistake, the big mess, the biggest mistake you have made' He shouted.

I looked down. 'Sorry' I just got one word to say. 'We are reaching there soon' Dad said.

The word 'we' moved me a little.

'We?' I asked. 'Who?'

'We, Priya's, Sam's and Priyanka's family' Dad said.

'C…'

'Contix?' Dad interrupted.

'City Hospital' I stammered. 'Dad I…' I said as the call hung up. I threw the phone on the floor the screen broke down into thousands of pieces. I sat down on the bench. I saw doctor coming towards us as I stood up.

'Doctor what?' I worried.

'See, she is responding now. But we can't say that she is totally out of danger. We have to keep her few more days under observation' He said.

I joint my hands before him saying 'Doctor, please save her. She is my life' I touched his feet.

'Hey, what are you doing? We are trying our best' He politely replied. 'Take care of yourself'

I noticed a nurse coming out of the room. A voice interrupted me. 'Sir, your appointments' it said. A ward boy came towards the doctor.

'Yeah, Please Excuse me' The doctor said as he disappeared.

I prepared myself to get into Sam's room. I cleared my face and had a smile, because I didn't want Sam to see me crying. Priyanka had already entered the room. I moved in. I noticed Priyanka telling Sam something in a strong voice. I moved close to him and stood there. He looked up at me giving me a 'what-happen-out' glance.

'Rohit, what I'm listening? Our parents…'

'Yeah, they know all this and soon will be here' I said. My dad's words 'you have shown your colours this then what after the marriage' echoed my mind. I'm really careless about Priya. Can I give the happiness she wants after the marriage? Will she will be happy with me?

I sniffed in as I came out of my thoughts of questions.

'Sam, you don't worry. We will get through this' Priyanka said.

'Priyanka, how is Priya?' Sam said.

'Doctor says that she is responding but not totally out of danger' I said as Priyanka looked up at me.

The tears from my eyes rolled down. Priyanka noticed me as she stood up. She hugged me.

'Don't worry, everything will be alright' She said.

'I'll not be able to live without her. My life will be of nowhere' I sobbed. 'I want to see her once. Please come with me. Please'

Priyanka looked at Sam. Priyanka released me as she held my hand and brought me out. We moved towards the ICU as a ward boy stopped up. I looked at Priyanka as she moved forward.

'Please let us in. We just want to see the patient once' Priyanka said.

'Ma'am she is under observation now and we don't have any permission to let anyone in' The ward boy said.

'See please let us in, we just want to see her. Just for two minutes' I begged.

'Okay, but only one can!'

I looked at Priyanka as she accorded me a 'go-now' glance. I crossed the ICU door as the ICU room felt silent, only the sounds of the machines were clearly sound-able. I stepped forward as there were curtains. I passed through them as I could see Priya lying on the bed. Her forehead had a wound, the cotton bandage rolled around her forehead and some pipes through her cute nose. I moved forward towards her and placed my hand on her forehead. I moved my hand through her forehead. Some hairs were spread through her face. I tugged them all back her ears. She suddenly opened her eyes and looked at me. Her eyes only had tears. I noticed her as I ran outside the ICU room to call out the doctor. 'DOCTOR… DOCTOR…' I shouted.

'What happed?' Priyanka asked holding my hand as I didn't noticed her.

The doctor ran towards me inquiring 'what happen?'

'Doctor, she opened her eyes and looked at me. She responded me. She…' I said as I couldn't control myself.

The doctor ran into the ICU room as he told us to wait outside. I moved here and there thinking 'she is back'. I looked at Priyanka and I smiled at her for the first time. I moved forwards towards her. She placed her hand on my shoulder as I smiled heartedly for the first time since the accident.

I sniffed in.

I stared at the ICU. Doctor soon appeared in front of our eyes. I ran towards him as all I could see was his eyes.

'Mr. Rohit, she is totally out of danger now. No need to worry' He said as his words felt like god appeared before me.

I joint my hands as I prayed god for this wonderful gift. I hugged Priyanka in cheerfulness.

'I'll tell Sam' she said as she ran towards Sam's room.

I wanted to talk to Priya. I want to see her cute eyes. I wanted to touch her.

'Doctor, can I meet her?' I requested.

'You can, but after twenty minutes' He said. 'Take care'

'Thank you doctor' I said holding his hands.

'Excuse me!' He said as he left.

I smiled at him.

I took my seat on the bench. I was happy for Priya. I looked in the corridor as I saw a strange thing. I saw Priya's mom running towards me. I stood up as I moved forward. She came close to me as she held my collars. 'Where is my daughter? Where is Priya?' She shouted. Priya's dad held aunty and bought her back. My collar was released.

Slap! Slap!

She accorded me two tight slaps on my right cheek and my face had five fingers printed on it.

'Where is she?' She shouted at me for the first time.

I pointed her towards the ICU. She moved as I moved forward to stop her. Priya's father stopped me saying.

'Stay off Priya and us'

I saw my parents entering the corridor. My sister had a strong hate for me in her eyes. I bend my head down in shame.

I sniffed in.

'Mom' I called her as my sister came forward

Slap!

I got another slap.

'Shame on you Rohit, how much I trusted you and you…' She stopped the mid-sentence.

'Didi, I can explain' I said.

'What will you explain now Rohit? You did everything already' Didi replied.

'You have to listen' I said as my dad moved forward towards me to give me another slap as Radhika didi stopped him. She looked up at me 'Dad, you be relax. You stay out of this, I'll talk to Rohit. You already suffer from Blood Pressure problems' Radhika didi said as my parents went towards the reception. I looked up at Radhika didi thinking, which sister loved me when I was a child, which sister cared for me like a parent, which sister supported me so much suddenly slapped me today. I held her hand as she said 'Rohit, what wrong?'

'Didi, it's was my mistake that I had been to a club' I said.

'Club?'

'Yes, I know that I shouldn't have been there' I said. 'I'm sorry didi, please don't tell this to mom and dad'

Radhika didi looked at me, baffled. She gave me a 'what-you-have-done-is-wrong' glance. I know she was right. I was so wrong. This would not be happen if we didn't have been to the daam club and drunk those fucking alcohols.

'Rohit, you have changed! Really!' She said. 'Tell me what had happen that day?'

I held her hand and brought her towards the Sam's room. I stopped her at the door. 'I was really unknown about all this. I really don't know that the clubs idea would bring us to the hospital' I said. I took her in as Priyanka stood up from her seat and Sam gave his full attention towards us. Didi moved towards Priyanka as she held her arms. She looked into her eyes. She had a question which says, 'What had happen that day?' Priyanka looked up at me as she started explaining the stuff that we had a day before. I moved towards a corner and stood there staring at the floor. The explanation went too long, I think about an hour. Priyanka explained didi each and every point. 'Rohit cares for her a lot. He loves her. He continuously cried from yesterday, and now when she is finally out of danger he smiled for the first time' Priyanka said.

My sister had tears in her eyes. She turned back towards me. She ran towards me as she hugged me. I felt good.

'Rohit please forgive me, not knowing anything I slapped you!' She said.

I sniffed in.

'I released didi as Priyanka moved towards us. We both smiled at her. She cleaned my eyes with her right hand. I thought of everything, that I had been from my childhood. I thought over my friends. I think, I have got strange friends, one side they teach me to kick off the problem which is before us now and on the other side they tell me to fight with the reality. I tightly hugged Priyanka.

'Err… we forgot Sam, how is he?' Didi asked.

'He is well now. He just has some fractures and nothing more' I said releasing Priyanka. 'Right Sam?'

He gave me an understanding nod.

Everyone broke down into laughter. The laughter meant something special to me. Something that I felt good for few minutes and glum when I looked my parents entering Sam's room. This time my dad looked a bit calm. He folded his sleeves as he walked towards me.

'What have you done this Rohit?' He said. He held my shoulders. We kept our eye-contact for few seconds as mom interrupted us.

'Are you okay Rohit?' Mom asked. 'I warned you before, don't get involved with that silly girl. See the results now'

'Mom, please stop!' I said politely. 'And you have said yes for her, what wrong now?'

'I only said yes because your dad and Radhika forced me. But now, I really don't agree. I don't agree. I don't want to you to get with this shameless girl for your whole life. Let her die'

I closed my eyes as my head echoed her last words. 'Let her die'

'Mom stop' I screamed so loudly that whole hospital could notice me. 'I don't want to listen a single word against her now'

'You shouted at me for that girl now? Yeah, it's really nice, I being your mom you support that girl?'

'Yes, because I'm right and what you say is wrong'

Slap! Slap!

I got another two slaps. My face almost turned red now. I looked up at Mom. I didn't had any tears in my eyes this time but I had some sparks which said 'you can get through this'

'I ashamed that you are my son. Get lost from our eyes Rohit. There is no home for you from today' Mom said.

'Really, what you say is right' I said as my dad leaned forward to give me one more. I caught him in my arms for few seconds and released him then. He gave me a look which he had never given before. I answered him with 'I don't need your company, I'm an adult now. I know my responsibilities and priorities' he came forwards as mom stopped him.

'We are really shameful. What sin have we done that we had got a son like you? No values, no respect. I don't know you now. I know my son when he was a child' Mom said as Mom held Dad's hand and brought him towards the door. They stopped the mid-way.

'Radhika, do you want to come with us or stay back with this stranger?' Dad said.

I looked up at Radhika didi as she looked at me. Our eyes met. But my eyes noticed something that I had not expected from her. She walked towards Dad. I started crying, I really couldn't control. Priyanka held me.

I shrugged my shoulders.

One week later…

While taking the side of my intimacy and supporting her, I neglected her and lost my home. I really don't know that I was right or wrong, but after some days this week was mugging my heart and I was feeling nowhere. The days I was suffering from were not good. I had totally suffered from murk days, when I get known to Priya…

I sat on the waiting chair outside the room in which Priya had shifted after her operation. There was no one for me there instead of those bloody empty chairs and the empty corridor frightened me more. I got up suddenly as I saw Radhika didi coming out from the room. I had left alone out as all of them were in. Priya said she wanted to talk to me when she is fully cured. I looked into Radhika didi's eyes as they said something good.

'Don't worry Rohit, she is all right' Didi said. 'Doctor says just one more day and she will be discharged'

I grinned.

I wondered of my Priya getting back to normal. I was finally getting out of this murk. I thought of having a night nosh with her soon. I heard a commotion as I looked at the door. My whole family (of course including Priya's) came out talking to each other. (I mentioned my family above means Priyanka's and Sam's parents after all my own parents left me and they were Priyanka's and Sam's were merely my parents now) Sam got discharged two days ago as he was freely talking and walking with us now. My brain was totally haywire the last week. But now my heart and my mind was recreated.

Priya's mom came forward to me. She looked into my eyes as she grovel. Priya's dad also came closer, but I didn't noticed him. I stood few seconds grovelling as finally Priya's mom said something.

'Rohit beta, I slapped you and told you to stay away. We both were really worried and could not control our mind. Please forgive us!' She said joining her hands. I looked up at her. I held her hands

'Err... aunty, why are you being sorry? It was me who was careless. And you slapped me because love your daughter and was worried' I said in a crying tone.

'Not more then you beta...' Priya's dad said.

He came close as he hugged me. The hug meant that I was somewhere wrong at my place. I was careless. He released me as my eyes were filled with tears. They soon rolled down. I looked up at both of them.

'Rohit, is everything all right?' Sam said.

'Yeah'

'Then why tears?'

'I got parents like these people' I said looking at Priya's parents. 'So, my eyes just watered'

I looked at each of them one by one. Their faces were filled with glee. I made myself the happiest person on this earth. Sam and Priyanka came forward to me whispering something…

'Rohit, good thing, your in-laws are good them mine' Priyanka whispered passing me a fruit. One of them was not enough as second started.

'I think you should get married to these people instead of Priya' Sam said.

I punched him playfully. All of them smiled at me as it made me laugh. I controlled myself.

'Feeling hungry, let's have something?' Priya's mom asked.

'Veg or Non-Veg?' Priyanka said.

♦

I was right outside Priya's room. All of them had gathered around me. I accorded all a 'don't-look-at-me-like-that' glance. Today I was finally going to talk to Priya. Yesterday night we met at the meal but haven't talked to each other a single word. I had a proportion able nosh yesterday, as I felt shy to eat more with Priya in the presence of Priya's parents. And over all that it played a balled song which made us all go in our own dreams. Whenever I looked at Priya, she broke down the eye-contact with me. I was unknown that why she did so? I think because of her parent's presence she did so but now I was totally gratuitous to talk to her. Her parents went up towards the reception to get the discharge formalities done and pay the bills. I was about to get into the room and talk to the belle in the world as Sam said 'We are back Rohit, we all are back' I gave him a smile and proceeded into the room. I stepped close to her as she sat onto the bed, her back towards me.

'Priya' I called out as she looked back at me and suddenly got up. I moved close to her. I realized that nothing was happen so far. We had not had any accident. I stared at her cute face and her extra cute pink nose.

She looked down without answering me. I held her.

'So, you finally came back?' She said releasing herself from me.

I said smiling at her 'what do you mean by finally?'

She made a face at me as if she hates me a lot from many years. I was pensive about what she has said now.

I baffled.

'So what would you like to have? Tea or Coffee?' She asked next.

I looked down at the floor.

'Priya, I know that I made a mistake, but I realize it…'

'Yeah, you realized that now. You don't know me right? Who is Priya? A stranger or an only nuttier in the world?'

'Priya, I can explain' I said.

'Rohit, you didn't answer me. Tea or a Coffee?'

I sniffed in.

'Priya, calm down. We will talk on this' I said moving close to her.

'No, I can't Rohit' She shouted. 'What you did, was just unacceptable from you. I had trusted you so much and you shown your colours'

I was unable to speak anything at this situation. Priya shouted the first time at me from when we met. I went closer to her and I held her. She pushed me away saying 'Don't touch me' She almost cried. The tears from her eyes rolled down.

'Rohit, it's not a joke. I had lend you my whole life, I had faith in you that my life-partner would never do anything like this. But today, you killed my faith Rohit. You really killed it' She said.

My eyes also cried but I controlled myself. I prevented her from her anger. We had reached the immitigable situation.

'Priya please…'

'Please get lost from my eyes Rohit' She shouted. 'And if you think that you can mend your fucking mistake then you are going into a wrong direction'

Priyanka and Sam entered in listening Priya shouting. They both stared at us as we were on the stage of break-up.

'What happen?' Priyanka asked as no one answered.

'And, what had you promised me that you will not drink at all' Priya said in a strong but crying voice. 'And you boozed at the club. I didn't say anything. I let it go as we were on the tour. But you served the alcohol in my drink? You already recreant and on that you added some alcohol in mine?'

'No, that's not the reality…' Priyanka said as Priya interrupted her.

'Priyanka, just don't interfere now. Please stay away with this'

Priya moved forward towards me. Before I could say something she slapped me on my left cheek. Priyanka moved forward towards her and held her. Priya held my hands saying 'These hands cared for me so much when we first met. But now…' She threw my hand down as she turned back. As she threw my hand in force her hand dashed on the bed. The blood popped out. She had a wound. I stepped forward towards her.

'Don't dare to touch me' She said showing her index finger.

I looked up at Priyanka and Sam. Priyanka stepped towards Priya and handled her wound. I kept alive my courtesy. She looked up at me sharing 'what-have-you-done' glances. My brain, my mind, my full body, my heart were all in indignity. Indignity, of the work which I had done so far. After doing this fucking shameful work I think I should be forced to be single, this apt for me. I have caused enough grieve to Priya. I don't want to cause more.

I swallowed the chocked gullet. They say, the language of eye speak better than the language of words. I looked in to Priya's eyes. Our eyes met. I was looking into her eyes of more, belle of the world. My eyes replenished again with tears. She broke down the eye-contact as her parents entered the room. She ran towards them. She hugged her father. I had accepted that hug when I entered her room first. She sobbed as her father made her look up at him. I could tell him everything and expound Priya's views but I was inarticulate before him.

'Dad, tell this person to get lost from my eyes' Priya said pointing towards me.

'What? What are you saying?' Her dad asked.

'I don't want to stay with the person who don't want to care for me' Priya said. 'And the person who doesn't care for himself what will he care for me?'

Uncle looked up at me. I looked in his eyes. Priya moved out. (Who knows that I was seeing Priya for the last time) he stepped close to me as he tapped my shoulders.

'Everything okay?' He asked.

I stared at everyone in the room. Sam, Priyanka, Priya's parents, all. I looked down thinking why Priya talked to me like that? She had never talked to me like that before. What made her? My behaviour? My attitude or my carelessness?

I baffled.

'Rohit, I'm asking you, what wrong?' He asked me the second time.

'She broke up!' I said. Tears rolled down my eyes. I closed down my eyes.

Priya's mom looked at me like she had never before.

'Why?' She inquired.

Sam and Priyanka just stood there and started at us.

I sniffed in. I didn't have any answer for her question 'Why?' I felt really contrite that I could not answer her question. I really had no answer for this.

'God knows' Sam answered.

I moved to a corner as I lie my face down as I stared grizzling.

'I'll talk to her' Uncle said as he started moving outside of the room.

I turned around.

'No uncle, if she truly loved me, she will come back herself' I bagged.

Aunty moved towards her husband as she whispered 'This girl is really…' something.

'She must be not serious. Just joking!' Uncle tried consoling me.

'I hope she is not serious and just joking' I said to myself.

'Well, let's get back to Mumbai. It's late' Uncle said.

Sam looked at me followed by Priyanka.

'No uncle, we have some work here. We will come later' Sam said.

'Aunty, you proceed, we will come' Priyanka said.

Priya's mom came to me as she held my shoulders. I was still sobbing.

'Rohit, take care' She said. 'And don't think so deep about Priya. I'll talk to her'

I gave her an understanding nod.

Priya's family was soon disappeared from my eyes. That means that my love was also washed out. Priya's face expressions said that she was serious and that slap? She had never slapped me before. I was waiting for, where my destiny would take me. I sat down on the bed in a no option way. Priyanka held me sitting beside me. I rested my head on her shoulder.

'Rohit, it's not time to sit and cry…' Priyanka said.

'It's time to fight against reality' Sam said.

13

I don't want to be a spoilsport between Sam and Priyanka. They were busy jogging in the park. We had hung out for a morning jog at the park. I really don't want to come all the way and doze away there. These both forced me to come along with them. I sat down on the resting bench. I was trying to maintain mellow atmosphere but I couldn't, my mind took me all the way to Priya's thoughts. The tree under which I thought was really silent as a foliage fell over me. It made me think more about Priya. The thinking remembered me of some momentous movement of mine and Priya. The movement which, Priya passed me the cheat at the railway station. The movement at which she and I was out for the candle light dinner for the first time. The movement when Priya was angry on my when I had missed a movie for few minutes. The movement when we were out on a date. The movement when I asked Priya for her life. The movement when I kissed her beautiful lips.

My eyes filled up.

I suddenly broke down from my thoughts as a five to six year old girl fell over my leg. I suddenly got up to pick her up. She started grizzling as her mother ran towards me. I stared at her as she had reached by us.

'Pranali, are you okay?' The mother said, caring.

I released the little girl thinking what would have Priya done if she have seen this girl falling? I looked at the little girl. 'Thank you' the mother said. I placed my hand on Pranali's head as she looked up at me. Da'am! Her eyes were so cute. They left as my mind clicked one more thing related to Priya. We had planned the same little cute girl after our marriage.

I sat down on my seat, this time catching my head.

I rebuked myself for my carelessness. My eyes filled up as they were wretched. I started reprimanding myself severally. I closed down my eyes as I saw my mom and dad playing with me when I was a child. I remembered how they bedecked my life that time and how is my life now. I made a short lift in my mind and started enumerating it. My parents were disappointed with me, Priya was upset with me. Both of them broke up and what endured? My fucking life? I think first I should discriminate myself with Sam and Priyanka, and then get started.

I sniffed in.

I slipped out my cell-phone from my track pants and dialled Priya's number. I thought that direct calling her would not work. I disconnected the call and typed some text.

HOW ARE YOU FEELING?
I'M JUST DYING HERE YA,
PLEASE MESSEGE ME BACK
I'M WAITING.

I didn't get any reply for my text. I placed my cell-phone on its original place. The situation made me feel in indignity. I closed my eyes as Sam and Priyanka ran towards me. I opened my eye as I stood up. They stood before me getting back to their breath.

'Have you jogged?' Priyanka asked.

'Yeah, I did' I lied.

'Let's move back to hotel' Sam said knowing my reply was mendacious.

They walked hand in hand and only I was who walked alone. If I was with Priya I would definitely had enjoyed this with her. I was behind them with fifty meters. Sam looked back at me.

'Rohit, come fast' Sam shouted.

I ran close to them. I was in my thoughts and I didn't know that when we had reached the hotel room.

♦

We all sat on the dining table having the breakfast. I really don't like *dosas* but my thoughts made me eat them with likeness. I ate silently as they both were busy chit-chatting with each other. For few seconds I felt that I was alone in this world wondering here and there. I took a glass full of water and took two big sips. I placed the glass back on its original place as Sam placed his hand on mine. Priyanka replenish my glass again with a jar. I looked into Sam's eyes, they said 'What's wrong? Why are you behaving like this?'

'What's wrong? Do you need anything?' Sam asked politely.

I shook my head.

I looked down into my plate. Priyanka was busy eating.

'Then, what's bothering you so much?'

'Priya's health!'

I was really bothered about her health because when I saw her the last time she seemed sick. I wanted to know her condition now. I thought over it as my brain begeted a new idea.

'Priyanka, will you help me?' I begged.

She looked up at me from her plate. I know I had prescind her from her breakfast.

She didn't said anything, just stared at me.

'Will you please call her and ask her for her health. I'm really worried' I said.

'Why not? Sure!' Priyanka said making her eyes big.

She got up from her seat as she picked up a napkin from the chair and made her hands limpid. She then stepped towards the bed and came back with her cell-phone. I gave her a 'good-luck' glance as she moved to the balcony fro by us. I was about to get up as Sam stopped me.

'Let her' He said.

I dropped my spoon in the plate and took a big sip of water. I closed my eyes and prayed god that she would say she is alright. I know that I have to retain reputation in the eyes of Priya. I have a deep reverence in my heart for all my friends. I got up as I moved towards the washroom to wash my hands.

I washed my face so that I could feel good. I came back to the table with my vacant heart and sat next to Sam.

'Rohit, take it easy. Priya will be back' He said.

I looked up at him 'No I know her attitude. Once she hate a person, she hates him her entire life' I wanted to say. I looked at the balcony as Priyanka was busy talking on the phone. I kept on staring at her. Once her eyes were on me. She broke down the eye contact.

'Sam, how do you feel?' I inquired.

He baffled.

'How do I feel means?'

'I mean, with your love with you?'

'Rohit, I know you are in deep…' Sam said as Priyanka interrupted us by coming close to us.

I stood up and looked at Priyanka. She stared at my eyes. Her eyes said something different and they looked worried too. She was playing with her cell-phone it mean something was wrong. She placed it on the table as I first spoke.

'What did she said?' I asked.

'Rohit, she is better now!' She said.

'And what?'

'Only the marks are visible. And nothing else'

I closed my eyes praying god for his astonishment.

'And what she said about me?' I asked. 'Have you told that I'm worried?'

'I did'

'Then?'

'She said… let…'

I squinted my eyes and stared at her.

'Let what Priyanka?' Sam said getting up from his seat.

Priyanka grovelled.

'She said let…' Priyanka stopped.

'Let what?' I said politely.

'Him go to hell' She said nervously. 'And she also warned me to cut contact with her'

I looked up at Sam throwing him an 'I-told-you' glance. Priyanka held my right hand.

'Rohit, please take care. I had not known that the situation would be that worse. The way she talked was very… she seemed serious' Priyanka said.

Tears rolled down my eye as Priyanka cleaned them. She rolled her hand from my head.

'Rohit, please don't cry' She said.

Sam stepped forward towards me as he hugged me. I repressed my tears as I released him saying 'Let us have our breakfast' Sam sat beside me staring all the way at me.

'Sam do you know any company which could give me a job?' I asked.

Priyanka and Sam stared at each other.

'Yeah we do' Both of them said in unison.

I smiled at myself.

'Priyanka, today I have no girl to share my feelings in Mumbai, I do not own any house there. Then what's the use of running back to Mumbai?' I said.

I would like to start my new inception from here. I have thought over this many times. When I saw Priya disappearing from my eyes, it felt like I was nowhere. Now I wanted to live a gratuitous life here in Goa with Priya. (If she comes back)

'Rohit, there are your parents!' Sam said.

'And this is my life' I gave him a sudden reply.

I looked up at them, it felt like I was talking to my parents. I cleaned my gullet as I was gossiping to myself.

'And if you think about Priya, I think she loved me and cares for me' I said lovingly. 'And I'll wait for her.' I said as I made both of them gratuitous from disentangle. They said that Priya was serious. But I don't think of it now. I do not grumble that Priya made a wrong decision because I know that she only and only pertain to me. The two of them were really jiggered at my answer. Priyanka's eyes lit up and Sam almost had tears in his eyes. This made my mind replenish again with positive thoughts. I heard a music played at a long distance. I think I know this song. It was not actually a song but a *gazal*. The instrumental score played the song '*Ek Pyaar Ka Nagama Hain*'. This mellifluous movement made me romantic. I was staring at the wall thinking all this.

'This is called true love!' Priyanka said.

I grinned at her.

'Rohit, but what the world will think? A young son left his parents for a…' Sam said as I stopped him his mid-sentence and I began.

'I really don't mind that what world mind, what you think is all right' I said. This was the thought which I had learned from my own mistake.

I was still strangling my mind by the aroma of the alcohol. I had promised myself that I'll avoid boozing from the day we had the incident. I was mugging my mind at the alcoholic part.

I wriggled.

I think that I had forgotten something, I had asked these guys that will I get a job here in Goa. I had cogitated myself at Goa many time and at last I got the result that 'I should do so' my life had arouse a new inception and a warm start to my thoughts. The thought beget into my mind that if I do the job then I'll have some money in my pockets and being them in our own pockets means having some respect. Here my thoughts were proportion able. I had not thought out of box yet. 'Idiot, if you don't do a job then the world will call you a person 'Skint'' I told myself.

'Don't you know anyone who could find me job in Goa?' I asked.

'Rohit I'm not a Goan or neither a knowledgeable person of Goa, but my friends are here. I'll talk to them and tell what works out' He said.

I was too glad to hear this. I retain my happiness within limits as I got another question.

'By the way, what type of job do you want?' Priyanka questioned.

I looked up in her eyes.

'Priyanka, mostly in sales and IT field' I replied.

Priyanka gave me an understanding nod.

I sniffed in as I rested my head on the chair thinking 'What type of life I'll be living after five years in Goa with Priya?'

♦

The new seed was about to be sown in my life. The idea of settling down in Goa was right, I think. Now I was puzzled that where this idea takes me to. I think mostly two to three days had passed I had not met my mom, but I felt low. Many children's in India or in the world don't have their mother, how do they fell then? One who has a mother is the luckiest person on the earth. Thinking all this I was walking on the streets of Panaji all alone. (I mean without Sam and Priyanka) I entered the Panaji Park as I saw a wonder, an eighth wonder of the world. I saw kids playing and running with their parents. How lucky they were. The parents were also engaged with their children's. No complaint, nothing. Only giving their full time to their kids. I was hopeful that my parents also kept that type of attitude but I was the unlucky person after all. Who will ask for this loser? Actually I'm not a loser in my life. I'm a loser in my love-life. I failed to keep it strong all because of the fucking alcohol. Who the hell had invented the alcohol first? If I really get I'm going to kill him first.

I looked at the beautiful sea right front of my eyes. The sound of it made me romantic. I saw a couple sitting at the benches chit-chatting with romance. I put my face down blaming myself for my mistake. My eyes had tears. I closed my eyes as a droplet rolled down.

I sniffed in as it made me control myself.

I cleared my eyes as I slide out my cell-phone from my left jeans pocket. I was a bit gruesome because I was about to send a message to Priya. I had a glee on my face. I think everybody should have smile on their faces, no matter if we are in a problem, no matter if it's a fake one because smiling changes our way of thinking positive. I stepped back as I sat on the bench all alone. I brought my phone close so that I could type. I brought my thumb meticulously towards the screen as I was fearful and ingeniously I was not in the state to type the message but I made myself to do so. I typed her a cute message which said 'My life is a cup of tea, but it had no sugar, it needs sugar and that's you' I presumed that if I send her this message then what will she reply me? Or will she ever reply? I was about to press the send button but I had a little point in my mind. I saved the message as a draft and I jumped into my phone gallery. It had lots of pics of me and Priya together. I felt like if I could see her here. But the pics of hers made me relax. I had so deeply concentration in the images, I could check the time. I checked my watch as it was 7:24 pm. The evening was silent. All the public from the park had been disappeared from my eyes.

I picked up my cell-phone and got up from my seat. My legs had pains but I made myself walk. I made my way outside the park. I reached the gate as the watchmen looked at me and smiled.

I accorded him a smile.

I made my way towards the lodge on the footpath. My heart suddenly felt that I should talk to Priya once. I had demarcate myself of thinking about her but my heart was not proportionalable at this stage. I had crossed the limits. I walked forward as I found telephone booth ahead of me. It contained a coin box. I entered as I dialled Priya's number. The ring started. My stomach had movements inside. Nobody answered the call. I tried the second time, nobody answered. I disconnected again and tried for the third time.

'Hello' the voice said. It was Priya.

I kept quiet.

'Hello, is someone there?' She said.

I closed down my eyes 'Yeah, there is a loser who wants to explain you his mistake, but you don't give him a da'am change' I wanted to say. As I was about to say 'Hello' the call disconnected. I was happy that at least I heard her today. I stepped out from the booth as my cell-phone vibrated. I noticed the screen. It said 'SAM'

'Rohit, where are you?' Sam said.

'Coming, on the way Sam' I said as I hung up.

I reached my cell-phone's drafts folder as I opened the message which I had typed few minutes ago. I dialled the recipient's number as my thumb stopped on the 'send' button.

I sniffed in.

I pressed the 'Send' button as I slide my cell-phone back at its original place. I started walking towards the Hotel, the message was been sent.

14

Dressing up smart was not daam simple. I was dressing up for my job interview. I was replete of joy and happiness. I had been dressed up in (Actually Sam and Priyanka made me dress) a white plain shirt and a black pencil pants with a black suit which Sam purchased for me the last night. It had been an astonishment for me. I stood before the mirror looking at my culpabilities in dressing. I couldn't find my blue tie. I was from a group of populace and I had not accepted a lot from others. What I get was enough for me. The aroma of the Fogg filled the entire room. I made my hair and put on spectacle which made me look more innocent. The blue eye lens also looked cute. I adjusted my hairs as the couple entered my room. I suddenly looked back at them, frightened. Sam had promised me that till and when I don't get ready they will not enter my room. But who will stop these, who bamboozle me. I looked at them and smiled.

'Doesn't he look handsome?' Priyanka questioned Sam.

Sam gave her an understanding nod.

'He is a gentlemen now' Sam said coming towards me.

He held my shoulders and looked straight into my eyes. My eyes were glistering and his were almost filled with water. He hugged me tight as his tears rolled down his eyes. Priyanka stepped towards me next saying 'don't forget me ya, I'm too a member of this group' we added her to our hug as we all three of us hugged.

'Best of luck' Priyanka said.

'Best of luck from me too' Sam said next.

I gave them both a smile. I think I was forgetting something. Yeah, I was. I was forgetting my daam tie.

'Priyanka, have you seen my…'I said as she interrupted me showing the same blue tie before me. I grabbed it from her hand but I really couldn't tie a tie. I returned over the tie as she stepped close to me. I bend down a bit matching her height. She hung the tie around my neck and pulled me closer which made her easy. She smiled at me. The tie was at its place and Priyanka was at its place with Sam. I looked at them as they were standing right front to me. The couple was so romantic. Sam held his camera in his right hand and clicked my pics.

'I think we should send it to Priya' Priyanka said.

'No!' I said suddenly.

They threw me a puzzled look.

'Why Rohit?' Sam inquired.

I grovelled. I didn't say anything.

Priyanka threw me a grubby look and Sam a 'what-happen' glance. They both looked at each other and smiled. It seemed that some Kichdi was being cooked between both of them.

'Rohit, you know that Priya is being getting engaged next week?' Sam said.

The thrones pokcd all ovcr my body. Thc hcart was almost in the state of mugging. I looked at them gingerly having frons on my head.

 Priyanka laughed as I got floored.

'Idiot, he is just joking! Don't take it seriously!' Priyanka said.

I ran towards Sam to catch him and he ran away from me. Priyanka held me mid-way saying 'Chill Rohit Chill'

I gaped at her thinking 'Are this people gone mad? Frist of all I'm a scary-cat and over that they plan non-sense things.

 I smiled at Sam.

'By the way have you taken you bio?' Priyanka asked.

'Yeah, I do. On my laptop' I said.

Sam stepped close to me and passed me Priya's photo. I took it and stared at it for few seconds.

'Keep it into you shirt pocket, as you could say she is close to your heart' Sam said.

I gave him an understanding nod.

'Sam I think we should leave now, it's quite 12:10 pm now. It's getting late' Priyanka said.

I put hung my laptop bag across my shoulder and got ready. We locked the room and stepped towards the taxi to reach the Padmavati Road at which the interview was. Sam stopped a taxi and we drove towards Padmavati road.

♦

The Padmavati road was full of IT companies from which one was called 'SIMNIXC' Sam had a appointment for the interview for me in the same. We stepped in into the company as the watchmen stopped us the mid-way.

'Whom do you want sir?' He said.

'We are here for an interview' Sam replied.

'Do you have... by the way who is the candidate?' The guard asked staring at Priyanka's body language. Priyanka threw him a dirty look.

'Me' I said.

The watchmen stared at me as if I was going to ask him for his urine sample.

'Candidates should proceed there' He said pointing to the upper corner at the first floor.

'There?' Priyanka asked.

'And other's wait here' The guard said showing them their waiting seats.

Sam stepped forward to me and placed his right hand on my left shoulder.

I sniffed in.

'Do well' He said.

I smiled at him giving him an understanding nod.

'Do well Rohit' Priyanka said holding my right hand.

I hate it when someone holds my hand in public area, but after all she was my cute sister. We shook our hands as I was getting fro and fro by them. I reached the first floor as there were already three candidates waiting for the interview. My number was fifth and I had to wait. I took my seat on the waiting chair. I closed my eyes and prayed god for my betterment. I brought my parents front to my eyes and touched their feet's. Radhika di herself appeared as she said 'All the best'. Suddenly God appeared saying 'Look Rohit, I know that you love Priya and have a reverence in your heart. I know that you both were with each other for a long time and had a broke up few days ago, actually she did. I know that you are supported by Sam and Priyanka who are themselves in your life. I know that you fought with your parents for Priya and I also know that you have thrown out of your house. And today this job interview, I will definitely help you with the interview. But you have to do a thing. You have to simply call her and tell her that you are at the job interview. I know she will talk to you'

The challenge was… 'But I have to accept it today' I told myself.

I brought out my cell-phone from my jeans and dialled her number. All the corridor was silent.

'Priya, look don't hung up' I said suddenly as she accepted my call. And I was really in confusion that she had accepted my call?

'I'm mot hanging up!' Priya said.

'How are you yaar?' I asked.

'Why do you need that, if you don't really care for me?' She said angrily 'And I have accepted the call to tell you that don't call me again and don't message me henceforth'

 I sniffed in.

'Listen, I'm at the job interview' I said.

'Whatever, I don't care' She said.

'Priya please, I'm sorry…' She hung up on my mid-sentence.

I placed my cell on my right lap and stared at it. A drop of water fell down on the screen. I closed down my eyes as the god appeared again 'That was nice' He said.

The forth candidate was in now and the next was me. The grave in Priya's voice today told me that she was serious about our relationship. But I know that she will return back a day or the another in my life all over again.

I sniffed in two to three times which made my mind active. This day was prominent for me in my life. And if I get the success today, it would be the most memorable day of my life. I rearranged my spectacles and got ready for the interview. I switched off my cell-phone and slide it under my pocket. 'Next candidate Please' the voice came from inside. I got up as I sidle towards the interview room. I was a bit nervous, but kept a strong believe that 'I will make it today'. I entered as I saw the panel of three people sitting right front of me.

'Good afternoon sir!' I wished.

They all smiled at me.

'Please sit down' the middleperson said which I think was my boss. He pointed me towards the candidate seat as I took my seat.

I read out the names from the name plate kept right before them. The first one was, Amol Kadam – Manager. Second, Yash Obiroi – President (Simnixc Pvt Ltd.) and the third name plate proclaimed Shobha Obiroi – Vice president (Simnixc Pvt Ltd.)

'Please introduce yourself' The manager said.

I introduced myself a bit nervously. 'My name is Rohit Pradeep Dcshpande. I'm from Mumbai…'

'Mumbai, then why are you seeking job in Goa?' The vice-president asked.

'Ma'am, I'm settling down in Goa' I said politely.

All of them stared at each other as if I had told them my girlfriend's name.

'Why?' The boss asked.

'Sir, family problems' I said.

They all nodded.

'Have you brought the bio?'

I unzipped my laptop bag and brought out my laptop. I switched it on and put on the Word file which contained my bio and ID Proof.

'Here' I said as I passed the laptop to them.

The boss took control over the laptop as he read the text as if he was reading a porn magazine. The three of them were discussing something in between themselves looking at my bio. I looked into their eyes, but I couldn't read them. Whatever it is, all I want only was a 'Yes'

'Good Mr. Rohit, your grades are good' The boss said.

'As this is an IT Company, in which field do you work? I mean, Software or Hardware?' Manager said.

My eyes lost somewhere, they just started moving here and there.

'Sir, I'm good at both and I have great interest in sales so if I get the sales and services department…'

'Sure, tell us about your family background! We mean what does your parents do?'

'My dad is an investment banker and mom is a housewife'

All of them gave me an understanding nod.

'Mr. Rohit, is this your first job?'

'Yes sir!'

All of them stared at each other. The Manager picked up the notepad and the pen and wrote something. People, both besides him nodded at the text he wrote.

'By the way sir, what are the working hours?' I said.

'Its 9:00 am to 7:30 pm' Ma'am said.

I gave her an understanding nod. We kept quiet for few seconds as they had reached the final decision, I think.

'Are you married or…?' Ma'am asked.

'No ma'am. I'm single' I said. 'Can I say something?'

'Sure why not?'

I looked into the boss's eyes, they seemed positive. I sniffed in as it gathered me some courage to speak out.

' Sir, I'm in a great need of job. Please...' I stopped at my mid-sentence.

They didn't said a word after that.

'I promise you that I'll work hard for the development of the company' I blunt.

'Mr. Rohit...' The boss said passing me the laptop back. 'What about the salary?'

I didn't answer anything.

'Rohit?' Ma'am called me out.

'Yes ma'am 'I said.

'We are offering you the package of six lakh per month for the post of the Software and Hardware manager of this company'

I lost my sense.

'Really? Thank you so much ma'am! Thank you sir!' I was unable to control myself.

It felt like God had himself appeared before my eyes. My happiness was not expressed in words now. I was daam happy. I got up from my seat as I touched their feet's. All three of them smiled at me. I was in no sense as I almost kissed the middle panel, I mean my boss. They passed me the letter which wrote 'Simnixc Employ Registration' onto it on which I have to fill out my details and submit it to the company. It was a job letter in other words. I grabbed it and kissed the papers. It was my life's first achievement. The success. 'You will soon earn too idiot' a voice inside me said.

'You have to join from 24th of Nov' The lady interrupted me from my thoughts. Today is 22nd. One day to go...'

'Sure ma'am' I replied happily.

I hung my laptop bag and rushed towards the door. I was unable to converge to myself in happiness. I moved towards the ground floor's counter. The backing of all the people in my life meant meaningful now. I screamed and danced and became a haywire. I was out of my control. Sam and Priyanka sat waiting for me to come out. They noticed me as they got up from their seat suddenly. Their face only had one expression, 'What happen?'

I ran towards them.

'Sam, I did it' I said as Sam hugged me. 'Sir Lakh a month'

The glee on their faces was more than anything in this world. I was now gratuitous from all the problems. I think, I should spew out all the thoughts now. I released Sam and hugged Priyanka as she tapped my back. I was jiggered that my life took me at a good place today. I released Priyanka as I loosed my tie an unhooked my top shirt button. I grabbed the pen from Sam's shirt pocket (without his permission of course) and stepped towards the counter. The counter speakers played mellifluous silent songs. I loved hearing silent songs when I'm in a happy mood. I filled up the form as I passed it to the receptionist as she put my data into the computer and took out a print out which printed all the information like, office timings, rules and days of work, etc. I took the paper and whispered 'thank you!' I tucked the paper into my pocket and stepped back at them.

'How do you feel now?' Sam asked.

I looked into his eyes as I didn't broke the eye contact.

'I feel like I'm out of this world now!' I exclaimed returning his pen.

He placed his right hand on my shoulder as we started moving out of the company. The cold wind dashed my face. I was not in my own world. I was somewhere where there was only joy and happiness. I was disposed to tell this to mom and dad but I couldn't. I thought I should tell them later. I repressed myself from doing so. I was pensive of making my own world by making my own rules in future. Sam tapped my shoulder.

'How about the Ice-Cream?' Sam said.

♦

'Err… Rohit take more roti, why are you pretending low?' Priyanka said putting a roti into my plate.

We were into the hotel room having our dinner. I was low, I remembered the time when I and Priya had dinners like this. I was low at her words. 'Whatever, I don't care' that was something ridiculous. This thing was eating my head like never before. And what had I done? 'First do everything, and then asking what I have done is funny' I told myself. I know that I had committed a mistakes but so big punishment from her was not done which could destroy my whole life. And after all I was not a foe to her, then why is she behaving like that? My mind procreated lots of questions more which answers I didn't have at all. Merely I had a thought which said 'You-Should-Say-Sorry' which all the way flashed in my mind, these thoughts were throttle. I was unable to breath my gullet was totally chocked. Today too I reproach myself of my mistake. A splosh flashed on my eyes which said 'Love'. The turquoise letters 'L-O-V-E' flashed as it was on Diwali rocket busting into the sky. I could not bear this anymore. I got up from my seat and stepped out in the balcony. I looked up at the sky, the aroma felt nice. I held the fence tight as Sam arrived.

'Rohit, what's wrong? Why did you come out?' He asked.

'Because, the thoughts eat my head every day!' I upbraided loud that my voice could reach Priyanka inside.

Sam looked up at me.

The stars in the sky were sparkling 'What if these sparks were in me?' I thought. Priyanka entered the balcony as she looked up at us as if we were fighting. She stepped close to us.

'What happen?' She asked.

I looked up at her then at Sam. I turned around as I didn't spoke anything after that, my back towards them. I got shocked as Sam placed his hand on my shoulder. I turned back.

'What happen? Anything wrong?' He asked politely.

I had no control over myself by telling him the 'Call' thing. The thought still pinched my head, the anger filled my head.

'Sam, I had called Priya before the interview' I said.

Priyanka stepped close to me as she held my right hand and made me face towards her.

'What happen then?' She said.

'I told her that I'm at the interview' I said nervously. 'First, I asked her about her health'

'Then?'

'She said I don't care for her anymore then which should I need her health status?'

'And what about the interview?'

I sniffed in.

'I told her that I was at the interview, she said she really doesn't care about where I am' I said crying.

Priyanka hit my right cheek playfully. 'Idiot, you care for her so much, don't you think she cares for you? She cares…' Priyanka said.

'No she doesn't, her tone seemed she was serious' I said sobbing.

Priyanka closed her eyes whispering 'Oh God…' She cleaned my face with her dupatta.

'And if you think that she is slapdash about you, then you are wrong' Sam said coming forward towards us.

'Who said?' I said.

'I'm telling, because I know more that how much you both love each other than your parents'

I gave him disappointed look.

Sam held my shoulders saying 'Hey, Chill. Don't think more about it, think about your future'

I gave him an understanding nod.

'After all you have a job now. Don't let this chance go from your hands now' Priyanka poked.

In few minutes Sam and Priyanka recreated me by telling me jokes and made some funny faces, I smiled at last.

They both looked at my happy face and smiled at each other.

'Rohit, let's have the dinner. It's waiting' Priyanka said.

I nodded.

The two creatures which destiny had gifted me were fantastic. I hope all could get these type of friends in their life. I had forgotten that I was in murk, these two had gave me the sunlight which made my life shining and bright.

15

This is my last day before my first job. It is 23rd Nov today, and my brand new life was going to start tomorrow. But life didn't meant life without Priya. Incarnation of love was still alive within me for Priya. We all sat down for the breakfast in the morning. Sam had ordered the breakfast as the room service boy served us to our room. Priyanka was still in the bathroom having shower. I cogitate about Priya, once again. 'Did she seriously broke up with me?' I asked myself. My life had become hell. Knowing that, that I had got a good job but what's the use of that asinine money if I don't have my love with me? Sam was busy arranging the plates as the romantic aroma filled the room. The waves of Dona-Paula beach made our movement more romantic. Priyanka was finally out from the bathroom. As I have already said, girls have a beautiful smell after bath. That was right. At last we all congregated on the dining table. Priyanka was busy drying her hairs with the towel. I loved the movement when Priya used to do it.

I grinned at Priyanka.

'Rohit, you look happy today. What's the matter?' Priyanka questioned.

'Nothing like that!' I said. 'I just remembered something'

Priyanka smiled back at me.

Sam served us the breakfast as we all finally settled down on the dining table. I looked up at both of them wondering how lucky they were to have each other and be together.

We had our breakfast for next few minutes. Today's day was full blank as there was nothing to do for us. Sam and Priyanka were daam happy but there was a bit of tension on their faces and that was all because of me. I really didn't like, that their love-life was being affected because of me.

'Guys, today we have nothing to do. Let's plan something' Priyanka said in an excited voice.

'I mean it' Sam blunt.

'What?' I said.

Both the creatures sitting before me stared at me.

'Rohit, tomorrow is your first day at work' Priyanka said.

'And you have today's day before it' Sam poked in.

'So, you have to enjoy it with us' Priyanka said.

'And we have planned something and you have to join us' Sam said.

They gave me no chance to say at least a single word. Just started speaking one after another. I just stared at their faces.

'Okay… okay… okay… calm down' I finally said. 'Tell me what…'

Priyanka's cell phone rang as it interrupted me asking her what the plan was. She brought out her cell-phone and whispered, 'Mom' and had lines on her forehead. Sam threw her a 'what-happen' glance. Priyanka accepted the call.

'Yes mom' Priyanka said.

We both stared at her as if we were watching a porn film and staring at the screen.

'What?' Priyanka said jumping on her chair.

We both looked at each other.

I shrugged my shoulders.

'Yeah, he is here' Priyanka said looking at Sam. 'Sure mom… okay'

Priyanka hung up the call and banged her phone on the table in excitement. She suddenly hugged Sam, I baffled. 'What was really going on?' I asked myself.

'Priyanka, what happen? What are you so…?'

'Sam, our parents are planning our marriage!' Priyanka exclaimed.

'What? Are you serious?' Sam said.

He got excited too. The happiness on his face made me feel good.

'They are going to exchange the kundlies tomorrow. We have to go back to Mumbai'

'When?'

'Tomorrow itself. Sharp at 10:30 PM'

I stared at both of them as I smiled. Their life was going to be set, finally. They were going to get married. They both really couldn't control their emotions. I rested back on the chair.

I grinned at both of them.

Sam and Priyanka suddenly looked at me. The smile on their faces was almost invisible. I leaned forward towards them.

'Sam, actually we cant go. We cant leave Rohit with his condition' Priyanka said.

'Yeah' Sam answered.

'Look, never do that! Are you both silly? I'm not a kid now' I said. 'And it's your marriage!'

'But Rohit…' Priyanka said as I interrupted her.

'You both will get a tight slap from me if you ever thought to do so' I said. 'And if you both have to reach there early in the morning, I think you should leave tonight'

They both looked at each other. Their face fell down.

'Hey, chill guys… you are going there for few days. You both have to come back. I want to disturb you more here' I said playfully.

Sam smiled at me.

'Come on guys… I'm not dying or something and…'

Priyanka placed her hand on my lips and stopped me from completing my sentence. I noticed the tears in her eyes. I smiled at her. I held her hand and got up from my seat. I placed her hand into Sam's right hand.

'Be happy always' I said.

'Rohit…'

'My dear brother and dear sister, we don't have much time. Go pack your bags. And you have planned something for me tonight then you will not get enough time to reach there. You will be late' I said.

'Rohit but…'

'Go, Priyanka' I interrupted.

'But…'

'Go!' I said interrupting Sam. 'And order fruits for us till then'

Both of them smiled at me, frowned actually.

♦

I baffled, why these two had brought me to such an expensive place? We were at the Hotel Paradise. The most expensive place in Goa. Priyanka made me dress in a gentlemen way. The hotel was bared nearby to the beach. We walked through the footpath. The fresh air of that evening made us feel relaxed. It was about 8:30 pm, suddenly an image of me and Priya walking along the streets in Mumbai flashed before my eyes. I smiled at my own thought. We all moved towards the gate of the Hotel Paradise as the guard welcomed us in. Priyanka looked stunning in her greenish saree. Sam and Priyanka moved towards the reception as I brought my legs a little back. I stepped back as I didn't wanted to be a spoilsport into their romance. They both looked really cute with each other.

'Rohit, what are you doing there? Come' Priyanka called.

I gave her an understanding nod.

They both had booked a table earlier for us. The waiter took us towards our table as Priyanka dropped her hand bag on the chair. She looked up towards both of us.

'Guys, I need to go to the washroom' She said.

Sam gave her an understanding nod.

We both took our places as the waiter asked us for the orders. I looked up at Sam.

'We will order in five minutes' Sam said as the waiter left.

I adjusted myself into the chair as it was not that comfortable enough. I brought out my cell-phone to check if I had any missed call or any messages as I had kept it on silent mode. I placed it on the table meticulously. I looked up at Sam as he was busy flipping through the menu card.

'You happy?' I asked Sam as the waiter served us the welcome drink.

Sam looked up at me, confused.

'Yes' He replied. 'I'm daam happy, after all I'm getting what I wanted'

I smiled at him.

'It's like dream come true. Priyanka and you will be together in few more months forever' I said.

'That's what I wanted'

Sam wriggled.

Sam looked a bit of puzzled. He was not ingeniously that way, but there was a thing that was bothering him too much.

I just wanted to know that what it was. My eyes turned towards the hotel entrance as I saw bountiful amount of people coming in. They all were couples. I remembered that night when we were in the bar. I diverted my mind towards Sam as I didn't wanted to remember it as it had ruined my life a lot already.

'Hey, I'm back' Priyanka said coming towards us.

Sam gaped at her like never before. There was an extra make-up then before.

'What?' Priyanka said taking her seat beside Sam.

'Nothing!' Sam said suddenly shutting his mouth.

I smiled at both of them.

I think that I should leave them alone. I thought about it because of the smile on their faces. I just don't want to be a spoilsport between them. Priyanka delectable to smile on Sam's jokes seemed that they both were happy with each other. I presumed to leave them alone. 'Idiot, what are you doing between them? Leave them alone' I told myself.

I looked up at them as Priyanka was busy hitting Sam playfully on his cheeks. I was now disposed to stay away from them. I really couldn't able to control myself as I got up.

'Guys, you both have fun, I'll wait outside' I said as if I was an international businessmen.

'Why? What's wrong?' Sam said.

'I have to make an urgent call, I just remembered' I lied.

Priyanka gave me a puzzled look.

I made my way towards the entrance door as I was out now. I looked around as there was a group of families had congregate on the beach for a birthday party. Children's were enjoying themselves into the beach poll lights. I made my way towards the beach as my mind arouse for a while. The fresh air on the beach and the sound of sea waves made me feel great. I sat down on the sea sand as I pushed my shoes out of my foot and kept them aside. I prescind from my family and the children as it made remember the promises that I and Priya made together.

I shrugged my shoulders.

A droplet rolled down from my eyes. My life was just turned into a hell. It was just like a quadripartite. Life was getting a new shape. But I didn't wanted so. I just want my earlier life back. I just want my Priya back. That's it.

I stood up picking up my shoes. I cleaned the sand from my pants and turned around to move back to the hotel. Sam and Priyanka walked towards me. Priyanka's eyes had tears as Sam's held anger for me. I stepped close to them. We stood face to face to each other as my body automatically felt loose and the shoes from my hand felt down. I hope they didn't have got the clue about why I had left them alone and was alone here at the beach.

'Guys, I was just…'I said as Priyanka interrupted me.

'Please Rohit. What's wrong?' Priyanka scolded. 'Why are you behaving like this?'

Sam placed his right hand on my left shoulder and moved me a little.

'If there is any problem share it with us' Sam said.

'We both noticed. You have changed these days. What's bothering you so much why are you behaving like this?' Priyanka said.

Their question started bothering me now. They both said the truth. There was a thing that was bothering me so much. I was really missing Priya. My life want Priya back, I couldn't survive without her. I have to answer their questions, but I felt indignity now.

'Because I'm missing Priya' I blunt. 'I really couldn't live without her'

Sam sniffed in.

Priyanka moved close to me. When I see these two in front to me, I feel relaxed. They have been epitomized me for love.

'Rohit, relax. Look, we will talk to Priya about this. We know how much you and Priya love each other. We all four had grown up together yaar. I and Sam promise you that we will not let you and Priya be divided' Priyanka said making me feel meliorate.

I gave her a disappointed look.

I was now about to cry. My eyes had already got tears into them. But however, I repressed myself. I trust both of them a lot. At last, only they two supported me in my lows.

'But, I had lost her. She doesn't wants to see my face' I said moving aside by Priyanka.

'Who said? We will sit and talk to her about this!' Sam said as he moved close to me.

'And listen Rohit, as we reach Mumbai we are first going to talk to Priya' Priyanka said. 'We all know she still loves you as earlier'

I gave Priyanka a fake smile.

Sam hit me on my chest playfully. Both of them had smiles on their faces. This meant whole world to me. These people are mine.

'Rohit, look take care of yourself' Priyanka said as she hugged me.

Sam hugged me next. It felt good.

'Don't worry, I'll take care' I said as Sam released me.

Priyanka's eyes watered. I cleaned them. 'I love my brother and sister a lot' I wanted to say.

'Thanks' I said.

'For what?' Priyanka questioned.

'For being for me' I replied.

Sam hit my shoulders. This time a bit hard.

'Don't be silly, I'll hit you if you say it again' Sam said.

We all grinned at each other. This movement made me feel like never before. Sam and Priyanka were the most prominent parts of my life. And now I have to get my most important and very prominent part back, Priya. I have to only get back Priya at any cost.

'Shall we move in? I have ordered the food and its waiting' Sam said passing me my cell-phone which I had left back on the table.

'Come, let's move' Priyanka said as she moved forward making her way towards the hotel.

Sam followed Priyanka.

'Wait yaar... I'm too coming' I said picking up my shoes.

I ran towards them.

♦

We all congregated on our table. Sam had ordered some Kolhapuri Chicken kind of stuff. Priyanka like this dish as the waiter too had recommended these two for this dish. Sam signed the waiter. The waiter arrived with the order.

'We would like to have fried chicken for starters' Priyanka ordered.

'Yeah... with extra cheese' Sam added backing Priyanka.

The waiter left as the romance between Sam and Priyanka started. I signed them clearing my throat.

Sam threw me an 'its-okay-Rohit' glance.

I smiled at them.

'I think there is a day tomorrow. You can make love tomorrow at your own room in A/c' I teased.

'Shhh... silly' Priyanka blushed.

'Such a dog' Sam said.

I was being a bit naughty this time. But I enjoyed their smile. We finished our meal in next few minutes as we suddenly left for the airport. I really didn't want to let them go fro by me, but I really had no option. They have to go for their marriage. I was really happy for them. 'One has to survive then one had to beget in his life without thinking about anyone else' but our case was a bit different, we could not like to beget, we only want was live in present…

♦

Lastly there was a time to say a 'good-bye' this was very gruesome for me. I meliorate my mood, as I don't want Sam and Priyanka leave the airport with my tears in their eyes.

'All the passengers are…' the security announcement started. I looked up at both of them. I hugged Priyanka as she whispered 'don't worry everything will be alright' into my left ear.

I accorded her an 'okay' smile.

'Take care' Sam said as the second announcement was announced.

They had left my presence. They had reached the check-ins. I kept on staring to them till they disappeared from my eyes. 'At last they were gratuitous to live their life' I thought.

I left the airport as I found a cab. 'No, I will not take a cab' I told myself. I decided to make my way to the hotel (4.5 km) walking. I started walking towards the hotel. I found number of belle on the road but no one looked a beautiful as Priya did. My mind already had lots of turmoil. Why was Priya doing this? What was she up to? Why she was avoiding me? A couple of questions popped out in my mind. The horns on the streets diverted my mind. There was a new start tomorrow. A new life. I was going to start a new life without Sam, Priyanka and of course Priya. But seriously I really didn't care about my life. All I want, all I prayed God was just a word, 'Priya'.

16

Inception of my first day of my new life was on. The new start was just arouse. I have to do everything today on myself as I had nobody to help me out. I had waved '*good-bye*' to Sam and Priyanka for their happy love-life. I was really happy for them. At one side that was good. I had obviate for both of them, else if they would be here then, Rohit do that... Rohit do this... crazy guys. The morning today was very tough for me. It made me do works that I have never done before. Priyanka did it when they were here, but now situation was changed a bit. We four of us had an intimacy between us once, but now the time had passed away. Our situations our priorities had changed. Destiny has grabbed Priya from my life. But I didn't blame my life for this, this conditions were made by me and I have to mend them. I was being a bit of emotional at this stage.

I had dressed up with the 'gentlemen-type' togs today as it was my first job and my first day at work. I had ordered the breakfast for myself which had to be arrived yet. I had purchased the package at the lodge which made me save my money, it was not more than five thousand bucks per month. I brought out my cell-phone from my left jeans pocket to make a call to Sam once before I leave for the job. I dialled Sam's number as someone knocked my door. I threw the cell-phone on the bed and stepped towards the door to unlock it. There I go, it was the room service boy with my breakfast.

'Sir, your breakfast' He said.

'Yeah'

I slide my hand into my jeans pocket and brought out a ten rupee note and handed it over to the page as a tip. I took the dish from his hand and locked the door. I came back towards the bed and placed the plate on the bed. I had my breakfast in next few minutes as it was already getting late for me. It was around 9:00 am. My office hours were from 9:30 am to 5:30 pm in the evening. It was complete nine hours of working. I hope the people here will be nice and friendly. I really didn't know that how they were, but I pray destiny to serve me the best.

♦

I reached my office at 9:15 am. Perfectly fifteen minutes earlier than the exact timing. I had hired a cab from the hotel to my workplace. I now stood in right front of the office building. 'SIMNIXC' it proclaimed on the gate. I stepped in as my eyes were searching the reception counter. I stared around as I found the reception where I can inquire about. I moved towards the counter as there was a hot and sexy girl addressing other guests. I felt anxious. I gathered some courage and stared straight into her eyes. She was busy with some other guests.

'Excuse me!' I spoke out.

She suddenly looked up at me.

'Yes sir, Ragini here, how can I help you?' She said.

I sniffed in.

'I have appointed for a job here. Today is my starting date' I said.

'Can I have you appointment letter sir?' She said.

I gave her a 'wait-a-minute' glance and dragged my hand into my carry case. I flipped through some papers to find my appointment letter. I brought out the letter and passed it to the girl, I mean Ragini. She buried her head into the letter as if it was a proposal from me for marriage. I smiled at my own joke.

'Yeah, there you go. Mr Yash Obiroi' She said passing me the letter. 'Mr Yash Obiroi, the manager'

'Where can I find him?' I asked.

'There upstairs' She said pointing towards the staircase. A notice board was hung at the start of the staircase. It said:

1st floor - Amol Kadam (Manager)
2nd floor - Nishant Manaotra (HOD)
3rd floor – Yash Obiroi (Chief of IT Department)
4th floor – Nisha Rawat (CEO)

I stared at the notice board. My target was on the third floor. 'Who the hell will go to the third floor by taking stairs? I thought. There was a lift right beside the staircase. I entered the lift as I pressed the button 3. The door automatically closed as the lift moved upstairs. The lift stopped as the doors opened. I was on the third floor now. I noticed the office proclaimed 'Yash Obiroi' on its door. I stepped towards the office as I entered in. An aged (around forty years of age) man sat on the chair with the apple laptop on his table. He had a greyish hairs. I read out the name plate on his table. He was the same, my boss.

I sniffed in.

'Shall I come in sir?' I requested.

My boss brought out the buried face from his MacBook and looked up at me. He noticed me from top to the bottom as if I was the only employ in the office dressed well.

'Sir, I am…'I was saying as he interrupted me.

'Mr Rohit Deshpande! Right?' he said. 'Come in, I was waiting for you'

I entered the cabin as I took my place on the chair kept before his table.

I sniffed in.

'So, welcome to Simnixc Rohit' He said.

'Thank you Sir!' I said politely.

I really didn't find any other word to say rather than 'Thank you'. My heart beats had suddenly gone fast.

'Shall I show you your work place?' He asked.

'Sure sir'

'Come!'

I followed him as he brought me to my workplace. It was a huge void place which had five rows. Each row had ten seats and each seat had a PC placed on it. It was like 'employ-less-paper-more' type of a place. There were lots of papers, files and other stuff in front of the each employ. I gasped at the place. I adjusted the carry case hung around my left shoulder as it was sliding down. Mr Yash placed me on my place and left. I had got the place at the last row, the sixth seat from the last. My boss had sent an employ to tell me about the work to be done and some of the do's and don'ts. I understood my work gingerly. Here came the lunch break.

There was a rule that no one should have their meal in the working place. Everyone should move to the office canteen. We all stepped in the office canteen. I had made some of the friends here. One of them was the receptionist Ragini. Neil, Karan, Jaydeep, Vaibhav, Pavan, these were the other five. We sat grouped on a circular table. Everyone ordered different dishes. Some veg and some were non-veg. We had a beautiful conversation. Everybody was friendly with each other. All the employ's here had a rapport between them. This was a good point. I was now relaxed and comfortable at my place.

'Guys, is this every day that you come here and enjoy or is this for today?' I inquired.

'Rohit, we all are just crazy!' Pavan said.

'That's our daily activity' Karan poked.

Pavan cracked some kind of joke as all of us broke down laughing. I suddenly remembered of Sam and Priyanka. I had not called the since morning. I slide my hand into my jeans and brought out my phone. I dialled Sam's number as the line was not lipid. I tried Priyanka's next.

'Hello brother, we were just calling you now' Priyanka said.

'Hey Priyanka, how are you? And where's Sam?' I said.

'Leave ours. How are you? And how's your first day? Have you ate something?' Priyanka started.

'Give it a break, how many questions you ask at a time?' I said.

'Don't act smart, I'll slap you one' Priyanka said playfully.

I love it when Priyanka and Sam talks to me in that way.

'So, what's going on there? Is everything good?' I asked.

'Here, everybody is crazy. Sam and I are daam happy' Priyanka replied as Sam grabbed the phone from Priyanka.

'Hey Rohit, what's up?' Sam said.

'It's quite good here. What about you?' I asked. 'Priyanka said everything is set'

'Yes, everyone is just da'am happy. The *Kundlies* matched and they are fixing dates' Sam said.

'Look, how fast we grown up!' I exclaimed.

'Brother, we all miss you. Especially Priyanka and Priya' Sam said.

'Priya?' I said. 'Have you talked to her?'

'Yes, we did. Actually she is here with us now' Sam said.

I sniffed in.

'What did she say?'

'She didn't react on what we said. She just didn't said anything'

I closed down my eyes as the image of Priya flashed into my mind. I just didn't know what to say next.

'Rohit, we will sort out things yaar. Don't worry!'

'Yeah'

I stared at my watch as it was 1:00 pm. The lunch break was about to over. My eyes were almost wet.

I sniffed in.

'Sam, I'll call you later. Actually my lunch break time had exceeded' I said.

'Sure, and don't worry. We will talk later about this' Sam said. 'Bye'

'Ba… bye' Priyanka shouted loud enough so that I could hear her out.

I hung up.

I could not really understand anything at this stage. Nothing was friendly for me. Priya was just disappeared from my life. She was hundreds of kilometres away from me. I wanted her back. I cleared my face as I moved back to the third floor.

♦

It was 5:30 pm. I really didn't felt that I had worked for nine hours today. I was so busy into my work that I forgot to notice the time. Time just flew away. I waved a *good-bye* to all my colleagues. Ragini left earlier today at 4:00 pm as she had some important work to deal out with. The boss was very nice and kind to us. This was the boss who understands his employee's. I packed my things and I left my workplace at 5:45 pm. I was on the streets of Panaji. The Goan's and the foreigners walked around. It felt like I was in a foreign country. The people here were behaving in incarnation. They live life their way. I didn't take cab, just walked on the streets of Panaji. I just wanted to feel the people around me.

My mind suddenly clicked something. I thought over to call Priya. I wanted to call Priya and share everything that had happen today. I brought out my cell-phone and dialled Priya's number.

'Hello…' the voice on the other side said. It was Priya.

I felt anxious.

There were two things. First, I really didn't understood that how Priya accepted my call and second, I really had no guts to talk to Priya.

'Hello…' Priya said again. This time a bit louder.

As it takes time to gather some courage and speak, I was about to speak something as the call was already hung-up.

I sniffed in.

I closed down my eyes as I stopped at my place. My body felt pale. The blood circulation was fast enough to match the speed of the Ferrari. 'I can't live without Priya' I told myself. Was Priya that angry on me? I know how Priya is. She is not that rude enough. Something is making her stay away from me. Is it the reality?

I opened my eyes.

I found only one thing prominent at this stage, 'Relations'. Firstly, I lost my parents, than my love. I really can't live without her. My mind started popping up with some stupid thoughts. I didn't paid attention towards it. I started walking my way towards the Hotel (Dona-Paula) beach.

17

Needless to say but, time just flew away. It had been a months since I had joined the work. Everything was settled down at its rest. I was feeling comfortable here now (not without Priya actually). The time span of one month would not bring much hike in my salary, but hardly ten thousand. But I was really happy with what I made. The amount of 6,10,000 was more than enough for me. But my fucking blunder mistake made Priya away from me and this salary was at the low level compared to Priya. I really didn't need this all the fucking thing. All I need is Priya. It was a Sunday today but Yash sir had called me to the office. I didn't know that what's the catch was. I really didn't wanted to get up and go. I didn't had any choice, picking up my cell-phone I called out Ragini. She picked up quickly at the second ring.

'Hello, Rohit' She said.

'Are you really going to go to the office today?' I questioned.

'Sounds silly but we don't have any choice' She replied.

'Did you have any idea that why sir had called us today?' I asked.

'No idea Rohit, maybe some extra work to work out with' She replied.

I sniffed in.

'Okay, let's meet then' I said as I hung up.

It was 10:00 am and I really didn't have mood to get up early and go to the office, but I didn't had any other option. I had to go. The passed months brought up my bank balance. I got ready for the office. I had ordered the breakfast. Dona-Paula beach seemed silent today. Each day seemed hell without Priya. Only I knew that how I was without Priya. She didn't even called me once in the past month. I had called once but she got a rude answer from other side, 'Don't call me again' it said. I feel like ending off my life. I just wanted Priya now. Nothing else.

I had my breakfast in next few minutes and left for the office. I was supposed to buy a bike for me, but I didn't. I usually used to take a auto to my workplace earlier and now to prefer to take a cab. I was agitated about what had boss planned for me. I hope that his plan was not challenging for me to work on.

I felt anxious.

The cab reached the office as I got down. I paid him two hundred bucks as it usually cost two hundred bucks from the hotel to my workplace. I started walking towards the gate.

I sniffed in.

'What are you looking for? Go get in!' I told myself.

As the long breath got me some courage, I got in.

♦

I sat eagerly waiting for Mr. Yash into his cabin. I felt anxious. I really didn't know what to do next. I preferred to only wait and see what my boss had plans for today. I almost got up five time from my seat to look if Mr. Yash had arrived or not. I thought over for the last month that if, I have made any mistake or what. But it was nothing like that. I looked back at the door as I saw boss entering the cabin.

I stood up suddenly.

'Sit, sit' He said taking his sit on his chair as I took my seat.

I sniffed in.

'Good morning, Rohit' He said.

'Good morning, Sir'

He smiled at me.

'Rohit, firstly, I'm really sorry that I'm disturbing you on the Sunday's' He said.

'No problem sir!' I exclaimed.

He started rearranging his table as if he had nothing to do else. I looked at him gingerly wondering what the catch was. His arranging of table was insistent.

'Rohit, did you know the Mumbai client?' He asked.

I suddenly started flipping the pages of my mind.

'Mr Sudeep, Sir?' I said as I recalled the client's name.

'Yep!' Sir exclaimed. 'You need to give a presentation to them about the financial increment into our products' He said.

I wretched. 'Who the fuck gives presentations on Sundays?' I brought a smile on my face burning off my anger.

'Today sir?' I asked.

'You need to leave for Mumbai tomorrow' He said 'This will also help you to understand Mumbai companies'

As I heard 'you-have-to-leave-for-Mumbai' I felt apprehensive. I really didn't had any guts to enter Mumbai at this stage. My stomach twinge. The sweat drops popped on my forehead. I picked up the glass from the table and took two big sips of water.

My boss looked up at me, jigged.

'Is there any problem?' He asked.

I don't know what made me say that there was a problem, but I had said it.

'Yes, I can't go to Mumbai!' I blunt.

I was in no sense. This situation made me be in indignity. I looked up at my boss. He stared at me.

'Rohit, are you alright?'

'Sorry sir, I…' I was not in the stage to speak up.

'Do you have any problem with Mumbai?' He asked. 'What is it?'

I looked up at him.

'Personal problem sir' I said.

He smiled at me.

I really didn't understand that what made him smile at me now. I threw him a puzzled look.

'What will you have? Tea or Coffee?' He said as ordered tea from his intercom.

'Sir, I'm sorry…' I stammered.

He threw me an 'it's-okay' glance.

I replenish myself with some courage and stood up. I turned around to leave the cabin.

'Missing Priya, right?' Sir said.

I stood at my place freeze. He rattled me a bit this time. I looked back at him, floored. I whispered Priya's name silently. My eyes filled up.

He signed me to sit back on the chair with hand gestures. I sat down.

'Sir how did you…'

'I know about Priya, right?' He interrupted. 'I'm not from those bosses who only make their employees work for their companies profit'

I brought out the hanky and cleaned my face.

'Rohit, I'm observing you from the past month. You work hard but something is bothering you. I researched about you. No matter how I got information about Priya, the thing that matters me is you' He said. 'I mean, look at yourself, you are half finished. Doesn't take care of yourself. That's not the solution for your problem'

I couldn't understood that what to say at this condition. My brain became vacant.

'You know why I only choose you to handle Mr. Sudeep in Mumbai?' He asked. 'Because Priya works in his company'

'Sir but…' I said as he interrupted me.

'Enough Rohit, I can't see you like this any more. I know this is the company trip but this is the personal holiday for you. Go get her' He said.

I looked into his eyes as I could not understand what to say next. I really felt like joining my hands before him. I loved his nature. He brought out his cheque book from his table drawer and signed the cheque of six lakh and ten thousand bucks under my name and tore it off.

'Rohit, this is the advance cheque for this month. Go get her back and take proper care of you and her too' He said.

'Sir I really don't know that how to thank you. Thank you sir!' I said as I droplet rolled down my face.

'No formalities please' He said. 'And listen, I don't want to see you here before fifteen days. Did you get it?'

I grinned at last. Hope everybody could get the boss like the one I got here. Calm, polite, understanding and emotionally developed. I really didn't know that what was going to happen next in Mumbai. Maybe destiny had planned something special for me. Here, I got to Mumbai…

♦

I logged into my PC and made a booking from Goa to Mumbai. I had a flight tomorrow at 2:45 pm. I had enough time for my packing. I decided to dress tomorrow in spick cloths as they could make Priya happy. She likes when I wear these type of cloths. I was eagerly waiting for her smile. It was her smile which made me fall in love with her. I was lastly going to see her after a full month. I didn't knew that how she could react tomorrow when she will notice me. The memories of mine and her splashed into my mind.

I grovelled as I noticed my hands. The hands which held Priya's hands into them once. My joy was immitigable. I couldn't really control myself. I only knew that I have to explain Priya about what all had happed that day. I have not done it purposefully. I know Priya will understand mc.

I sniffed in.

I started packing up my things for tomorrow. I suddenly thought over to call Sam and Priyanka and tell them that I'm leaving for Mumbai tomorrow. I moved towards the dining table and picked up my phone placed on it. I sat on the chair and dialled Priyanka's number.

'Good that you remembered us, we almost thought that you have totally forgotten us for a while' Priyanka said without saying a 'hello'.

'What up?' I said.

'All set, we have planned engagement next month' She said.

My face had a smile.

'Really very happy for you, May God makes you happy and secure with Sam'

'Hmm… how about you?'

'I'm the same as usual, incomplete'

This made me emotional. This made me cry. Priya was now emotionally attached to me. Priyanka heard me sobbing.

'Rohit, I'm really sorry. I should have not asked you this' Priyanka apologized. 'I'm sorry'

'No sister, you don't have to feel sorry' I said. 'The absence of Priya made me cry'

'We had talked to her about you many times'

I sniffed in.

'What did she say? Does she asks about me?' I inquired, unable to control myself. 'Does she asks…?' I said.

'Shhh… take a break, that's not for now. Will tell you later' Priyanka interrupted me.

'Actually I'm leaving for Mumbai tomorrow' I said. 'There is an official work so…'

'What?' Priyanka shocked. 'Are you serious?'

I thought, was Priyanka surprised or shocked by this? I really couldn't understand anything.

'That's great yaar, I'll make sure that Priya will fall for you this time' Priyanka said.

'Really?'

'Brother, trust me!'

'It's being difficult without Priya. I really want her back' I said. 'Please, please help me'

'Are you mad Rohit? Remember how you made Sam and me come together? Now that's our turn'

'Love you sis!' I said. 'By the way where is Sam? Is he around?'

'Yep, he is here. Should I call him?' Priyanka asked.

'Accha, Priyanka listen' I said. 'See a good hotel for me. Actually I didn't have any house in Mumbai to live in now. Priya is upset and Mom and Dad… you know. Please help me with this. See a good one. No matter how much it costs' I said.

'I'll slap you one tight! And if there is my house, why will you stay in a hotel? You are accommodating with us' Priyanka said angrily.

'Sis but…'

'No arguments Rohit. I said no? That's final' She said. 'You want to talk to Sam? Wait he is here'

'No let it be, I'll call him later' I said. 'And please don't tell anyone that I'm coming for Mumbai, Priya nor my parents. Please!'

'Don't worry, I won't'

'Love you!' I said as I hung up.

Even my life had given me only sadness, destiny had gifted me the buddies like Sam and Priyanka. I didn't know what tomorrows day will bring to me, but I knew that tomorrow will be a blast. Priya was finally going to be before my eyes after a month. There was nothing better than this, nothing better.

Mumbai

18

My flight landed at Chatrapatti Shivaji international airport. The heartbeats of mine were a bit high at the stage. I rotated my eyes around to see if Sam and Priyanka were here to fetch me up (as if I was a small kid). I stared around as I found them both already holding-up from me. I noticed them but they both were busy fighting with each other. Looking at them from a distance, realized what's the true amity between two people is. They deliberately moved towards me and their eyes were finally onto me.

Priyanka hugged me followed by Sam.

We released as our eyes met. These both creatures looks at me as if it was their first time they were looking at me. I stared at them the same way. I could clearly notice their eyes. Their eyes had tears into them. I could feel their love for me. My eyes were wet automatically.

'Hey guys, what up?' I said calmly.

Priyanka smiled at me as my eyes turned towards her.

'We should ask you the same!' Priyanka said. 'I mean, look at you. You are not our Rohit that we had left earlier'

I looked at Sam as he threw me a 'she-is-right' glance.

'What is it Rohit?' Priyanka said. 'Look at yourself, you're almost down'

I smiled at both of them as they stared at each other, baffled.

I sniffed in.

'Sam, I think I know the reason!' Priyanka told Sam.

'What?' Sam asked.

My eyes were busy staring both of them as if they were a salesman and implementing high cost then the MRP rates.

'Priya! Rohit is missing Priya a lot' Priyanka said. 'Right Rohit?'

I didn't answer.

I was really lucky that I obviated from Priyanka's bloody questions else she would have been started here itself.

'Everything will be all right' Sam said placing his hand on my shoulder.

'And that too, very soon' Priyanka followed. 'Chill brother'

Priyanka brought a smile on my face.

Sam carried my one of the bag. I begged him but that was of no use. Sam really won't listen to anyone instead of Priyanka. We stepped out of the airport as Sam placed my luggage into the car. We stepped into the car. Priyanka took the driving seat and Sam beside Priyanka. I took the back seat. I wanted to ask Priyanka if she had booked a hotel for me as I had well-versed her yesterday.

'I hope you had booked a hotel for me? I told you yesterday' I asked.

'You really need a Slap Rohit' Priyanka said looking back at me.

Sam turned towards me.

'Why had you told her to book a hotel room? Do you have any problem with us?' Sam blunt.

I really had no words to say. I was floored what to say next.

'No, it's not like that…'

'Then what is it Rohit? No rooms will be booked for you in the hotels. You are living at my place. I've already arranged a room for you' Priyanka interrupted.

'Rohit, we know that you can't feel relaxed here now, but trust me you will be. Don't just worry bro. We are here for you. Priyanka, me and Priya too. We are all here. And frankly everything will be alright. We can discourse and sort the things out' Sam said.

I felt anxious as I heard Priya's name from Sam. I leaned over to ask Sam about Priya. But how can I really ask directly?

'Sam, how is Priya?' I grilled.

'Well, see it yourself. She is here at Priyanka's place. And consequently she is there to help out Priyanka in functions'

'What?' I jiggled.

'Relax Rohit, she is not going to make out with you or something' Priyanka said as she grinned at her own joke.

I relaxed back. I closed down my eyes thinking all the way about Priya. I was thinking of, I was finally going to see my love. Priya is finally going to be before my eyes. She meant whole world to me. She was a popsy at which only I could stare. She was mine. My eyes could only peer her off there. The murk from my eyes and my life could finally disappear.

I sniffed in.

'Well, Rohit how was the flight?' Sam asked.

I precipitously opened my eyes and leaned forward.

'Good, thinking all the way about Priya' I blunt.

'Control a little brother, we are on the way. We'll reach soon' Priyanka teased.

We all broke down laughing. I patted slightly on Priyanka's shoulder. I remembered college days, seven years earlier. I could only see the picture. The time just flew away. We didn't realized that how fast we had grown up. I replenished my mind with that of our college days.

'We have reached guys!' Priyanka said as she zeroed the car.

We have finally reached our destination. We stepped out and stood steady. My eyes searched only for Priya and remembering old thoughts, old life.

'Let's move in Rohit' Sam said.

I felt anxious.

I didn't say anything as Sam moved towards me and held my hand. He pulled me towards the entrance door.

'Sam, my bags?' I said.

'They will be in your room' Priyanka said.

'And my laptop?' I said as Priyanka held another hand and pulled me in.

'Come for now, they will manage' Priyanka said.

We had finally stepped into Priyanka's house. I could see everyone making arrangements for the engagement. I could notice four Pandit's.

'Come' Priyanka said as I moved in.

My eyes only rotated in search of Priya. Priyanka noticed me and smiled.

'Searching for Priya ha?' Priyanka teased.

'She is upstairs' a voice from behind said.

I turned around to check out who was it. It was Priyanka's mom. I touched her feet's.

'Hello aunty, how are you?' I inquired.

'We are good. How are you? Everything good?'

'As usual!'

'I learned about your parents! Look, don't get depressed. We will sort out things and feel yourself relax here.'

I gave her an understanding nod.

Her friend called her out from behind as she left. I turned around. Sam moved forward towards me.

'Take shower! You must be tired. Have something. We can talk then' Sam said.

'And listen, hurry up. Priya is waiting' Priyanka teased.

Priyanka took me towards my room upstairs as my luggage was already into my room. My floor had two rooms. I thought another one was of some guests. I was going to have Priya with me soon, sounds interesting and heart-warming. I took shower the next few minutes as I got faultlessly ready. The day today felt delectable. I presume to be brought some gifts for Priya, but I failed to. I know Priya had high-temper on me but it was me who have to get over her. I really need to expound her the reality. I really have to…

♦

I moved downstairs at the hall. Priyanka's mom said that Priya was upstairs, but she was not there. I hope she was downstairs. Priyanka and Sam were enthusiastically waiting for me. I moved towards them.

'What happen? Why are you both…?' I said.

'Shall we go?' Priyanka said interrupting me.

'Yeah, we should definitely leave now' Sam said.

I stared at both of them.

'Can I know where are we going?' I said.

'Don't want to see Priya? We are going for Priya' Sam said.

Fear filled my body. I really couldn't think anything.

'Priya?'

'Yes, Priya. Come' Priyanka said as she took me towards the garden. The wind blew as it relaxed my warm body. It felt good but cold too.

I felt anxious.

I noticed a girl sitting on the bench making her back towards us. I think that was Priya.

Yes! She is it. She was Priya!

'Priya… Priya…' Priyanka called her out.

Sam placed his hand on my shoulder as I looked up at him.

'You are here, Priya is her. It's time to sort out things' Sam said.

We exchanged 'okay' glances. Priyanka signed us to be close to the bench. Sam joined Priyanka who stood face to face with Priya.

'Priya, we had got a gift for you!' Sam said as Priya got up.

Priyanka made her turn towards me as our eyes met. Priya was finally in front of me. We stared at each other. Her eyes had tears. Mine too. Sam and Priyanka stood aside as they made us some space. Priya's eyes filled up. I could clearly notice. I slowly moved towards her, closer and more closer.

'Priya…' I was really wordless.

She moved away from me. I didn't know why she did that.

'Stay away!' Priya blunt. 'I don't want a man who don't really care!'

Sam and Priyanka stepped forward towards us.

'Priya, what are you…' Priyanka said as Priya interrupted.

'Enough Priyanka, please leave me alone. I had already moved on' Priya said.

I continuously stared at Priya's eyes.

'No! You have not. And if you have really, why did your eyes have tears?' I questioned.

Priya didn't made any eye contact with me. I really wanted to give her an elucidation on what had really happen that night.

'Sam, tell this man to leave, else I'm leaving' Priya said.

Sam looked at Priyanka then at me. I moved forward towards Priya as I held her right hand. She pushed me back. She started crying. She had a wry face.

'Don't touch me! You have already lost the rights!' Priya cried.

The droplet from her eye rolled down. I really couldn't understand what to do next.

'Priya, I love you! Don't you love me?' I said. 'I know you do'

'No, I don't love you! Got the answer? Now please leave!' Priya said.

'Priya!' Priyanka screamed.

'Just look at him. Look at his health. He is almost down. He is like all the way asking me about you from the past month. Have you ever tried to call him once? No! You didn't. He loved you a lot and still loves you. And we all here know that you too love him the same way. Then what are these distances Priya? What is making you stay away from Rohit?' Sam said.

Priya hugged Priyanka tight as she cried on her shoulder. I really can't see Priya crying anymore. But what can I really do? I was helpless. I really couldn't do anything. I just freaked out at Priya's sayings. She really didn't cared about me anymore. I didn't know that what was making her away from me? Was it life or Priya herself?

'Priya, please. I can explain' I said.

Priya didn't say anything. She just ran inside. Priyanka followed her. I really felt contrite about Priya's condition. I have to make her feel good. But at first, I have to explain her about the night. I stood needlessly on the garden lawn. I couldn't think anything. My body was lifeless. I really can't live without Priya. I wanted her back. I want my life back. I fell down on my knees as Sam ran towards me. He held me.

'Sam, what I had thought and what all had happen?' I said.

'Please be calm. Everything would be good. We just need time' Sam explained.

I hope that everything will be good. I hope Priya would come back to me. I hope that I could hold her in my arms once again. Sam patted my back. My eyes were continuously watering. But I know one thing, everything will be sorted out because I know how much Priya loves me.

♦

I sat pointlessly at the poolside all the way thinking about my fate. What would it all be without Priya? This emptiness made me think of suicide. I was now ingeniously meant to do the same. I was thinking to suicide off. I could not live the mellow life without Priya. I was again grieving Priya by being in her eyes. I had northing now. Priya, nor my parents. What should I do alone? It's better to die off.

Oodles of fucking thoughts came to my mind. This caused anguish.

I sniffed in.

A small boy about of nine years ran towards me as he dashed over. He fell down as I held him up. I made him sit next to me. I looked up at his face. He looked really cute.

'Are you okay?' I said.

'I'm okay, Thank you!' The boy said in a childish way. 'By the way, you are Rohit bhaiya?'

'How did you know my name?' I baffled.

'Priya didi told me about you!'

'Accha… and what did she said?'

'She said that you are very nice and care for everyone'

I smiled at the boy thinking if Priya had said this? I was really happy to hear this. But I was still unable to understand that what was making Priya away from me?

'By the way, I'm Roy. The mom lovingly call me as Bunny at home' The boy said.

'Hello Bunny!' I said as we shook hands.

The boy stood up. One of his friends called him as he left. I saw Priya into the boy. I didn't know how but I saw the same. My cell-phone vibrated as I brought it out. It showed me the 'Birthday Remainder' notification as I tapped onto it. Daam! It was Priya's birthday tomorrow. I had fucking forgotten about it. I have to get a gift. I really have to. I came back on my home screen and dialled Sam's number.

'Come here at the poolside' I said.

'Why?'

'Just come fast'

He didn't say a word for a second.

'Okay, we are coming' Sam said as I hung up.

I stood up as I started making rounds, thinking of what gift I should get for Priya? Sam and Priyanka were here, at another minute. I brought them aside.

'Guys, its Priya's birthday tomorrow!' I exclaimed.

'What? Are you serious?' Priyanka said.

We stared at each other as if we were dealing with a horror film.

I sniffed in.

'Yep, seriously!' I said.

'Have you planned anything? Plan something special' Sam said.

'I'm thinking to buy her a gift. Something expensive. She loves branded goods' I said as I looked up at Priyanka. She seemed to be discerning something. Her eyes rotated as the sharpies lights rotate into the concerts. I leaned over to ask her if she has a special idea.

'Priyanka suggest something' I said.

'How if we plan a dinner? You will also get some time together' Priyanka advised.

I looked at Sam then at Priyanka. I threw them a 'let's-do-it' glance.

'Ok, that's perfect' I said. 'But will Priya come with me?'

'Don't really worry about it. I'll make her up for this' Priyanka said.

'Get ready guys. We have only twenty minutes. We have to leave' Sam said.

We moved towards our rooms and got ready in few minutes. I thought, I should make this night very special for Priya. I should tell her everything about the night. She would definitely understand me. She will forgive me. She will…

I reached at the parking five minutes prior to Sam and Priyanka. I stood there pointlessly for five minutes. Rest of all arrived, Sam, Priyanka and of course Priya. I checked

Priya from top to bottom. She wore modish togs in which she really looked dashing. I looked into her eyes, but she didn't made any eye contact. I suddenly looked towards Sam, avoiding my eye contact with Priya. He signed me to get into the car. The aroma of Priya's hairs filled the car. I really want to hold her tight but couldn't do so.

'Can I drive?' I said.

Priyanka looked up at me, baffled.

'Why not!' Sam said passing me the keys. We exchanged our places.

We all reached the car as Sam sat beside me and both girls took the back seat. I gave a start as we drove off.

'Well, where are we going?' I inquired.

'Rohit, drive towards Hotel Love Birds. That's the only romantic hotel in Mumbai' Priyanka said.

Sam and me stared at each other. I adjusted the upper mirror so that I could clearly see Priya.   Daam she looked so cute. Her nose was so cute that one could take it home. I really want to kiss her, but the circumstances pulled me down. Priya noticed that I was looking at her through the mirror. She looked at me for a second, our eyes met. She threw me a dirty look. I broke down the eye contact. I concentrated on the road. We had not spoken a word throughout the drive from Priyanka's place to Hotel Love Birds. All of us sat quietly as someone has punished us. I parked the car. We got down as we entered in. The hotel seemed expensive. One of the waiter took us towards our table. The table was decorated with heart shaped balloons and surrounded with red roses. Priyanka took her seat beside Sam and Priya had no choice rather than taking her seat beside me. Priya sat beside me in a no option way.

I sniffed in.

I placed my hand on the menu card to lift it up as Priya unknowingly placed her hand onto mine.

'Control guys, you have rest of the night' Priyanka teased as Sam laughed at it.

Priya suddenly lifted her hand from mine. She got anxious. This sign shows that she still loves me and still cares for me as before. I passed the menu card towards Priyanka to see what special we should have today. These two people were backing me perfectly to bring Priya close to me again. Hats off!!!

'Girls, we have an impotent work, we just remembered!' Sam said. 'We will be back in twenty minutes'

'No, you both are going nowhere, you are sitting here with us' Priyanka scolded.

Sam signed Priyanka with 'try-to-understand' glance. It seemed that she had understood.

'Come back soon' Priyanka said as we left.

As we left Priyanka looked up at Priya as threw her a dirty look. Priya looked at her, floored.   Priyanka seemed in furious mood.

Priyanka sniffed in.

'What's wrong with you Priya? Why are you behaving like this?' Priyanka questioned.

'Like what?' Priya said being innocent as if she didn't know anything.

'Why are you treating Rohit like that?' Priyanka asked.

'Like what?'

'Look Priya, we all know, you also know it well. Rohit is already hurt a lot. Look at him, he had lost himself somewhere. Why are you hurting him more? Please for God's sake, stop this. He needs you'

'But I don't need him' Priya said heartlessly.

Priyanka threw her a dirty look.

'What's wrong with you?' I know you love him a lot. Then what are these distances still maintained?' Priyanka blunt as Priya's eyes filled. 'Look your eyes filled up. That shows how much you love him'

Priya broke down. She cried. Priyanka controlled her.

'Priyanka, what do you think? I don't love him? I love him more than anything in this world.' Priya said. 'I love him more than myself.

Priyanka stared at Priya.

'Then what are those distances? Do they really mean anything before your love?'

'Priyanka, he had already lost his parents because of me. He left them for me. And I didn't want Rohit getting away from his parents because of me. They also love him equally' Priya said picking up a tissue.

Priya cleared her eyes.

'So you…'

'Priyanka, relations matters. I don't want Rohit to break down, I don't want him to be a looser in life. I want him to be successful and if that's me who is a thorn to his life, I will back off' Priya interrupted.

'Priya he is already broken down without you. He is half over. Don't you care for him?'

'I do. I know how I had been alone without him for a month. Yes, that's true that I was distraught with him after the accident. I learned the truth afterwards. But all I know that he had left his parents for me. And I really couldn't bear that one'

Priya's eyes filled up. Priyanka got up from her seat and sat beside Priya. She hugged her whispering 'everything will be all right'

'You know, I should not tell you this one but listen. You know where Rohit has been now?' Priyanka said releasing Priya.

'He had been to get a gift for you for your birthday tomorrow.' Priyanka said.

'Really? He remembers my birthday?'

A droplet trundled down Priya's cute cheeks. Her makeup had all vanished. She had a wry face.

'Priya, he never forgotten you! He was always yours and will be yours forever. And tell me how many more day you are going to continue this?' Priyanka said.

'I really don't want to do this. I really can't see him disturbed. But I have to do this till and when Rohit don't patch up with his parents.' Priya cried.

'Please Priya, control yourself. You would like if Rohit sees you like this?'

'I have hurt him a lot Priyanka' Priya said. 'Promise me two things'

'What?'

'You will not talk to anyone about what I had told you now. You will not even tell Sam'

'I promise you Priya'

'And second one, you will take care of my Rohit. I know he needs me but... He needs someone. Please stand by him. Please!' Priya said.

'Nice to see you back, don't worry about Rohit'

Priya broke down again. She tightened her lips to control her herself from crying, but she cried loud from inside. Priyanka passed her a tissue. Priyanka held her.

'Priya, get to the washroom. Freshen up' Priyanka said.

Priya nodded as she moved towards the washroom.

Life had made our love different. We love each other like hell. God knows it but he still keeps us away. I don't know why, but I think he had planned something special for us.

We entered the hotel entrance. We had got a titan golden watch for Priya. Sam had purchased same for Priyanka. The balled played as it made my mind fresh. We reached our table. I couldn't find Priya there.

'Where is Priya?' I boggled.

'She had been to the washroom' Priyanka said pointing towards the washroom door.

I relaxed.

'Well, what have you brought?' Priyanka inquired.

'That's a surprise madam' Sam started.

Priya walked towards us. She took her seat beside Sam. Sam sat opposite to me and Priyanka. I could clearly see Priya's face. The black spot on her forehead was clearly visible. I noticed her. She seemed different like something had happen. Priya grovel as I looked at Priyanka throwing 'what-had-happen' glance. Priyanka nodded regarding 'nothing'

I sniffed in.

I wanted to ask Priya, if she was all right. But I practically couldn't do it. Next few minutes went making jokes and remembering previous memories. We ordered our dinner soon. 'Life would be so easy without problems' I thought. I hope Priya would like the gift. That one was especially for her. I had proclaimed her name onto the watch. I prayed god for only one thing, 'please give me my Priya back'. Things seemed smaller than Priya. I really didn't want anything. All I want and all I could pray for was 'Priya'

♦

We all stood in the hall looking at each other's faces. This was too late night. Sleeping time. We were two of us on my floor. I wanted to ask Sam that who was the other one on my floor?

'Sam, who is the guest on my floor?' I asked.

Sam smiled at me. I got floored.

'Rohit, I and Priyanka are very naughty already, you know. We had purposefully placed Priya and you on the same floor. So that you could…' Sam said. 'Understand the rest'

'You…!'

'Why is there a problem? If yes then say, we could change the rooms' Priyanka teased.

I threw her a flying kiss.

I moved upstairs as Priya was already in her room. I felt anxious to enter her room. I really felt something different. Her door was locked. I moved forward gathering some courage. I knocked the door. Once, twice, thrice… but no answer. I knocked it the fourth time as Priya opened the door and stood right front to me. For few seconds she stood silent staring at me. I replenished myself with some courage. She tried to shut the door as I pushed it off. I entered in as I looked the door from inside. I held Priya tight as she tried to free her off. I pushed her over the wall and held her arms.

'What are you doing?' Priya said.

'I should ask you the same. What are you doing Priya? Why are you doing this to me?'

'Leave me!'

'No, I'll not. Else what?'

'Else, I'll shout and call people'

'Really? Call them. I really want to see that how loud you are'

Priya really didn't spoke a word, shouting was the far away thing. I knew she would not do nothing that could hurt me.

'What happen? Call people.' I said.

Priya stood quite. Her eyes filled up. This were the tears that mentioned love for me. The tears she couldn't control.

'Rohit, please leave my room. Please leave me alone. I have moved on.' Priya cried. I released her.

I stood two steps away from her. I couldn't just think anything. I could not have just a word.

'Priya, I love you. Don't you remember the movements that we had spent together? Don't you remember the promises?' I said as tears filled my eyes.

'Priya, please don't cry. If it's hurting you, I'll leave the room' I said. 'But please don't cry'

I kneeled down on my knees. I held Priya's feet's. I was almost crying. I was doing the thing that I had never done before.

'Priya, I beg off you! Please come back. I really can't live without you' I sobbed.

Priya moved aside. She was unceasingly crying. It was me who made her cry.

'Rohit, get up and leave' Priya said sobbing. 'Please don't do this!'

She really didn't seemed serious. There was a thing making her do this. But what was it?

'And if you really can't live without me then don't live' Priya said vehemently.

As I heard the last words of Priya, I was helpless. I stood up and left the room. Priya ran and locked the door from inside. I turned around and stared at the door. I heard the sound, Priya was sobbing. She cried for me. But the thing was I made her cry. Priya said 'Don't live' that's fine. If that gives her happiness, I was completely agreed to it. I really don't want to spoil tomorrow's day. This was a new start. A new morning and here came Priya's birthday.

19

'**H**appy Birthday Priya' I said mentally as I got up from my bed. The first morning thought was of Priya.

I sniffed in.

The blanket was still rolled around my body. I had no intentions of getting up so early at 6:00 am, but there was Priya's birthday and all I know was I want Priya in front of my eyes the entire day. 'You are going to quit your life Rohit. That makes Priya happy' I told myself. I thought about it a long time. The warmth in the blanket still filled my body. I threw the blanket as I jumped out of the bed. I ran towards the door to see Priya was there or not? I couldn't find her there. I thought over to go and wish her but dropped the idea thinking of something special to work out with. I came in to get fresh and dress quite good today. My face delimited only smile today. Priya had brought it to me. The door smashed hard as I looked back. I felt anxious. It was Priyanka.

'Haven't you got ready yet?' Priyanka said.

I smiled at her.

'Just got up madam. Will work out soon' I replied.

Priyanka stepped towards me as she pulled my left ear.

'Ouch...' I screamed.

'Priya is waiting for you and you are wasting your time?' Priyanka blunt.

'What Priya is waiting *for me*?' I said tracing more on last two words.

Priyanka made her face expressions like she had mistakenly told me. I got floored. She smiled at me.

'I mean, don't you want to wish her?' Priyanka said. 'Get ready fast'

She walked towards the room door. I felt that she was hiding things from me. She hadn't made any joke which was risible, but she had hid a thing from me.

'Priyanka?' I called her out as she stopped the mid-way. She turned up towards me.

I can clearly notice the water popped on her forehead.

'Is everything all right?' I said. 'I mean, had Priya talked to you about me something and that you are hiding from me?'

Priyanka sniffed in.

'Rohit, I know she loved you. And trust me I will make her came herself and patch up' She said coming towards me.

'Please make her come back to me' I begged her. 'She is my life'

'I will! Don't you trust me?' Priyanka said placing her hand on my shoulder.

She smiled at me.

'I do'

My eyes were filled with water. All I could see was only Priya before me. All I could feel was Priya. All I could live my life for was Priya. My love.

'Now get ready and come down fast. Priya is already in the kitchen' She said tapping my shoulder.

I gave her a smile.

'Good, get down fast. We are waiting!' She said as she left the room.

♦

As I got down I noticed the preparation done for Priya's birthday. The hall was decorated full of flowers and garlands, looking at the venue this birthday party will really go tawdry I guess. I moved down the stairs as I saw Sam sitting on the sofa. Priyanka was busy instructing the decorators what to do next. My eyes rummaged for Priya. I couldn't find her. 'She must be in kitchen' my mind told me. I moved towards Sam and sat beside him.

'Good Morning' He said looking at me.

I gave him a smile. My eyes were still searching for Priya. But I couldn't find her.

'She is not here. She is with Priyanka's Mom in kitchen cooking' Sam blunt.

I looked at him as he smiled. I was confused.

'He cannot live without her a single second' Priyanka joined in.

She sat next to Sam. She made a face at which anyone could bust out laughing. I laughed at her hard. Sam stared at me.

'Good to see old Rohit back who could smile always' Sam said looking at Priyanka.

I stared at both of them.

'What?' Sam and Priyanka said in unison.

'Nothing' I nodded.

The sofa where we sat were not at all comfortable. They were sudorific. They should really change them.

'Why are you not changing these uncomfortable sofas? I said.

Priyanka stared at me.

'What's wrong with them now?' Priyanka questioned.

'They are so uncomfortable!' I exclaimed.

Priyanka nodded at me.

Sam was busy with his iPhone playing *Candy Crush* on it. Priyanka and I looked at each other exchanging 'he-would-not-change' glances. Priyanka snatched the phone from Sam as it flew and directly smashed down onto the floor and broke down into millions of pieces. Poor iPhone, I guess. Priyanka looked up at Sam with her sorry face. I looked at Sam. He was not angry on her.

'Sorry Sam, I was not…' Priyanka said as Sam interrupted her.

'Relax *Jaan*, I'll get a new phone'

'I'm really sorry'

'But I'm not angry with it…'

Priyanka's face fell down.

'What was decided, the thing would be anything. We would not say sorry or thank you to anyone of us' Sam said. 'You broke the promise, I don't want to talk to you'

Priyanka cut the distance and moved close to him. She placed her hand on his shoulders.

Sam shrugged.

Sam stood up jerking off her hand from his shoulder. I stood up.

'Please, I would not make such a mistake again' Priyanka begged.

'What will I get if I forgive you?' Sam said playfully.

'Anything you want but please forgive me' Priyanka said in a childish way.

'Okay, kiss me right here on my face'

'Here?'

'Yeah, do you have any problem with that?'

Priyanka glanced at me as I gave her a 'go-ahead' look. She held Sam's face as she kissed him on his right cheek.

I sniffed in.

Priyanka almost had tears in her eyes. Sam noticed it.

'Why are you crying?' I was just joking baby!' Sam said.

Priyanka stood quite. A droplet rolled down from her right eye.

'Say something *Jaan*' Sam said as Priyanka hugged him tight.

Sam held her.

'Chill up yaar. I was just joking' Sam said.

Priyanka hit Sam's chest playfully. The scene was going on in front of my eyes. I smiled at myself looking Sam and Priyanka's unbreakable love for each other. All I could feel was love filled in the air around me. The love for which I was still waiting.

'Guys get ready for the party' I said.

♦

It was around 11:30 am when all was set for the birthday party. All the arrangements were done as well. I liked the heart shaped ice-cream cake which was decorated proclaiming Priya's name on it. Priyanka was upstairs into Priya's room making Priya up. I begged Priyanka to dress Priya like never before. Sam and I stood near the kitchen puffing the balloons for the party. Needless to say but Sam and I had blew more than hundred in last few minutes. My eyes only waited for Priya to come down as I haven't seen her from morning. We had dressed up earlier so that girls could get enough time to get dressed up. Sam had dressed up in *desi* kurta and I was in formal blue blazer. Priya likes me when I dress up in American style. I noticed Priyanka coming down the staircase. While she was crossing by the kitchen I pulled her towards me. She too dressed good and looked pretty.

'What's going on? Has Priya dressed?' I questioned.

'Yeah, I have dressed her up as you said. Pretty like a princess' She replied.

Sam smiled at us.

'Just few more minutes and you will see her yourself' Sam teased.

'Priyanka, will you do me a favour?' I said.

Priyanka higher her eyebrows.

'No!'

'I'm serious, can you please bring her to me before she goes on the stage? I want to talk to her, please' I begged.

Priyanka came close to me.

'Rohit, I will try. She is still angry with you'

My face fell down. Sam placed his on my shoulder to encourage me.

'I have to get her downstairs as all the hosts are here' Priyanka said. 'See you around'

I sniffed in.

We moved towards the stage area. I waited for Priyanka to come down with Priya. And to bring her close to my heart all over again. All the head turned towards the staircase waiting for the birthday girl to come. My heartbeats started to beat faster than usual. I had brought the gift properly wrapped in the gift paper. I hope Priya would like that. My eyes rolled to the table kept beside me. It had the decoration material on it. I stared at the blade on the table. I picked it up and placed it into my pocket. I didn't know what I was doing but I have to do it. The wait had finally gone down. I saw Priya coming down from the staircase wearing a blue coloured saree. Her pink nose made her look even prettier the usual. Priyanka brought her towards me as she stood five seconds before me staring at my eyes. It really felt well. Priya made her way towards the stage. All the people turned their eyes onto the birthday girl. Priyanka came near us and stood beside Sam and I. Sam had control over the mic to make an announcement.

'Guys, today we are here to celebrate the birthday of my cutest and dearest friend Priya!' Sam announced.

I was continuously staring at Priya. Not a single second had gone when my eyes were off Priya.

'Let's make the day of birthday girl more special' Sam added next and gestured Priya to cut the cake.

'HAPPY BIRTHDAY TO YOU…!' The song started.

I didn't sing as my eyes didn't allow me to look away from Priya even for a second. She didn't looked at me even once. This made me cry but I controlled myself. Priya was really ingrained in my heart. I really love her a lot and miss those days when she was with me. The cake was cut, the birthday song was sung. 'What was next?' I thought.

Sam and Priyanka came up to me together. Sam covered me as if I was a criminal and the cops were here to catch me.

'Go, give her the gift' Priyanka said.

I felt anxious.

'Rohit, go man. This is the time' Sam said.

I looked at both of them as I sniffed in.

I put my hand inside the blazer and brought out the gift box. I stared at it for a while.

'Should I go now? She will be irritated if she sees me right now. And I don't want her mood to be off at this time' I said in a serious voice.

Sam came close to me and placed his right hand onto mine.

'Bro, go now. We are here to handle the rest. We are too coming with you on the stage' Sam said.

I looked up at Priya. She was busy accepting the birthday wishes from other guests. Priyanka threw me a 'shall-we-go-now' glance. I nodded in agreement. I dared this time and stepped on the stage followed by Sam and Priyanka. I was finally in front of Priya. She looked directly into my eyes which made me more anxious.

'Happy Birthday baby' I said handing her the gift box.

She didn't said even a word. Her eyes were filled with water. My eyes were fixed on her face.

'May your all wishes come true' I added.

She kept the gift box aside and turned towards Sam. She looked up at Priyanka next.

'I'm tired, shall I go rest for some time?' Priya said.

Priyanka nodded in agreement.

Priyanka looked at me next and threw me an 'I-will-handle-it' look and went up towards Priya. Sam followed Priyanka. I was alone in the market of guests. I had learned a thing today that Priya really hates me a lot. There was no reason of me to live any more. My eyes filled up. My heart cried. I had lost in my life. My body had goose-bumps which meant failure. I was failed. My life wasn't in love, it had come to an end.

♦

'Why did your eyes had tears on the stage when Rohit wished you?' Priyanka questioned.

Priya broke down. She couldn't control herself just cried hard. Priyanka stood up from the bed and held her. She hugged Priya to make her feel better.

Priyanka and Priya were in Priya's room upstairs. The party had got over at 3:00 pm. The clock had reached 6:25 pm now.

'Priyanka, I could see Rohit almost lost. His is like finished' Priya cried.

Priyanka tapped her back.

'It's all because of me. He all the way loved me a lot and what did I do to him?' I had only hurt him since long' Priya added.

Priyanka held her hand and sat face to face.

'Priya, I'll tell you seriously. He is just dying for you, I mean look at him his health had gone down' Priyanka said.

Priya broke down again.

'I really love him a lot Priyanka, more than myself. I just don't want to hurt him more' Priya cried.

'Priya, control yourself. Will you be happy if Rohit sees you in this state? He will be hurt right? Can you see you hurt?'

'I can't hurt him more. I really can't'

Priyanka smiled at her. She made her look up and made her smile too.

'I want to go talk to him' Priya said.

Priyanka smiled.

'Why are you smiling?'

'Because you gave Rohit back his life' Priyanka replied. 'I'm really happy'

Priya got up to leave as Priyanka held her hand and pulled her back.

'First have a look at the gift. See what Rohit had gifted you' Priyanka said handing her my gift box.

Priya unwrapped the box as she saw the golden titan watch I had gifted her.

'Wow! That's cool' Priyanka teased.

'Shut up! My darling had gifted it to me. That's very special to me'

The box contained a letter which I had added into the box. I was about to end my life off.

'What's this letter about?' Priya asked.

'How would I know? May be it be a love letter' Priyanka teased again.

Priya smiled at her as she opened the letter. The letter said:

Dear Priya,

I know that this is a stupid thing I'm making but I have to do it through. I really love you a lot Priya. I really cannot live without you a single second now. You would get a better person than me who would care more than I did as your soul-mate. All I want is to you be always happy. Always have a smile on your face.

Remember you said that, 'if you can't live without me than don't live' Yeah, I'm doing the same. See you the next birth. I really love you a lot Priya. But when you don't talk to me and ignore me it hurts. When you didn't even look at me that hurts. When you scream at me that hurts. ☹ I'm ending my life off. But I would be always be smiling for you, always be with you. Hamesha Kush Reahna Priya! Love you! Love you a lot!

Yours heartbroken,

Rohit

'Rohit' Priya screamed out as she had a suicide note in her hand.

She really couldn't believe her eyes. She had all broken down.

'He can't do this' Priya said.

Priya and Priyanka ran towards my room as the door was already open. The blood had spilt all over the room. I had cut my wrist with the same blade which I had picked up from the table downstairs. I was losing my consciousness. But I could see Priya coming towards me with her half-squinted eyes. My body already had a huge blood loss. I was unable to move any of my body parts.

'Rohit, what have you done?' Priya said holding me up.

She cried for me. Priyanka held my hand and tried to stop the blood but it was of no use now. I want Priya to hear something from me before I die.

'I…Love…You' I stammered.

'No, you can't do this to me Rohit' Priya cried.

It was late enough now. The blood loss was huge. I had no sense. I shouldn't have been to try a suicide but I really can't bear the loss of Priya in my life.

20

All of them stood still like a statue waiting for the doctor to come out of the ICU. Sam cried for the first time, Priyanka couldn't believe herself that I have tried to commit suicide. Priya was almost down. She uninterruptedly cried from Priyanka's home to the hospital holding me in her arms. But I had no option rather than suicide. What else would I have done if my love wasn't with me?

'Priya, control yourself. Everything would be all right!' Priyanka explained.

Priya hugged Priyanka and broke down hard. Sam came closer to them. She cried hard as her eyes were almost red now. If I could seen Priya in this state I could never have been forgiven myself for what I had done to her.

'This is all because of me. He was in depression all because of me' Priya blamed herself.

'Don't blame yourself Priya. He will be alright' Sam said placing his hand on hers.

The atmosphere outside the ICU was not good. All of them including Sam had tears into their eyes, and that was all because of me.

Sam had informed my family and Radhika di about this. They were on the way to the hospital.

'Sit Priya' Sam said as he made Priya sit on the setter. Priyanka sat next to Priya. Sam noticed the doctor coming out from the ICU. He signed Priya and Priyanka. They suddenly got up and stared at the doctor's face.

'How is he now?' Sam inquired.

'The blood loss had made him unconscious' The doctor said.

All of them stared at each other.

'He is out of danger no, my Rohit is all right. Right?' Priya said.

'Due to the blood loss the complications are still there. But you need not have to worry. He is out of danger. He will be alright' The doctor said.

'Thank God' Priyanka relaxed.

Priya had a cute smile on her face. The smile showed that how much she loved me. Sam and Priyanka smiled at each other.

'But we have to keep him under observation for two days. Then you can take him home' the doctor added.

'Thank you doctor, thank you so very much' Priyanka said as he left.

Priya was glad. She was happy for me. Sam brought out his phone to spread the news everywhere among relatives.

'Guys, I'll come seeing him once' Priya said as she left for the ICU.

She stepped inside. I was still with no sense. I was still unconscious. I had no idea what was really happening. Priya came closer to me as she sat next to my bed. She placed her hand on my forehead. She leaned over and kissed my forehead. She had tears.

'Baby, I love you a lot. Get well soon no, with whom will I talk? I want to talk to you. I want to apologize for what I had done to you. I want you to kiss me. I want you to hold me tight' She said.

She held my hand tight. A droplet from her eyes rolled down as it fell on my hand.

'Remember our dates? How romantic they were?' Priya cried. 'I want you to make love to me. I want to name my life as yours'

She touched her forehead to my hand. She really felt sorry. She cried only because she loved me a lot.

'I really love you baby' She said again.

Sam and Priyanka stepped inside the ICU followed by Radhika di. Priya stood up suddenly. She was shocked noticing Radhika di.

'Priya, are you all right?' Radhika di said as Priya ran towards her and hugged her.

Priya buried her face into her shoulder. She tried to regulate herself. Radhika di hugged her tight.

'Radhika di, this is all because of me. I am responsible for all this' Priya cried.

'No baby, that's not you. Everything will be all right. Rohit loves you a lot' Radhika di explained. 'And look at you, you really need rest. Come with me home and rest'

'How can I rest? Till and when Rohit doesn't get well, I'll not have food nor rest'

Sam and Priyanka stared at each other. They cried for me. In this parlance Priya's eyes were red. She loves me a lot. She cried for me.

'Guys, let's make him take rest and let's move out of here' Sam said pointing towards the door.

All of them moved out of the ICU. Mom and dad had not come still. I don't know why, I hope they still hates me for what I had done to them. As Priya moved outside the ICU she noticed my mom and dad standing near the bench. She sniffed in as she walked aside of them. Mom moved towards Priya in an angry mood as Priyanka pulled my mom aside and brought to a corner.

'Please aunty, not now. Priya is not in the state to answer you. She loves your son a lot!' Priyanka said.

'If she loves him then she wouldn't have left him to die' mom replied angrily.

'She had done it for a reason. And…'

'Fuck off her reason. And Priyanka I had not expected this from you. You are taking the murderer's side' Mom interrupted.

All of them stared at the fight between mom and Priyanka. The situation was out of its control.

'How dare you to call her a murderer? How could you? Do you really want to listen that why she did it? If you want to then please listen'

Mom stared at Priyanka.

'She had done it for you. Remember Rohit had left you for Priya? She didn't wanted that because of her, Rohit should be away from his parents. Priya all the way avoided Rohit so that Rohit could hate her and come back to you. I'll tell you one thing, I really don't understand their love. They love each other a lot. They know to love and also can handle it themselves' Priyanka said.

Mom had tears in her eyes.

'You know what? I think because of this attitude Rohit had taken a right decision to leave you and got to Priya that time. You never tried to understand him. His dad supported him, but you… Never! I beg you to please leave him alone for few days. Give him a break' Priyanka added.

A droplet from my Mom's eye rolled down. My mom looked at Priya. She really want to apologize to Priya. She felt sorry for what she had done to Priya. Now the things were in complete mess. Could the fight between mom and Priyanka would made things back to normal? I had hurt all of them a lot. I really felt sorry for what all I had done. But nothing was in my hand, I have to walk where fate takes me.

2 Days Later…

I had been brought home (Priyanka's home of course). I could feel and see what all was happening but couldn't move as my body strength was not good enough still. I had been kept in the room where Priya would stay upstairs. As I was brought home with a hospital appointed nurse I hadn't seen Priya anywhere. 'Had she left me or what?' I thought. I have to take this situation shrewd. I wanted to get up and look for Priya, but I couldn't get up from my bed. The nurse entered the room as she stopped the saline.

'They are over?' I inquired.

'I'm giving you few injections now' the nurse said.

I threw her an 'Okay' glance.

'These could give you sleep as they are high doses' she said.

'Hmm'

I closed down my eyes as the nurse injected the serine to my left hand. The nurse collected the empty injections as she left the room. The doses made me sleep as I went off the sleep.

◆

Priya sat next to me holding my right hand into hers. I had went off to sleep. Priya really cared for me. She was slightly looking at me.

'Baby, get well soon no, I want to talk to you' She cried.

Priya sobbed.

'I know I had hurt you a lot, but trust me I love you a lot baby. Please forgive me no, please'

Priya got up and kissed my forehead. She kissed my nose next. The door opened hard as Priya looked back at the door. Priya noticed my parents entering the room. She couldn't look at my mom as she didn't had more courage to do so. My mom came towards my bed as Priya moved aside looking down (still don't have courage to look up at my mom) Mom sat next to me. She placed her hand on mine. She didn't cried but kissed my hand. She loved me. My dad came to me the next movement. He smiled looking at me. Priya was about to leave the room as mom held her hand getting up. She came close to her. Priya broke down. She really couldn't control.

'Beta, why are you crying?' Mom said making her look up at her.

Priya didn't said a word.

'Priya, I know I was wrong with you. I've seen how you cared for Rohit just now. I and Pradeep were watching you from the door gap. We learned why you avoided my son for so long. Only for us. Priya we both are looking for your future with Rohit. We want you to be our daughter-in-law. I want you to be my daughter'

Priya looked up at Mom.

'Please forgive me beta' Mom said joining her hands before Priya.

Priya suddenly held mom's hands and brought them down. She looked at my mom nodding in disagreement.

'Aunty, what are you doing? You were always right at your place. And please don't feel sorry'

Mom cried for the first time before Priya.

'You love my son?'

'A lot aunty'

'Will you really be with him in his all the good and bad times?'

'See giving me one chance. I will not let you complaint'

Mom smiled at Priya. She slide out the golden bangle from her right hand and gave it to Priya. Priya stared at my mom. She hugged her. 'Always be happy beta' Mom whispered. Dad came close to Priya.

'Bless you beta' Dad said.

Priya felt blessed. Priya touched mom's feet followed by dad. Mom made her stand. My parents stared at each other.

'Priya can I request you something?' Mom said.

'Sure Aunty!'

'Aunty? Still angry with me? I thought you have accepted me as your mother'

'Okay Mom!' Priya smiled.

'That's like a good girl' mom said.

This made all of them smile.

'Beta please don't tell Rohit that we were here'

'But mom…'

'Please beta, that's a request' Mom interrupted.

'Okay Mom'

'We will leave now, we shouldn't wait here anymore' Dad said.

Priya gave them an understanding nod. Dad smiled at Priya.

Mom and dad moved towards the door to leave. They left the room as Priya smiled at herself. Priyanka stood to the door. She looked at Priya as she too stared at her. Both of them smiled at each other.

Priya sniffed in.

The atmosphere felt loveable. Things were sorting out, but I was unknown about all this. Priya ran towards Priyanka and hugged her in excitement.

'I told you everything will be all right' Priyanka said.

'I just want to pray for one more thing'

'What?'

'I want to pray for my darling to get well soon'

Priyanka smiled at her.

◆

Priya went downstairs to get my medicines. I was still in deep sleep. My doses were been finished. Doctors had strictly instructed Priya that I still need complete bed rest. The point at which I had cut my hand was dressed up properly. I can get up and walk now. My eyes opened as I was feeling a bit better now.

I sniffed in.

I got up from my bed as I moved to the side table of my bed and got the water glass. I took two big sips. I placed the glass back to its original place. My hand still had a slight pain when I move it hard. I stepped into the balcony to get some fresh air. The cold breeze dashed my body. It really felt good. I closed down my eyes to feel Priya into the air. I suddenly opened my eyes. My life was inoperable. 'Why had God given me a second chance?' I thought. I wanted Priya back. 'She had left you Rohit' my mind said.

I stepped inside the room. I really myself didn't know that what was I doing but I was trying the suicide for the second time. I picked up the pen kept into the pen-holder on the side table. As I was about undress my hand and poke the pen into the injury and tear out the hand the door suddenly opened hard. I looked up at the door. I noticed Priya coming in with the medicine bottles. She had found me attending the suicide for the second time. She ran towards me as she grabbed the pen from my hand and threw it away.

'How dare you? Are you mad? What were you doing?' Priya screamed.

I only stared at her. I was speechless.

'Say something! Haven't you thought of me? How could I live without you?' Priya cried. 'And if you want to die please kill me first. Kill me first...'

My eyes had tears.

'Priya!' I said.

'What? Please kill me no'

'You are...'

'I hate you Rohit, I really hate you a lot' Priya cried hard as she hugged me tight. I hugged her back in response.

'Why Priya? Why? Why have you done this to me?' I sobbed.

Priya released me as she stood before me. She cried hard, she felt sorry. Her tears were rambunctious. I held her face and made her look at me.

'Why baby?'

'I had to do it. I had no other option. You rejected your parents for me Rohit, and I couldn't separate a son from their parents' Priya cried.

'You must have at least talked to me once Priya'

'How could I? I had no courage *Jaan*'

Tears from my eyes rolled down. I couldn't believe my ears. Priya loved me and my family too much. I really couldn't believe that I had a misunderstanding that she all the way hates me.

'Can you imagine how much it hurt me when you started avoiding my calls? How much it hurt me when you avoided me? How much it hurt me when you were being rude to me?'

Priya placed her left hand on my face. She really felt sorry. I could see her wry face.

'I'm sorry Rohit… I'm really sorry' Priya cried.

I really can't see her crying. I really couldn't see her wry face. I held her and brought her towards the bed. I made her sit down. I held her face next and made her look up at me.

'Please Priya, stop crying' I said politely.

She held my hand and stared at me. She could feel me.

'Promise me you will never leave me alone' I said.

'I love you baby, I would never leave you alone. I will be with you till the last breath'

I smiled at her as she too responded with a smile. I hugged her. It all felt romantic. It all felt like I was in heaven.

'I love you' I said.

'I love you too baby' She replied.

She held my injured hand releasing me.

'Does it pain?' She asked.

I didn't answer for few seconds. Just stared at her beautiful eyes.

'Not really!' I lied.

'Lie, you can't hide anything from me, you know. I could feel your pain' she said and smiled.

'Get well soon *Jannu*' She said as she kissed my face.

Priyanka entered the room unknowingly. She moved towards us as she gave us a smile.

'O...how... Romance and all ha?' She teased.

She was knowing that thing between us both were all sorted out. She knew that we had patched up. She knew that our life was back to normal.

She smiled looking at Priya next.

'Come down dinner is ready' She said as she left smiling.

My life was back to normal. It was full of happiness. It had a reason to live. It was all because of it, a word, 'Priya'

'Don't worry, I'll not waste your time. I'll get you the plates here' Priyanka said re-entering the room.

I smiled at her.

♦

It was around 8:30 pm as the plates were served into our rooms. My eyes couldn't really get away from Priya. All I noticed was her hairs. Her cute pink nose. Her wet lips. Her eyes. I stared at her face.

'What?'

'Nothing, just looking at your face'

'You really missed me lot no?'

'A lot Priya. I really couldn't live without you'

'I'm sorry baby. Please forgive me'

'You shouldn't be sorry. I should be'

Priya held my hand tight and brought it close to her face as she kissed it.

'You are my darling. I love you' Priya said.

I smiled at her.

Priyanka entered the room with two glasses of cold drinks. She placed it on the glass table kept in front of us.

'I had blew the candles. This dinner should be special to you. Switch off the lights and the candles would play romantic' Priyanka said. 'And Priya have something now. You hadn't had anything form two days'

I suddenly looked up at Priyanka then at Priya.

'One minute, Priya you haven't had anything from two days?' I questioned.

Priya didn't said a word. Just tried to hide her feelings from me.

'Don't lie, I could sense you!' I added.

Priya's eyes filled. I made her look up. She stared at my eyes.

'Why Priya?' I asked.

'Rohit, I could answer this' Priyanka said. 'She had fasted for you, she decided that she would not have food till and until you don't get well'

Priya threw Priyanka a 'keep-quite' glance. I looked up at Priya as she got up from her seat. I held her hand as I jerked it off.

'Sis, give us five minutes please' I said.

'Take your time. I'll wait downstairs' Priyanka said as she left our room.

I turned back to Priya as she looked into my eyes.

'Priya have you…'

'Please *Jaan,* let's not spoil this night. Let's fight some other day' Priya said.

I smiled at her.

'You would never change no? It's really difficult to win against you' I said. Priya made me sit back on my seat. We had our dinner in next half an hour. I made Priya eat first. The candle light dinner really got romantic as Priyanka said. I could sense the love in air.

♦

We stepped out into the balcony. The cold breeze felt romantic. Priya made me remove the shoes and told me to feel the coldness. It really felt good.

'Priya, have to say something!' I exclaimed.

Priya stared at me paying her full attention.

'Thank you!' I said.

'For what?'

'For giving me my life back. It was really not happening without you'

'I'm all yours Rohit. I really don't need anything from life now'

I stared at her beautiful lips. I really felt guilty for what I had done.

'If you are still angry on me you can slap me as you had slapped me in the hospital that time' I said as I bend down to match her height.

She held my face as she placed a sweet kiss on my right cheek. She kissed my forehead. She gave a smile to me. The smile meant whole world to me.

'I'm really sorry Priya' I apologized.

'Shhh… I only want to hear I love you from you. No sorry, no thank you, nothing' Priya said.

'I love you' I said.

'You are my darling' She said pinching my nose playfully.

I moved close to her as I held her. I pulled her close to me as our bodies touched. We both only stared at each other's eyes. I could feel her breath on my face.

'*Jaan* what is someone comes?' Priya said politely.

'You really think that someone can still come in between us?'

'No one can divide you from me. We are one love. One soul' Priya said.

The wind brought us the cold breeze which made us more romantic. The doors were locked. I really couldn't control myself anymore. I had felt Priya after a so long time. I wanted to make love to her. I wanted to feel her more.

'I want to make love to you' I said looking into her eyes.

'You don't need my permission for that' Priya said.

I slowly brought my mouth close to hers. Our lips met as I kissed her. I kissed her after a long time. She kissed hard in response. I held her face for support. I held her up in my arms and brought her into the bedchamber. I made her sleep on the bed and moved towards the light switches. I switched off the lights as the candle lights played romantic. The candles were still lit. I slowly moved towards Priya as she smiled at me. I sat beside her as she sat up straight. I held her face as she stared at me.

'You are the most beautiful girl in the world' I said.

She smiled at me. The smile meant whole world to me. She grabbed me close to her as our lips met all over again. We embraced. I grabbed her upper lip with my teeth and kissed it first. She didn't protest just allowed me to do whatever I was doing. I slide down towards her lower lip. I kissed it next. Our tongue met as we kissed hard.

'You have never changed. You are the same, my earlier Rohit' Priya said.

I made her sleep on the bed as I slide my hand to her back and unzipped the Kurti chain. She held my shirt collars and grabbed them towards herself.

'Love me hard' She said. 'No mercy on me now!'

I placed a kiss on her forehead. My right hand slide into her Kurti as now my hands were almost on her breast. She unbuttoned my shirt next. She made me take off my shirt as I took it off. She unhooked my jeans next. 'Life would be too easy without hooks' I thought.

'You are only and only mine' Priya said.

I smiled at her.

She took off her Kurti as she threw it far away at a corner. She had worn a transparent bra. I kissed her forehead, then her nose, then her lips, then the whole body till her toes. I slide down her bra straps with my teeth. I kissed her bare shoulders. She took off her bra as she hugged me tight.

'Thanks Priya!' I said.

'For what?'

'For making this movement special'

We smiled. Her cloths were off the next movement. She signed me to remove my jeans. Our streaming bodies met as I took the charge.

'Ouch…!' Priya exclaimed. 'Slow baby, don't go wild'

I smiled at her as she playfully hit my bare chest.

'Do you have a condom?' I inquired pointlessly.

'Should a boy have it or a girl?' Priya asked. 'But don't really worry, I have got one for my darling'

I stared at her.

'From where have you got it?'

'I kept one for you. I planned this evening days ago. I planned to give you a surprise. But you broke it' She said as her hands reached the side table's drawer.

She brought out a packet as she handed it over to me. Our love making session lasted for hours. I only could see was Priya's cute face. I had only loved her my entire life. I only love her and will be loving her. She had tears in her eyes.

'Priya?'

'I'm really da'am happy' She said. 'Be mine always Rohit'

'Always darling'

We slept pointlessly on the bed. Priya slept in my arms hugging me tight. The double bedded blanket covered our warm bodies. The wind blew as the cold breeze smashed our faces. The wind brought a romantic feeling with it. This romantic wind was that romantic that we really didn't know that when we had went off to sleep.

21

It was around 6:00 am as all the candles in the room were lit down. The room felt dark. I looked at Priya. She still slept in my arms the same way as she slept last night. I held her head and made her sleep on the pillow. I jumped out of the bed. I got dressed up first. I picked up the water jar kept on the side table and poured a glass for me. I took two big sips and placed the glass at its original place.

'Good morning baby' Priya said in a childish way as I turned back at her.

I accorded her a smile.

'You look cute in bed' I said.

'And you wild in bed' She replied suddenly.

I ran towards the bed and jumped on it. I hauled the blanket from Priya's warm body as she held it tight.

'Hey, what are you doing?' She said.

'Taking off the blanket!' I replied.

'I'm not dressed'

'So? No one is in the room. And when I am concern I could see you bare….' I stopped the mid-word.

She took a pillow as she threw it towards me playfully. I moved close to her and kissed her forehead.

'I'll get a coffee for you' I said as I was about to get up. Priya held my right hand.

I looked up at her.

'You are not going anywhere. You are a patient. I'll get it for us' Priya said.

'Baby you get ready I'll get it' I protested.

'But…'

'Get ready Priya… I'll just come back soon' I said as I got up from the bed.

I moved downstairs towards the kitchen. The emptiness downstairs seemed that no one gets up so early in this house. I prepared the coffee for me and Priya. I slide out the drawer and brought out the serving-plate. I placed the jar and the cups into it and stirred upstairs. I stepped into the room. I placed the tray on the bed as I locked the room behind me. I couldn't find Priya anywhere. I found the washroom door open as I stared at it. Priya was dressed up in dark blue Kurti which made her look more eye-catching.

'Priya' I said.

She looked back at me. I didn't say even a word only stared at her eye-lined eyes.

'What happen?' she said.

'Nothing, just looking at your cute face' I replied.

'Can I get a morning kiss?' Priya begged.

I held her as I placed a kiss on her right cheek. We sat on the bed, gossiping, chit-chatting and making jests. Hot coffee at cold atmosphere, each sip of the coffee made our movement even romantic. The smile of hers, her talks, and her gestures, all made me fall for her all over again. Life meant complete. I really couldn't feel the pain in my hand. All I could feel was an angle, a word, Priya!

♦

We all four of us sat on the sofa in the hall downstairs, amusing. All of them looked really happy. Especially Sam and Priyanka. They were about to get married in few months. What else they want? They got the life partner they chose for themselves. I was happy for that. I had got my life back. It all happen because Priyanka and Sam meddled into my life to sort out things. But still I had pain in my heart that how would I expound my parents? I had hurt them a lot. My face fell down.

Priya noticed me.

'What happen dear?' She said placing her hand on mine.

'Nothing! I lied in an innocent way.

She understood that something was not right. She placed a kiss on my face to make me feel good.

'Guys, we have something to announce' Sam said.

I and Priya paid full attention towards them.

'Are you planning your honeymoon?' Priya teased as we broke down laughing.

I shrugged my shoulders.

'We had got a placement in France!' Priyanka exclaimed.

We both stared at Priyanka as if we had never seen them before.

'What? That's worth celebrating and you are like telling it so simply?' Priya said.

Priyanka got up from her seat and sat beside Priya.

'We will be in different countries Priya, we have to settle down in France' Priyanka said.

My face had already fell down. As Priya listened 'two-different-countries' hers fell down too. We both looked at each other.

Sam stared at me.

'Not happy no?' Sam said.

I smiled at him.

'What are you saying? I'm really daam happy with you. Your life is about to settle. But I'm a bit low, you guys are leaving us' I said.

I looked up at her.

'When are you leaving?' I asked.

'The marriage night' Sam said.

I looked at Priya, as we exchange fake smiles. I was happy for Sam and Priyanka. Priya became emotional. I controlled her. She hid her tears from Sam and Priyanka.

'Not here Priya' I whispered in her right ear.

I looked up at them.

'Have you planned something for engagement?' I said changing the topic.

'Have you got her a ring? Or forgot?' Priya entered in.

Sam smiled at Priyanka as she blushed.

'Your engagement is in two days and you haven't got her a ring still?' I questioned.

'I did get one' Sam said.

'And one more announcement, you both should not see each other till the marriage. It's the ritual' Priya said as she got up from her seat.

'Yes, I'll make sure that you both could have two different rooms tonight' I poked in.

Priyanka threw us a dirty look.

'But what's the need? I mean…'

'That's the ritual' I interrupted him.

Priyanka's mom stepped towards us. She looked at me as she gave me a smile.

'Good to see you both together again beta' She said looking at me then at Priya.

'Never break her heart!' She said looking back at me.

I looked at Priya.

'Never aunty' I said as Priya held my hand.

'Come for the lunch, it's served' She said as she left.

Sam and Priyanka moved forward towards kitchen. Priya held my hand tight gesturing me to stay back with her.

'Come' Priyanka said looking back at us.

'Yeah, just two minutes. We'll just come' Priya said as they left.

Priya stared into my eyes. I really didn't understand anything. I was helpless. I looked into her eyes.

'What?' I said.

She didn't say a word for few seconds.

'What's wrong Rohit?' Priya questioned.

I felt anxious. It seemed that Priya had sensed me. If she goes into a conversation, I really had no answers for her.

'About what?' I pretended to be innocent.

'You know about what' Priya said.

I looked away from her as I really had no answer.

'Eye contact!' She said.

She made me sit on the sofa and sat beside me. She made me look into her eyes. I had no option rather than telling Priya the truth.

'Priya I…' I stopped.

'What is it making you uncomfortable Jaan?' Priya asked in a romantic way placing her hand on my shoulder.

My eyes filled up. I was really missing my parents. I want them to love me. I want to share this to Priya but I really couldn't. If I tell her, I'll made her mood go off. But what can I really do? I have to tell her.

'I'm missing my mom' I blunt.

Priya's eyes watered. She only looked at me.

'Baby, we would sort out things. Things would be good' Priya said.

'How? You know my mom is against you. She would never accept you. Never!' I said.

Priya smiled at herself. I didn't knew why she did so.

'I have got a surprise for you!' She exclaimed.

'What?'

'Not for now. Wait till the evening'

I looked down. I had no idea what Priya was talking about.

'Don't worry. We will sort out things. Don't you trust me?' She said.

I waggled.

She hugged me as she whispered 'I Love You'. I hugged her tight.

'Well, is today's dinner going to be something special like yesterday or have you planned something else?' I asked.

She smiled at me.

'Shut up!' She said hitting me playfully on my shoulder.

♦

Priya had brought me to hotel two twins. I had no idea that why she had suddenly planned the dinner. I was glad to be with her here. She had reserved the table for us. The manager took us towards our table.

'Please have a sit!' he said pulling out the chair for me.

We took our seats. The rounded table had a candle lit between. Staring at the candle I remembered the last night. It all recalled before my eyes, the romantic movements between us.

'What will you have sir?' Manager said.

Priya looked up at me. She threw me a 'what-will-you-have' look.

'Get us full of Kolhapuri Chicken' I ordered.

The manager left. I looked up at Priya as she had a smile on her face.

'That's my favourite too' She said.

My eyes were not competent to divert from her. She had worn a red coloured dress with red extra high heels which made her look more beautiful.

I sniffed in.

I slide my hand into my left jeans pocket and brought out a red box. I had purchased a diamond ring for Priya. Hope she likes it. It really felt good as I had purchased it from my first salary for her. I opened the box beneath the table to take a glance at it once. 'It would look dashing in Priya's hand' I told myself. I brought it up as I placed it before Priya. She stared at the heart-shaped box.

'This is for my darling' I said.

She picked up the box as she opened it. I could see the diamond reflecting on her smiling face. She looked up at me next.

'You'll not place it in my hand?' Priya said.

I picked up the box as I plunked off the ring from it. I held Priya's left hand and placed it in her ring finger. It made Priya's hand more beautiful.

'Good no?' She said showing me her hand.

I smiled at her.

'It would be costly!' Priya said.

'Not really'

'I love you'

I threw her a flying kiss. I noticed her left hand which worn the same watch which I has gifted her on her birthday. She remembered it.

'You remember the gift?' I said pointing towards the watch.

'That's really cute' She said kissing it.

The waiter arrived with our order. He started serving our plates. Priya was busy staring at the ring which I had gifted her few minutes ago. I was really eager to know that what surprise she had planned for me. Should I ask her now? 'Go for it idiot' I told myself.

'By the way, what's the surprise?' I inquired.

'Not for now, wait for few more minutes' She said cutting the roti.

I sniffed in.

'Have it' She said pointing me towards my plate.

We had our meal in next few minutes. The candle light made our mood more romantic. Life earlier was strange. It first separates me from who I love the most and then makes us meet again. I was thinking about my parents. How will I apologize to them for what I had done to them?

'Get the bill please' I shouted at waiter.

'So, how did you feel? A candle light dinner with me?' Priya said.

I stared at Priya.

'Really good, but I'm still curious about the surprise!' I said.

'Oh… you can't really wait no?' Priya said.

I nodded in a no option way.

We paid the bill as we moved out of the hotel. Priya smelled really good. Her aroma always makes me fall for her all over again. We moved towards the parking as we got into the Fortuner. Priya took the driver's seat once again.

She drove the car out of the hotel.

'Where are we going?' I asked.

'Towards your surprise!' Priya exclaimed.

I slide down the window and let in the breeze.

'Please close the window, my hairs…' Priya said placing her left hand on her hairs.

'Your hairs look good when they blow' I said.

I peeped out of the window. I stared around. The streets where Priya drove seemed familiar to me, but I couldn't recognize it at once.

I stared at the dashboard and ordered my mind to recognize the place.

"Daam" she drew towards my house. I suddenly looked up at her.

'What are you doing?' I asked.

'Curious about your surprise?' She replied.

I really couldn't understand what Priya was doing. I was floored. She stopped the car before my house as she stepped out.

'Come out! Let's get in' Priya said.

'Priya but…'

She came close to me as she opened the door for me. She held my left hand as she pulled me out of the Fortuner. She shut the door hard. We both walked towards the main door. I really didn't want to do so but Priya made me do it.

'Priya, I can't do this' I said.

She looked into my eyes.

'You trust me, right?' She said politely

'Of course I do!' I said.

She knocked the door. One, two, three…. Nobody answered the door as Priya knocked for the fourth time. Ramu Kaka answered the door. As he looked at me then at Priya he got surprised.

'Are… Rohit baba… please come in' he said.

I looked at Priya as she threw me a 'let's-go-in' glance. I held her hand tight.

'Jaan, you can do this. Please, for me' Priya said.

Priya made me step in as we were in. We sat on the sofa. I started at my own house as if I was a stranger. But it felt good when I stared at each and every thing in my house. My memories were refreshed.

'Sir… Madam…' Ramu kaka called out.

Mom and dad were upstairs into their room. I felt anxious. I threw Priya a 'let's-go-from-here' glance.

'Take to your mom Rohit' Priya said.

I sniffed in.

I heard the footsteps from upstairs. I stood up from my seat. Priya too got up. It seemed that my parents were coming down from the staircase. I had seen them after so long. My mom stared at me when she first looked at me. Dad stood close to my mom. Mom had tears in her eyes. My eyes filled up. I didn't know what had happen to me, but it happen. Priya stood a step far from me. Mom ran towards me as she hugged me tight as she broke down.

'How are you? Are you Okay?' She asked.

I only stared at her. I had no words to say.

'Do you have meals on time? How is your health?' She started.

Her questions were never ending. I could see the love for me into her eyes. A droplet from my eyes rolled down on my cheeks.

'Mom?' I said the first word.

'I really missed you beta' She said.

I couldn't really control myself. I fell down on her feet's. I held her feet's tight.

'I'm sorry mom' I sobbed.

She held me and made me stand up. She stared at my eyes. She smiled at me.

'My son has grown up today!' She exclaimed.

Priya looked at us from a corner. Her eyes were too filled up. I looked at her. She smiled at me to encourage me. Dad moved close to me. I was about to touch his feet's to apologize but he held me. He hugged me tight.

'God bless you beta' He said

'Priya, is really perfect for you. She really cares for you and us too' Mom said.

I baffled.

'Did you know, we hand been at Priyanka's place?' mom said.

'No' I floored.

'We met Priya there. She cried for you. She didn't had anything. She didn't slept for a while. Priya cared for you as a mother cares for her child. She cares for you a lot beta' Mom said.

'She didn't told you about this because we had told her not to tell you' Dad said.

I looked towards Priya. She moved close to me. She smiled at me. The droplets rolled down her eyes.

'We want you both to get married' dad said handing Priya's hand into mine.

He blessed us.

'Be happy always' Mom said.

Mom smiled at us. All I could see in her eyes was love for mc and Priya.

'Priya, I'm really sorry for what I have done with you so far. I really couldn't ascertain your love for my son' mom said joining her hands.

Priya moved forward towards mom as she held her hands and put them down.

'Mom! Don't do this. I'm your daughter. You don't have to feel sorry' Priya said.

Mom smiled at her.

Priya turned at me as she pinched my cheeks playfully.

'Got the surprise?' She said.

I really had no words to say. All I could do was, feel Priya with me.

'Priya, can I request you something?' mom said as Priya turned towards her.

'Yes mom' Priya said.

'Spend time together so that you could be together for some time' mom said.

Priya and I exchange glances as we smiled. Life seemed as a dream. All the dreams have come true. Things have been sorted out. My parents were with me. My love was with me. My friends were with me. Life meant full of love. It all seemed as a dream, a dream that came true.

'Stay here for tonight, its late now' Dad said.

'Dad but…' Priya said

'No excuses please.' Dad interrupted Priya.

Mom smiled at us.

'Good to see my children's growing up' Mom said.

♦

'Pass me the juice please' Mom said pointing towards the juice jar.

We sat for having our breakfast into the kitchen. The dining table looked complete. Mom and dad sat another side and Priya and I exactly opposite to them. Priya passed the juice jar.

'So, Sam and Priyanka's engagement in two days?' Dad inquired.

'Yeah' I said.

All I could say was 'yes'. I really couldn't tell them more about it as we ourselves had loose end.

'That couple is meant for each other' Mom said.

I looked at Priya as I smiled at her. She suddenly looked down as she was blushing before my mom.

'Mom, why don't you guys join us tomorrow on our date? You both can get time to spend together as well' Priya said looking up at Mom then at Dad.

I looked up at them.

'No, it's you who should spend time together' Mom replied.

'Yes, she is right' Dad poked in.

Priya held my hand beneath the table. I looked up at her. She gave me a 'what-to-do' glance. I didn't respond anything. I was thinking about Sam and Priyanka. We will be in different countries soon after their marriage. They were the pillars to my love-life. I would really miss them a lot.

'Rohit!' Priya whispered. 'What happen?'

I nodded.

Priya was daam happy. Destiny, our fate had planned the safe and happy future for us. Life was a puzzle for me. Hints like Sam and Priyanka really made it easy to solve it.

22

The day today was special for me as well as Priya too. I want to make her day even more special.

'Get ready Rohit, we are late!' Priya screamed.

We were at Priyanka's place last night. The arrangements were to be done of tomorrow's engagement program. Rest things were all set, the decorations were not done and I and Priya had decided to decorate the place our way.

I got up from the bed as I moved towards the washroom. The mirror in the washroom reflected my lazy face into it. We were getting really late as it was 9:30 am now. I want to intrigue Priya's day today. I got ready as fast as I could. Priya had brought my breakfast into my room as I looked up at her. I picked up my plate as I started. My cell-phone beeped as I got a message from Priyanka. Priya came close to me holding two hangers each in a hand. The hanger held two beautiful party togs. One was blue and another was black.

'Jaan, I really couldn't decide which one should I wear. Help me out of this' Priya said in a childish way. 'Blue or black?'

I was busy messaging Priyanka. She had asked me to get red coloured heart-shaped balloons for the function tomorrow.

'Red!' I said pointlessly.

'What?'

I looked up at her. The red balloons made me say 'red'.

'That's good. I have two colours. One is Blue and another one is black' She said.

'Oh… baby blue will be good' I said directly to control the situation.

'Good, don't pay attention to me. It's better if you get married to your cell-phone rather than me' She said as she left for the changing room in haste.

I smiled at her. She really looks cute when she fights with me. I messaged Priyanka a 'done' remark.

I sniffed in.

I threw the cell-phone on the bed and got up. I moved towards the changing room. I entered the room as Priya was dressed in blue dress. I moved close to her. She made a disappointed face at me. I held her shoulders and made her face towards me.

'Oh… so you remember me?' Priya said. 'I thought that your cell-phone is your girlfriend'

'If my cell-phone is my girlfriend then who are you?' I said.

She didn't say a word after that. She stood silent.

'Well, your cheeks are inviting me to kiss them' I flirted.

She had a smile on her face.

'If they want so, go ahead' Priya said.

I kissed her cheeks, her nose, her eyes, and her forehead. I looked at her. She stared my eyes.

'You look really look cute when your hairs are open' I said.

'Well, in that case they will be open for today' Priya said.

'Shall we get naughty tonight?'' I said.

'And who will do the decorations? The decorators are here!'

'Who cares for them?'

'You are really silly' She said as she pushed me off playfully and walked out of the room. She looked back at me as she threw me a flying kiss. The kiss landed on my lips, which felt really good.

'Come down, I'm waiting for you' She said.

♦

I walked towards the driving door as Priya stopped me holding my right hand. She pulled me back.

'What?' I said.

'You are not driving! Give me the keys' She said.

'Thank you madam, but I'm driving'

'No! You are not! Your hand will suffer Jaan' She said. 'You are not well still'

She grabbed the keys from me as I couldn't do anything. She stepped into the Fortuner. I had no option rather than going and having my seat next to her. I really couldn't fight with her as it has no meaning. She wins every time.

I scratched my head.

The starter had put on as she drove the car. I wanted to flirt with her. When I do so she really looks cute. I looked at her at once and thought for something new.

'Priya, haven't you used the lips-stick today?' I said.

She looked at me.

'I have. The red one' She said.

'But I really couldn't recognize it!'

'Really?'

She made the front mirror towards her face as she checked for her make-up. Her lips moved Zig-Zac as it made them look more delightful.

'If you say, my love-bite can make them red. No need to use the expensive lips-stick' I flirted.

She looked up at me as she hit me playfully on my shoulder.

'So cheap Rohit' She said. 'You would never change!'

'You really want me to change?'

She took off her hand from the gear and placed it on mine. Our eyes met. I signed her to look straight and drive safe.

'If you change I would never bear it. I love my darling, who could find ways to flirt with me' Priya said.

I smiled at her.

She drove towards Andheri (West). We had planned to get a *Sherwani* for Sam and a *Lehenga* for Priyanka. 'The showrooms on the streets of Andheri (West) are worth watching' Sam had told me about this once.

I only stared at Priya for few minutes. We laughed, we flirted, we smiled, and Priya blushed as the car drove. We reached. That was really true, the showrooms on the streets of Andheri (West) were worth watching. I slide my window down and searched for some expensive showrooms.

'That one will be good' Priya said pointing towards one of the showroom.

'Let's check it out' I said.

Priya drove the car towards the showroom as we entered the parking. We parked the car as we walked towards the entrance. The security guard on the main gate greeted us with a smile. We entered in as the cold breeze smashed our faces. We searched for the *Sherwani's* and *Lehenga's*. I moved towards the men's section as Priya towards the ladies. I had selected a white coloured Sherwani for Sam which cost fifty thousand bucks. I signed the sales boy to pack it for me. I made my way towards Priya. She was busy flipping through some designer *Lehenga's* for Priyanka.

'That one could be good' Priya said pointing towards the red one.

'That's really good'

'Pack this!' Priya ordered at sales boy.

The sales boy placed our order as he took it to the counter. We moved along towards the counter as the cashier greeted us with a smile. I carried out my credit card from my wallet.

'Here' I said handing over the credit card to the cashier.

She swapped the card and made the payment. We grabbed the bags and made our way out of the showroom.

'We got good' I said entering the parking.

'Hmm'

I placed the bags in the back seat. I held Priya and brought her close to me.

'Well, no one is in the parking. Any chance?' I said.

'You're mad!' She said as she pushed me away.

'Think about it!'

'Shut-up Rohit'

♦

We spend our morning shopping things for Sam and Priyanka. We shopped enough. I had really flirted enough with Priya as she was tired. I was really a nutcase. It was around 6:30 PM. The evening felt romantic. We were at Marine Lines. The beach carried a romantic atmosphere. We walked along bare-footed as the cold sand really felt good. Priya walked holding my hand. I held her shoulders.

'Priya, what happen? Why are you so silent?' I asked.

She looked up at me as she smiled.

'I'm not silent, just thinking about our future together' She said closing her eyes.

The sea wave's sound made out movement more special. The cold sand brought a spark into us. The evening really made my mood go more romantic.

'Rohit?'

'Hmm'

'I love you'

'I love you too baby'

I held her tight. We walked further. The people around us felt happy as us. Some of them were children's, some were families and some were couples. I noticed the couples, the way they loved each other.

I sniffed in.

Priya pointed me to sit down on the cold sand. I smiled at Priya. I made her sit first. We placed our shoes aside as I sat next to her. I held her as I put my arms around her. All we could see was the romantic sunset.

'How romantic!' Priya whispered pointing towards the sunset.

'That's really romantic' I said kissing her forehead.

Priya hugged me tight. She buried her face in my chest. I heard her sobbing. I didn't know that what made her do so.

'Priya?' I said as I made her look at me.

Her eyes filled up. She cried. I really didn't know why but she did so. I made her look into my eyes.

'I'm sorry Rohit. I'm really very sorry' Priya said.

'Priya?'

She buried her face in my chest again.

'I'm really sorry for what I have done with you' She said. 'I'm really lucky that I have got a life-partner who could love me so much'

'Please don't cry, it makes me cry too' I said as she cried hard. 'Please Priya'

I made her look up at me.

'Swear to me if you cry now' I said.

She stared at my eyes. Her eyes were still wet. I threw her a 'don't-do-this' look. I made my grip tight.

'Why are you doing this? Let my cry for you'

'No!'

'Why?'

'Because, I really can't see you crying'

She controlled herself as she held my right hand. We looked up towards the sunset as the sun was half set. The reflection in the sea made it look more stunning.

'Can I say something?' Priya said.

'Hmm'

'You should have not behaved like that way with your mom, the way you have behaved past few months' Priya said.

'What else could I have done? I was really unable to live without you' I said.

She sniffed in.

'Rohit, life is not of one single day. You can't sort out things in a single day. You have hurt them a lot. You thought that they don't love you. But they do Rohit. You hated them for mc, right? And if you really hated them, then how could you miss your mother that day?

I didn't utter a single word.

'Do you have any answer?' Priya asked. 'Rohit, relations matters in life. These relations are very precious. Try maintaining them not spoiling them' 'My parents really love you a lot Priya'

'I know baby and not only me, they love you the same'

'See, it takes years to have good relations with each other. But a second is enough to lose it off' Priya explained.

I smiled at her. I love the way she explained me. I loved the way she talked to me. I hugged her tight. The sun had gone down as the lights lit on the streets of Marine Lines. It had really a beautiful look.

'Let's leave!' Priya said.

'Sure'

We got up as we held our shoes in our hand. The night walk on the beach felt really romantic. We walked towards the footpath as hundreds of couples walked through. I checked my watch, it said 7:10 PM. Priya held my hand tight as we walked.

'I'll miss this evening!' I said.

'Me too' She said making her grip tighter.

We walked forward as we found a telephone-booth roadside. There was no one around. I brought Priya behind the booth. We placed our shoes down as I moved close to her.

'This evening should never end' I said.

'You also think the same?' Priya said as she gave me a cute smile.

I moved close to her as I held her face. Our lips met as we kissed. We kissed at the footpath. We kissed as there was no one around. We kissed as that was the last day of my life. We kissed...

23

The decorators didn't understand the thing, we tell them once. The decorators were still in progress. I and Priya were busy instructing them about the decorations to be made. But these people were snotty. Sam and Priyanka were making-up for the program today. We have to go and make them up, but these decorators, to no avail have their work incomplete still. We made our way towards the pillar as we instructed them to decorate it with the red roses which could make the atmosphere more romantic.

'These people are head-ache' Priya said, almost tired.

I smiled at her.

A hand from behind tapped my shoulder. I looked behind. Ragini!

It was Ragini from my workplace. I stared at her for few seconds wondering what she was doing here.

'Hey!'

'Hello Rohit' She said shaking her hand with me.

Priya threw her a dirty look. It was right thing that, someone had said well 'When someone talks to their boyfriend the girl gets possessive about her boyfriend' there was the same thing with Priya now.

'Priya, this is Ragini, from my workplace' I introduced.

'Priya! Have heard a lot about you from Rohit' Ragini said.

Priya gave her a fake smile.

'How come you are here?' I inquired.

'Oh… Yash sir is coming today for Mumbai' Ragini said.

'Anything important?'

'Nothing, he learnt about you. I mean your suicide attempt'

I looked at Priya. I didn't say a word for a movement.

'Suicide? How did he know?' I asked.

'Well, I don't have the answer. He is really happy for you Rohit'

'Happy for?'

'Your patch-up with Priya'

I got floored. How did he knew this all? I couldn't really understand anything. Ragini stared at me as she sensed my confusion.

'Actually, sir had called you once but your friend attended the call. He had a talk. I think he had…'

'Oh… Sam' I understood.

Priya smiled at herself. She too had the same wavelength as me. Her mind too clicked Sam's name at first.

'Okay, bye for now. Have some official work. Take care' Ragini said.

'Bye'

She left as I looked up at Priya. She made a childish face at me. I pinched her nose playfully.

'You are really an princess' I said.

'I know it baby'

'Let's work. We have a lot's of work still' I said.

'I'll go up and get Priyanka ready' she said.

'Come fast, I'll miss your cute nose' I said.

'Miss me too'

I smiled at her.

She left as I moved towards Sam's room. The smell of the decorated flowers filled the hall. I pushed the door as I stepped in.

'Can I come in?' I bleated.

Sam suddenly looked back at me as he greeted me with a smile. The preparations were already done. I stared at Sam's hand. Sam held the heart-shaped ring box in his hand. The guest were to be here in one hour and Sam haven't dressed yet. I moved forward towards him.

'Get ready Sam, we're getting late I guess' I said. 'Priyanka is waiting'

Sam's face went red. He blushed.

'Oh… blushing and all ha?' I teased.

'Rohit, can I say something?' Sam asked.

I listened to him.

'You're not happy with us moving to France, right?' he said.

I sniffed in.

'Are you serious? You really think I could be unhappy?' I blunt.

He smiled at me.

'Will you miss us?' He asked.

'Never!' I replied according him a smile.

He came close to me as he hugged me tight. I patted his back. I had tears in my eyes. I would really miss them a lot.

'Be happy always' I said.

He hugged me even more tightly. This movement made us become emotional.

'Hey, we are getting emotional. It's not the time. Get ready, the function is about to begin' I said releasing him from my hug.

I gave him a smile. I got him ready in next few minutes. I handed him the engagement ring. The music downside began loud. The hosts were all arrived. I could see the happiness on Sam's face. We stared at each other for few seconds.

I grinned.

'Let's go' I said.

♦

The hall was beautifully decorated. All the hosts were arrived as expected. The hall played the song '*Teri Jhuki Nazar*' from the movie '*Murder 3*'

The stage was decorated as heaven. I had placed the red-coloured heart shaped balloons as Priyanka had told me earlier. I had rolled them around the pillars. The couple names on the stage were decorated with flowers and red roses. I and Priya stood along with the hosts. My future in-laws were arrived as they greeted me with a smile. My parents were yet to be arrive.

'Has Priyanka got ready?' I inquired.

'I made her dress in a beautiful white dress' Priya said. 'What about Sam?'

'He is ready!'

She gave me an understanding nod.

Sam and Priyanka came down as a couple, hand in hand. All the heads turned towards them. All smiled at them. Both of them entered the stage staring at us. We greeted them with a wide smile. They took their seats on the sofa placed on the stage. The rituals were made by the parents. Sam's mouth was full of sweets as he was impotent to eat further.

Priya smiled at him.

I brought out my IPhone from my left jeans pocket as I opened the camera. I clicked the pics of them. Priya grabbed the iPhone from my hand to click the pics from different angles. I could notice Sam and Priyanka, I could notice the smile on their faces, and I could notice how happy they were. Priyanka looked at me and signed us to come on the stage. I held Priya's hand as we moved towards the stage. I stood beside Sam and Priya beside Priyanka. We passed them the rings. The rings were exchanged as the audience clapped. Sam kissed Priyanka's hand next which made the hosts go mad. They both stood up.

'Got engaged finally' I teased.

Sam smiled at me. Priyanka hit me on my shoulders playfully. The rings twisted a happy atmosphere among us. I took the control over the mic.

'Let us all request the couple to perform Salsa' I announced.

I made them dance on the floor. The track played '*Tum hi ho*' from the movie '*Aashiqui 2*' which made the salsa romantic. All the couples among the guest danced around them. Priya made me dance with her. She only stared at my eyes.

'Control yourself Priya' Priyanka teased.

Priya blushed.

'Not now Sis, she is being romantic' I said.

♦

The couple was reinforcing the day in different way. They both had planned a special dinner for the family members. The party was planned on the roof. The roof was too decorated well. It was decorated too well as if they both were veteran in decorating. The engagement was very triumphantly done. We really didn't know that when these creatures had planned something for us.

'Where are others?' Priyanka asked.

'They're coming' Priya replied.

Our families were invited for the dinner. A long table had been served with food. We took our seats. Sam and Priyanka sat at the corner seat of the table. They stared at their engagement rings and smiled. They held each other's hand.

'May they have a successful future' I said.

Priya held my hand being romantic. I held her in response. We could feel the warmness.

'They look really cute with each other' Priya said.

I sniffed in as I held her hand tight. The movement felt phenomenal. Love makes us change. That's the great thing that I have ever seen.

'Well, we are here' Mom said coming upstairs on the roof.

We suddenly released out hands from each other and sat up straight. I felt anxious. Sam and Priyanka were up from their seats.

'You guys can carry on' Priya's mom teased next.

'Aunty come, have your seat' Sam tried to change the topic.

Priyanka moved the plates and acted to serve them.

'Drama queen, keep the plate down. We all were staring you from few minutes there' Sam's mom said pointing towards the enterance.

We all broke out laughing. We took out seats as the waiters served us the food.

'Finally!' Sam's dad said.

'Yeah finally' We all said in unison.

The non-veg smell filled our nose. We all started. The cold breeze at night is really good to feel.

'Your daughter is making me do what she wants aunty' I complaint.

Priya looked up towards me.

'Well, get comfortable to it, you both have to spend life together' Priya's dad said as all of them busted out laughing.

Priya kicked my leg beneath the table. I looked at her as she smiled at me. The movement I saw Priya's wet lips, I really wanted to kiss them for sure.

'Well, Priya always makes Rohit do things' Sam teased.

'How mean Sam!' Priya said.

'You do!' Sam foisted.

I held her hand.

'But...'

'I really love you for that' I interrupted Priya picking up the leg piece next.

All of them busted out laughing. We had our dinner, chit-chatting, making jests, and remembering movements that we had spent together. All the families looked really happy. It all seemed as a dream. Each of the person here loved everyone present at the movement. We finished our dinner in few minutes. My life had given me what I really wanted. I really love my life for that.

'Beta, I had got something for you' Dad said looking at Priya.

'What is it dad?' I inquired.

'A gift from a father to a daughter'

He brought out a blue coloured square box. It was the same blue coloured box which I had seen in dad's office that day. He handed it over to Priya.

'What's that?' Priya said opening the box.

It was the jewellery set. It was really daam precious. Priya stared at the set for few seconds.

'We all love you beta' He said.

She looked up at me as I gave her a smile.

'That would be really costly' Priya said.

'Not more than you!' Dad said.

Priya had tears in her eyes. She really couldn't think anything what she had to do next. She looked at each one of us.

'We are really lucky that we got a son like Rohit' Priya's mom said.

Priyanka came forward towards us. She held Priya and made her look towards her.

'I said that everything would be back to normal. See that's done' Priyanka said with a smile.

'You would have a great future with Rohit' Priyanka's mom said.

Priya cried. She turned towards me as she hugged me tight. All of them stood around us.

'I love you Jaan' she said releasing me.

I shrugged my shoulders.

'Dad your daughter is being romantic' I told dad.

'I am, because I love you a lot' Priya replied.

All of them broke down. Priyanka moved towards the table as she picked up the bunch of cards kept on it and handed one for each. They were the marriage invitation cards. I slide it out of the envelope. They looked really pretty.

'Congratulation! Both of you' I congratulated them first.

They greeted me with a smile. I stared at the card as I could only see the proclaimed words which read:

S A M
Weds
P R I Y A N K A

'Do come all' Sam joked as all of them broke down.

Sam hugged Priyanka as we stared at them. It all felt good. It all felt romantic. It all felt like a dream... a dream that had come true.

ONE MONTH LATER

24

The day has finally risen up. The day which finally made our dream come true. It felt like we were right onto the heaven. I really couldn't control my exaltation. All the decoration, all the arrangements were systematically arranged by me and Priya. 'This marriage would really drive people crazy' I told myself and grinned. This day really brought a spark among us. This was the day we actually were waiting for. Our families were busy arranging the arrangements for the rituals. I saw Priya at a distance as she was busy addressing the guests. The arrangements were all done. The house was decorated beautifully. The *Mandap* was decorated full with flowers. There were around seven to eight hundred hosts invited for this marriage anniversary. Greeting them all over was not possible for Priya. I thought over to join her. I slowly moved towards her taking the precaution that she wouldn't see me.

'Greet me too' I said kissing her right ear.

She turned towards me in reflex.

'Rohit?'

'What?'

'Not here, we are in public' She said looking around if someone noticed us.

I smiled at her. Her face went red, blushing. I looked around to see if someone noticed us, I too felt anxious. I grabbed Priya's left hand and brought her into a corner. I only stared her eyes.

'*Jaan*, what are you doing?' She said looking up at me.

'Can I kiss you?' I requested.

She stared at me making her eyes even bigger.

'You're crazy, let me go I have to greet people'

'And when will you greet me then?'

'I've reserved today's night for it' She said as she pushed me back. She walked away from me.

She made a childish face at me throwing me a flying kiss.

'Go, get the arrangements done Rohit' She said.

'They are already done'

She came close to me. She placed her right hand onto my left shoulder.

'Get the photographer and the make-up man' She said.

'They are already here darling'

She hit my shoulders playfully.

'You would never change, Right?' She said. 'But I really love the way you are'

She heeled up her toes to match my height and kissed my nose.

'Let's move, else I couldn't control myself anymore' I said.

She smiled as she grabbed my hand. We walked towards the entrance to greet our guests. The each person we greeted brought us a feeling of love.

♦

I stood in the balcony upstairs. I saw my mom arranging the stage. Our eyes met for a second as we smiled at each other.

'What are you doing there? Come help me out with this' She shouted.

'Coming Mom' I shouted back as if I stood on a rostrum.

All the members were busy arranging things. I leaned over to go and run into Sam and Priyanka once. I looked down as my eyes searched for Priya. My eyes rolled from left to right. I found her talking to my dad about something.

'Priya?' I shouted as she looked up at me.

I signed her to come up. she walked towards the staircase. Sam and Priyanka were match-maker in our life. We are really gratified to them.

I sniffed in.

Priya walked upstairs. I turned towards the staircase as she walked towards me.

'Have you talked to Priyanka and Sam?' I asked.

'Not still, shall we talk now?'

'Now?'

'We have to get them ready too. The make-up man has already reached Priyanka's room'

I signed her to walk towards them. I walked forward as Priya held my hand as she pulled me back.

'Wait here, I'll be back in one minute' she said.

'Where are you going now?'

I baffled.

'Just one minute' She said as she ran towards her room.

Where had she gone now? It's really impossible to understand her. I waited at the balcony staring at the people downstairs. 'I would really miss those two creatures' I said mentally. I would miss those movements that we had spent together.

'Let's go!' Priya said as I looked behind at her. She came with two bags. The bags contained the *Sherwani* and the *Lehenga* that we had brought for them.

I shrugged my shoulders.

I stared ta Priya for a second. I really had thought right few minute ago. 'It was really unable to understand girls'

'Take this' She said handing me one bag.

I didn't say a word, just stared at her beautiful face.

'What?' She said.

'Nothing' I said. 'Just staring at you'

'Not again baby, it's already late' She said as she grabbed my hand and pulled me forward.

She moved towards Priyanka's room and signed me to be quick for Sam's.

'Be quick, the *Mahurat* is on its way' I said.

'Funny!' She blunt. 'Shall I go now?'

'Please, madam' I said.

She left as I stared at the bag which Priya had handed me. I thought all the way about us four. I, Priyanka, Priya and Sam, all four of us together. I would miss them a lot, but I was really happy for them.

I sniffed in.

I made my way downstairs towards Sam's room. I stared at his door as it brought memories before my eyes. They were really perennial. I controlled my emotions as I pushed the door in. I stepped in slowly with light steps. I rolled my eyes throughout the room as I couldn't find Sam anywhere. I placed the bag on his bed. I suddenly perceived the steps behind me as I turned back.

'I was searching for you, and you are here!' Sam said.

'You haven't got ready yet?' I said.

He smiled at himself.

'I was waiting for you. You will make me up today' he said coming forward.

He brought out his cell-phone and threw it on the bed. I picked up the bag.

'What's that' Sam said pointing towards the bag.

I brought out the *Sherwani* as I threw the bag back on the bed. Sam stared at the *Sherwani*.

'This, we want you to wear this at the marriage' I said.

Sam smiled at me.

'What was the need Rohit? I mean…'

'Brother, not today man… you would leave for Europe within few hours' I interrupted looking into his eyes.

Sam came forward towards me as he took the Sherwani from my hand and placed it on the bed. He looked straight into my eyes.

'No matter how many time you say, but I knew that you are not happy with us moving to France' Sam said 'I also know the reason, it's because you love us a lot'

I didn't say anything.

'Nothing like that Sam' I said.

'If it's bothering you so much then we could cancel it' Sam said.

'No!' I exclaimed. 'There is nothing greater then you both being happy to me. I would miss you guys, a lot I guess.'

Sam had tears in his eyes. I didn't wanted to make this movement emotional. I didn't want to spoil this evening.

'This is not for now, forget it all and get ready first' I said.

I picked up the *Sherwani* and handed it over to him. I tried to parch the atmosphere. He dressed up with the *Sherwani*. He really looked dashing. I gave him a smile as it brought a cute smile on his face too.

'That's good, Priya really have a great choice' Sam said.

'Actually that's my personal choice' I said.

'Oh… Really?'

Sam stared at the *Sherwani* like never before. I could sense that he had liked it very much.

'I really love it' Sam said.

I smiled at him.

I looked at the bag which I had thrown on the bed. I picked it up as it contained one more gift for Sam. I brought out a rectangle-shaped gift wrapped with blue gift-paper.

I sniffed in looking at the gift.

'That's one for you!' I said handing it over to him.

He started unwrapping the package. I hope he likes it too. I looked into his eyes. He brought out the gift. It was the group of pictures which we had clicked in our Goa trip. This could definitely help him recalling his memories.

'Unbelievable!' Sam exclaimed.

I checked for my watch as it said 8:10 PM. It was getting late for *Mahurat*. I signed him.

'I'll stare at this every day when I will be in France' Sam said.

I accorded him a smile. Life will be really difficult without them. But I had one more pillar with me, Priya!

'Let's move' I said.

'Sure'

◆

Priya was busy dressing up Priyanka. She looked beautiful of all. She was not our Priyanka anymore. She was a *'Dulhaan'* Priya was making-up Priyanka for the marriage. The make-up man helped her through. The 'Mehendi' on her hand and on her feet glowed up, after all she was getting married today.

'You look really a princess' Priya said adjusting Priyanka's necklace.

Priyanka's eyes went wet. Priya noticed.

'Hey, what happen?' Priya asked.

Priyanka hugged Priya tight. She cried. She really couldn't control herself. Priya held her.

'Priyanka, don't cry. Your make-up will vanish'

'Let me cry Priya, I would really miss you and Rohit a lot'

'We will too miss you guys' Priya said. 'Look, how fast we had grown up'

Priya held her and made her sit on the bed. She cleaned her face as she made her up all over again. This was the happy movement. This was the movement of love. It really doesn't felt that the marriage was about few minutes later. We really didn't know that how the days had passed. We didn't know, how fast the things sorted out. Life had played a game with us, the game of love which also taught us the right meaning of 'relationship'. I remember Priya's words.., *'Relations matters, maybe with your parents, with your friends, with your loved one, they should be all maintained equally'*

'Nervous?' Priya asked.

'A lot!' Priyanka replied.

Priya stared at Priyanka and gave her a smile.

'Let's go!' Priya said.

Priyanka didn't say anything. She blushed.

'Come on Priyanka'

Priya held Priyanka as they both walked out of the room. They walked through the staircase. I and Sam already stood at the *Mandap*. I could see them both coming downstairs. I looked at Sam as he stared at Priyanka with his mouth open.

'Control yourself Sam' I teased.

Sam smiled at me.

All the eyes into the hall turned towards Priyanka as all had a smile on their faces. Priya brought her into the *Mandap* and made her sit before the '*Havan*' I made Sam sit next to Priyanka. Priya signed me to come close to her. I moved close to her as she held my hand and brought me at a distance from the *Mandap*.

'The Groom and the Bride's parents should come forward' Pandit-ji announced.

Their parents moved forward as they sat next to them. The mantra's started. I and Priya were at a distance watching all this. Priya held my hand tighter.

'Finally they are there' Priya said.

'The smile on their faces is everything' I said.

Priya smiled at me.

'Click some pics. We would upload it on Facebook' Priya said.

I brought out my cell-phone and turned on the camera. I started clicking the random photographs of, some happy movements, some tears, some romance...

'I just love this movement' Priya said.

We both only stared at them. We only stared at their happiness.

'How romantic' Priya said pointing towards them.

Sam was setting the '*Mangal-Sutra*' to Priyanka. Priyanka close her eyes. She cried at the movement nobody noticed, I did. I smiled at her.

'We'll really miss them' I said.

'A lot, I guess'

The mantras went on as we only stared at the movement. Both the parents held their children's hand into theirs. They passed them the garlands. The garlands were bartered. Priya cried. She buried her face into my chest.

'Priya control yourself, we have to wave them smiling' I explained as I held her tight in my arms.

All I could remember at the movement was the first time I met Priyanka, I remembered our grades at the prelim exams. I remember how I made Sam and Priyanka meet. I remember the movements we spend together in Goa trip. I remember how these two creatures helped me sorting out my problem. I remember our madness we made. My eyes filled up. A droplet rolled down my eye. I was actually seeing what I wanted to see from years. I saw the seven rounds. The seven promises taken by Sam and Priyanka. They took the seven promises of their life. It really felt romantic.

I sniffed in.

I slide my hand into my pocket and brought out the flight tickets and their passports. I stared at them. A droplet rolled down and fell on the passport.

'Rohit, let's not get emotional. You said we have to wave them smiling' Priya tried to control me.

I controlled myself. We were hysterical at the movement. The marriage was successfully got over. The smile on Sam and Priyanka's face told me that how happy they were at this stage.

'Let's not wave them here' I told Priya.

'What? Then…'

'At Marine Lines' I interrupted.

I waved my hand to Sam smiling at him. The marriage photographs were been clicked. Sam signed me to come on the stage for the photo shoot.

I only smiled at him. All the people around me felt romantic. The music was put on as they danced around. My mom signed Priya to come up. Priya looked up at me.

I threw Mom an 'okay' glance as Priya stride towards today's couple.

They took the blessings of their elders as they blessed them for their happy future together. Their relatives, their friends, their families, the guest's greeted them with hugs. Priya threw a flying kiss at them.

I brought out my cell-phone and composed a message to Sam

SEE YOU AT MARINE LINES,
DON'T BE LATE, YOU COULD,
MISS YOUR FLIGHT.

♦

The cold breeze at Marine Lines brought a spark within us. It was around 10:05 PM. I and Priya had reached the Marine Lines. We sat on the benches. Our car was parked at a distance. Priya seemed happy. She really couldn't control her happiness. She held my arms and rested her head on my shoulder.

'Rohit?'

'Hmm'

'What happen? You look down?'

I didn't say anything.

'Look at me' She held my face and made me look up at her.

I had tears into my eyes. I was happy one side for Sam and Priyanka but unhappy another side of Sam and Priyanka leaving us.

'Rohit, please don't cry' Priya said. 'Look at me'

I looked up at her.

'We had got everything we wanted in our life. Our friends got married. We will be getting married in few months, everything is as per us. What else we want?'

I sniffed in to control my emotions.

I slide my fingers through her hairs. I could see the pale black spot on her forehead which was because of the accident. I stared at it.

'I'm really sorry Priya. I'm responsible for that accident' I said.

Priya held my arms tight as she looked up at my eyes.

'Leave it baby, it's over. You don't have to feel sorry for it'

'I do'

She came close to me and placed her ear on my chest which could make her hear my heart beats.

'Rohit, I love you a lot' she whispered.

I kissed her forehead. I closed down my eyes as I could feel her.

'I had got something for you Priya!' I said.

'What? Is it something special?'

'Yes, it is' I said as a car drove towards us.

We stood up from our seat as we stared at the car.

It was Sam's car!

The car stopped before us as Priyanka and Sam stepped down. We stared at them. They slowly walked towards us.

We greeted them with a smile.

'So, finally got married ha?' I teased moving close to them.

'They are planning their honeymoon Rohit, don't disturb them right now' Priya teased next.

We all broke down laughing. I slide out the passport and the flight tickets from my left jeans pocket. I smiled at them showing them the same. Priyanka hugged me tight. She broke down as I held her.

'I'll really miss you guys, Rohit' Priyanka cried.

I smiled at myself thinking about a great future together.

'But I'll never miss you' I said. 'Because if I do so, I would definitely break down crying'

I moved towards Sam as I stared into his eyes. I handed him the passport and the tickets. I greeted him with a wide wry smile as I was about to cry. I hugged him tight as I was unable to control myself anymore.

'Be happy brother' I said releasing him. 'And be in contact. We want regular calls'

Priya came forward as she held Priyanka's hand. Priyanka embraced her as Priya gave her a smile.

'Will miss you both' Priya said.

'We too'

I checked my watch as it was 10:30 PM now. It was really late for them for their flight. I looked at Priya as we exchanged 'we-will-miss-them' glances.

I sniffed in.

Sam hugged Priya. They both exchange a joke within themselves. I smiled at them.

I moved towards Priyanka as I stared at her.

'Whenever Sam's ask for a kiss give him one' I teased.

She smiled with her wet face.

'It's getting late brother' I said turning towards Sam.

'Yeah' Sam said checking for his watch. We exchanged our last glances.

We moved towards the car as Sam took his seat on the driver's seat. Priya held Priyanka and made her seat right besides Sam.

'Have a happy and safe flight' Priya told them.

I placed my hand on Priyanka's head and gave her a smile. I looked at Sam next and stared at him. We waved them a happy good bye as the car moved. Priyanka waved us with her head out of the window. The car went far and fro as it was totally disappeared. They left, but left us behind the huge treasure of memories. The memories which couldn't be forgotten. I turned towards Priya as I smiled at her. Her beautiful face looked even beautiful and cute today.

I stared at her.

'Now?' I said.

'Now What?' Priya asked.

I slide my hand into my pockets and brought out a platinum ring. I kneeled down on my knees and stared at Priya's beautiful eyes.

'Priya, I really love you a lot and want to marry you. Will you marry me?' I proposed.

Her eyes had watered. She cried. She cried for me. This was the day I waited for so long. I stood up showing her the ring. She ran towards me as she hugged me. I hugged her tight as I felt her. I could feel world full of romance.

'Well, you promised me the night today' I teased as she threw me a flying kiss.

'I'm all yours Rohit! I really love you a lot' Priya said.

I held her hand as I placed the ring into her finger. I looked around as there was no one around. I wanted to feel her, I wanted to kiss her, and I wanted to love her.

'Come, let's walk' Priya said as she held my right hand.

We walked through the path of marine lines, hand in hand, feeling each other, remembering the memories.

'Never leave me alone darling' Priya said.

'Never'

We both really couldn't control our exaltation. We were da'am happy. We had learnt something from our life. Our life took us from the path of love. It showed us the real meaning of relationship. We learnt a meaning. The cold breeze dashed our warm bodies. The insects charming sound made our movement even romantic. My life was completely in love. I could simply say 'MY LIFE IN LOVE'. I had the greatest feeling ever. This was the magic, the magic of love. Someone had said this really well, 'Life makes love happen'.

Epilogue:

'*T*he book will be finally out tomorrow' I said picking up my cell-phone from the desk.

We were at my office at Andheri East. I had invited all of them for a book launch party at my office.

'Baby, give us the books, we wanted to read it' Priya said as I ignored her.

'Please Rohit' Priyanka begged next.

'Please yaar' Sam started.

I smiled at both of them.

'No! Not now. At the book launch' I said.

All of them threw me a dirty look. Priya stood up suddenly.

'Don't talk to me!' Priya said as she stepped out in haste.

I smiled at her.

'Don't talk to us too' Priyanka and Sam said in unison.

I stood up suddenly to stop them. No one could stop these mad guys. We were really crazy, all four of us. Finally our real life story was been made in a book which the whole country could read.

'Listen Guys, how about an ice-cream? It could make your heads cool' I shouted coming out of my cabin.

All of them looked back at me. All made a face at me, I baffled.

'Err... sorry no' I said.

'We got the book Rohit' Sam said showing me the book.

I baffled, how did they get the book?

I ran towards then as they made me run throughout my own office.

'Run baby run...' Priya said playfully. She actually teased me.

Acknowledgements:

I really met a lots of people around the globe. I would like to thank those people who had met me in my life till now. Each of them had played a very important role of motivating me in my work. My life has gave me everything I want, I would like to thank my life and especially to them who had gave me a chance to live such a precious life, My Parents.

I have a lots of people to thank to, in particular I would like to thank to:

1. First of all I would like to thank to my parents for giving me this beautiful life, I'm living now. And for their blessings too.
2. God, who was every time after me with his blessings. The person who has gave me strength to think.
3. My lovingly Mama, Vijay Bisure who have continuously motivated me and is still inspiring me with his work. I would really like to thank him for everything he had gave me.
4. My educational institute Amboli Public College and Junior College of Science, Amboli for their knowledge, the people who had trained me so good and for those people who had made me what I'm today.
5. Chetan Bhagat, who always motivated me during my writing and who inspired me to write and who made me who I am.
6. Nikita Dubay and Praveen Obiroi, Amazon Seller Central, who gave me beautiful comments on my manuscript.
7. My relatives for their support for me in my work and for the love they had shown towards my work.

8. Rajashree Powar, being a motivation mother she inspired me on writing a story that could change people in different ways.
9. 'Adittia Powar Group' on twitter and other social networks, for making my manuscript worth reading and giving wonderful comments.
10. My extended family on Facebook and Twitter for giving so precious likes on my book. My extended friends on Facebook and Twitter.
11. My younger brother Athrav, who says' 'it's OK' during my low.

And at last, all you the readers for choosing me, for choosing my story to make yours.

Welcome to MY LIFE IN LOVE.